THIS IS NOT
A LOVE SONG

THIS IS NOT A LOVE SONG

KAREN DUVE

Translated by Anthea Bell

BLOOMSBURY

First published in Great Britain 2005

First published in Germany by Eichborn AG, Frankfurt
am Main, 2002 under the title *Dies ist Kein Liebeslied*

Copyright © 2002 by Karen Duve

Translation copyright © 2005 by Anthea Bell

The moral right of the author and translator has been asserted

The publication of this work was supported by a grant from the Goethe-Institut

Bloomsbury Publishing Plc, 36 Soho Square, London W1D 3QY

A CIP catalogue record for this book
is available from the British Library

ISBN 0 7475 7239 9
ISBN–13 9780747572398

1 2 3 4 5 6 7 8 9 10

Typeset by Hewer Text UK Ltd, Edinburgh
Printed by Clays Ltd, St Ives plc

All papers used by Bloomsbury Publishing are natural,
recyclable products made from wood grown in well-managed
forests. The manufacturing processes conform to the
environmental regulations of the country of origin.

For poor Heinrich

*What follows is fiction. Places and incidents
have very little to do with real places and events.
Books and films are only loosely quoted.
And no reference to any of you is intended.*

When I was seven I swore I'd never fall in love. When I was eighteen I fell in love anyway. It was just as bad as I'd feared. It was humiliating, painful and totally beyond my control. My feelings were not returned, there was nothing I could do about it, and my own attempts to fall out of love again nearly sent me round the bend. When you realise you're going crazy the best idea is to keep quiet about it and pretend you're in perfect mental health by behaving like everyone else. All the other girls had boyfriends and sex and careers, they went to parties, they travelled, and they spent five whole days looking forward to the weekend. So I went to bed with men too, and I went to bars with women, I failed to make the grade in various jobs, I was bored out of my mind at parties and elsewhere, and I carved patterns on my upper arms with a potato-peeling knife on Sundays. Meanwhile Bayern Munich football club won the German championship eight times. All the people I knew bought watches with digital displays and swapped their flares for tight jeans or tapered pants. Iran denounced the USA as the Great Shaitan, and MTV began its programmes with 'Video Killed the Radio Star', by the Buggles. British soldiers marched into the Falkland Islands, Soviet soldiers marched into Afghanistan, American soldiers marched into Grenada. All the people I knew turned in their digital watches again in favour of normal watches with hands and a dial, and bought Walkmen. Reactor 4 of the Chernobyl nuclear power station scattered radiation all over Europe, we were advised not to eat wild mushrooms for the next twenty years, and for a whole two years we actually didn't eat as many mushrooms as before. The Soviet Union withdrew from Afghanistan again, the Cold War came to an end, and when no one believed the Berlin Wall would ever fall, it did. Models got thinner and more famous all the time, computers grew smaller and the hole in the ozone layer larger, joggers trotted out only early in the morning and late in the evening in summer, and the man I loved moved to London. We had the Gulf War, the Balkan War, the Chechen War, and America intervened in Somalia. Civil wars broke out in Uganda and Liberia and Georgia, and Azerbaijan fought Armenia. And the hit songs still carried on about love. And men and women kept on having babies and going to marriage counsellors and therapists and getting divorced. Personally I never felt that any of this had anything to do with me. I was holding my breath all the time, so to speak, waiting for my cue, waiting for the words that should be spoken before I came out on stage from behind the curtain and joined the action. But life went on and on, the words weren't spoken, and the years piled up like dirt and dead leaves in a gutter. One day, Thursday 20 June 1996, to be precise, I decided that this had to come to an end one way or another, either a bad end or one that I couldn't really imagine. And I went to a travel agency and bought myself an air ticket to London, the way someone else might buy a rope.

So now I'm sitting in this plane. In a window seat. The aisle seat is occupied by a young man in an eye-catching pale-blue suit. He's leafing through a free copy of a weekly magazine. Luckily the seat between us is empty, or perhaps the flight attendants made sure it would be. Because I now weigh a hundred and seven kilos, and my thighs, stuffed into their khaki fabric casing, are spilling out under the arm-rests and on to the next seat. So no one could sit there anyway. I hate my legs. I wish they were different. It would be a lot easier going to see someone you love who doesn't love you back if you had slim legs. Not that I think they'd change his feelings for me all of a sudden, but if I had slim legs I could bear not being loved better. A female voice over the loudspeaker, backed up by a flight attendant doing a mime act, explains that in the unlikely event of a sudden loss of pressure we should pull the oxygen masks towards us like *this*, and fit them over our mouths and noses before helping our clumsier fellow passengers to get the elastic strap over their own ears. The elegant woman in the row ahead of me is showing her elegant daughter a photo in *Vogue*. She's wearing an old-rose suit jacket with a green chiffon scarf. I imagine some colour consultant palmed it off on her. Her blonde hair is cut in a crazily asymmetrical style, stopping just above her ear to the left of her parting and coming down to her chin on the other side of her head. Of course the long side keeps falling into her eyes, so she has to push it back with her forefinger as she reads. Her gazelle-like daughter bends over the magazine. Behind me three men are discussing Paul Gascoigne at the tops of their voices. I bet they're on their way to the semi-final of the European Championship in London – England versus Germany. They're the kind of men I hate most, the kind who sit in front of the TV making faces and yelling, 'Come on, shoot! *Shoot!*' I like Paul Gascoigne, though. He reminds me of that racehorse Meteor, the steeplechaser. Meteor was

3

surprisingly overweight for a top athlete too, slow and undisciplined, but he left all the others standing. The football fans behind me are making more digs at Gascoigne. Then they laugh stupidly, agreeing with each other, so they never get to hear where the life-jackets are and how to reach the emergency exits in a hurry. In the unlikely event of our having to ditch in the English Channel they'll run the wrong way, trampling all over the elegant woman and her daughter, getting tangled up with each other's legs and blocking all the escape routes, while I have to sit jammed into my window seat, watching the water inexorably rise up the pane outside.

We taxi to the runway, soft music floats down from the roof, scraps of melody that are immediately blotted out again by assorted engine noises. It's hard to make out what the music is, but anyway it's not the kind you'd want to be the last thing you heard before dying in a plane crash. In my view 'No Milk Today' by Herman's Hermits would be about right. The Hermits start very sadly, rising to melancholy excitement as the wing catches fire, and in the midst of the most dreadful despair – strings, the whole works – you suddenly hear the pointlessly hopeful ringing of a bell.

It may not sound like it, but I really like flying. I consider myself amazingly lucky to be living at the end of a century that's invented so many miraculous machines. No one from my own cultural background would particularly envy me my air ticket or my old mail-order TV set. But a mediaeval ruler would have given half his kingdom to be in my place now.

A blue and green map appears on the screen, with a little white plane moving jerkily along a dotted line running from Hamburg (marked in red) to London (also marked in red). The scraps of music break off entirely. Instead of them, the captain addresses us over the loudspeakers. His name is

4

Hermann Kahr or Tahr, and before wishing us a pleasant flight Captain K. mentions the favourable wind conditions and says the temperature here in Hamburg is eighteen degrees. Well, what he actually says is: 'The temperature here in Hamburg at present is eighteen degrees Celsius, but the wind-chill factor makes it feel more like sixteen degrees.' He's probably picked it up from TV, this silly new habit of distinguishing between the real temperature and what the wind-chill factor does to it. As if everyone feels the same to the exact degree Celsius. You could perfectly well apply the same distinction to other areas of life: statistical risk of crashing in this plane one in ten million; mind-chill risk one in twenty. They calculate the statistical risk from this airline's accident record, the safety standards at Hamburg Fuhlsbüttel and London Heathrow airports, and the fact that we have to fly over water. The mind-chill risk that I personally feel is calculated from my misgivings about the whole idea of this trip, my suspicions of Fate in general, and films I've seen. While the plane drones on, gathering thrust, I run my favourite scene from *Alive* through my head. *Alive* is a film about a real-life air accident when a rugger team from Uruguay crashed in the Andes. Some of the players survived and had to stick it out for seventy days in the icy cold before they were found. They ended up shaving flesh off the frozen corpses of their fellow passengers with shards of broken glass, and then eating it. In the film one of the survivors sets out to fetch help and asks the others to leave cutting up his dead mother till last. But I'm not thinking of that scene now, I'm thinking of an earlier one, when the plane crashes into a mountainside and breaks apart in the middle. The front part races on through the air without wings, and instead of the engines all you suddenly hear is the hissing, howling airflow.

The passengers, strapped in, are rigid, clinging to their seats, the skin of their faces is flapping, their gums are bared, there's this huge gaping hole behind them, their badly stowed hand baggage whirls through the air, the slipstream tears out the rows of seats at the back of the plane one by one, and the real risk and the mind-chill risk are exactly the same.

We're racing down the runway. The pale-blue young man beside me is ostentatiously reading the business section of his paper. As a frequent flyer, he's trying to let us know that he's not impressed by any of this. And it probably really doesn't impress the poor guy any more. We've left the ground behind us. We're airborne. We're actually airborne. Twenty-eight per cent of all air accidents happen while the plane is gaining height.

My first boyfriend was called Axel Vollauf. Axel was fair-haired and thin, with big round eyes that were always wide open, as if he'd once had to watch a massacre, or a meteorite hitting the earth, and the look on his face had stayed put ever since. Our love affair was cheerful and unspectacular. We were in the same class and we walked to school in the mornings hand in hand, Axel in his brown anorak and the yellow bobble hat provided by the Road Safety organisa-tion, me in a dark-blue blazer with an embroidered crest on the breast pocket. The crest included my initial, an ornate A for Anne. I'd lost my Road Safety headscarf the day after I started school. We always met and parted at the same road junction, where we made a date for the afternoon, which we spent under a rhododendron bush in my parents' garden. I had opened an animal hospital on the mossy ground under-neath the rhododendron, in dappled sun and shade. At first I ran it on my own. I was both doctor and nurse, while Axel just watched. Then he wanted to be a doctor too, and when he was a doctor he said I had to give up one of my careers. 'You can't be a nurse *and* a doctor,' said Axel, fixing his large eyes on me. I decided to abandon the medical profession so that I could still wear my nurse's cap. It made no difference to our division of labour. I performed the operations, because they made Axel feel sick, and Axel assisted me as he had before and tidied the mossy carpet of the hospital ward. The beds were made of orange cigarette packets. We had to keep replacing them because they soon got soggy with the overnight dew and the dampness of our patients. The beds were for frogs. Barnstedt had an unusually large frog population. They hopped up from the still undeveloped water-meadows beyond the gardens and flung themselves straight at the brand-new motor-mowers chugging across the newly laid turf of our neighbours' lawns. Not a house in our street was more than five years old. People were building like crazy, creating durable assets for themselves, laying the foundations of a happy family life and keeping the grass cut short. They ran up debts and trusted that they and the economy would both go on getting more and more prosperous. Sometimes my mother told my brother and sister and me how the neighbours opposite had lunched on a single sausage every day for two years, so as to save money to build their house. Herr Lange ate two-thirds of the sausage and his wife ate the rest. And if my mother embarked on the story of this shared sausage she inevitably went on to tell us how our father had built our house himself.

'Your father has held every brick of this house in his hands – every single brick,' she said.

We were the most efficient nation in the world. That's why

7

other nations hated and envied us. The houses we built all had fences, a square, glazed-brick patio by the front door, and a panoramic window at the back. Small birds broke their necks flying into it.

My hospital had a bed for birds too: a cigar box which I had upholstered with a handkerchief and a mattress made from a chocolate box. The frogs slept on grass.

Axel and I spent most afternoons there, waiting. While we waited we listened to each other's chests, hit each other's knees with the rubber hammer, and got ready for the next operation. We set out the plastic scalpel, toy syringe and cotton-wool buds on an orange box, but the only things we actually used – a real pair of scissors and a roll of sticky tape – stayed hidden in my medical bag until we needed them. I'd had to steal them from my mother's kitchen drawer because I wasn't allowed to use sharp scissors by myself yet, and sticky tape was so expensive. My father lay on a garden recliner on the terrace, asleep. He had a mysterious job which I didn't understand, and which had no proper name. At school, when we had to say what our fathers did, I didn't know. But anyway mine only had to work until early in the afternoon. Then, if the weather was fine enough, he would pick up his folding recliner, go round behind the house he had built himself, smoke Ernte 23 cigarettes and fall asleep over the *Hamburger Abendblatt* while the sun tanned him browner and browner. He would begin this routine in March, putting on shorts while other people were still wearing gloves, and he followed it every afternoon and weekend of good weather, all through the spring and summer and right into the autumn. He slept lightly, a restless sleep. Like us, my father was waiting for the sound of a motor-mower. He hated motorised lawn-mowers. He hated the noise they made. The first thing you heard was an unsuccessful attempt to start the mower, the brief stuttering of an engine that immediately cut out again, and often a second and third attempt before the regular droning noise began, whereupon my father would jump up, prowl along his fence and peer over hedges, conifers and rhododendrons to see who the culprit was this time.

'Weigoni,' he snorted, folding his arms over his chest. 'It's in the Weigonis' garden. People aren't supposed to mow their lawns at lunchtime.'

Then I would put my nurse's cap on and pick up the medical bag. Axel followed me, carrying a little wicker basket. Most of the gardens had no fences between them and the undeveloped water-meadows beyond, so we could move from neighbour to neighbour without any difficulty. Herr Weigoni knew what we wanted. He nodded to us over his droning mower as it emitted fumes, and made an inviting gesture which meant we were welcome to search the section of lawn he had just been mowing for injured frogs. We weren't allowed to walk in front of the lawn-mower and rescue the frogs first. Herr Weigoni was afraid we might get our feet caught in the blades. Axel held the basket and I put the frogs in it, frogs without arms and legs, big fat frogs with greyish intestines bulging out of their stomachs, and arms and legs without any frogs attached. When we got back to my parents' garden our basket was full and Herr Weigoni was still mowing. The smell of cut grass and petrol filled the air. By now my father had taken refuge indoors, but he came out again every ten minutes to see if the noise had stopped. Axel tipped our patients out on the orange box and counted the limbs we had found. I dealt with the stomach wounds first. Since the frogs with stomach wounds had stopped moving they were the easiest to treat. I stuffed their intestines back into the stomach cavities.

'I could never do that,' Axel always said in tones of mingled admiration and disgust, pulling a length of sticky tape off the roll and holding it out so that I could cut it. I stuck the tape over the wound and put the patient in one of the orange beds. The wound would burst open again at once, letting a transparent fluid seep out. Sticky tape didn't stick well to the frogs' damp skins. I would put another strip over it and then pick up the next frog. The patients with amputated arms and legs were wriggling like crazy. I seldom managed to stick their limbs back on, so I just put the frogs to bed. They struggled out again at once and limped off under the rhododendron with any legs they still had. We didn't bother them any more after that, we just put the chopped-off legs, hands and feet under the bush in case the frogs wanted to come back for them later. This was the frustrating part of our hospital work: by next morning all the patients had either made their getaway or were dead. I don't remember that we ever cured a single one of them.

It wasn't just my father with his lawn-mowers – all of us in our family had something we couldn't stand. My mother hated shrill female voices. More precisely, it was probably the voice of my grandmother who lived in the partly converted loft of our house that she hated. But she never said so straight out. All she said was:

'Those screeching voices, I just can't bear screeching female voices. How's anyone supposed to work with that racket going on?'

My granny couldn't stand the noise of the men who came into her little loft bedroom by night. She said men came up there night after night in secret, pulled her hair out, took the lids off her saucepans and banged them on her tiled kitchen walls. The most startling part of this story, perhaps, was the fact that my granny didn't have any saucepans, or any kitchen either. She didn't cook for herself at all, but ate downstairs with us.

My elder sister hated the twittering of birds. When she was doing her homework, using crayons in different shades to colour in the rivers and ranges of hills on a map, or whatever other homework they gave her in Class 4, she would suddenly chuck her crayons on the floor and say crossly: 'Those wretched birds! How am I expected to work? They keep screeching the whole time.' My sister hated not just the twittering of birds but any kind of noise that I made too.

Personally, to this day I can't stand the sound of someone squeezing a sachet of baking powder and rubbing it until it squeaks, not that it has made a vast difference to my life. My little brother was the only member of the family who didn't hate a particular noise. What he couldn't stand was the feel of pearl buttons. My mother always had to cut all the buttons off his pyjamas and sew up the places that were supposed to be buttoned. However, he loved coins. He had a money-box that my father had brought back from a conference in Finland. It was a small, transparent plastic globe with a key to open its base, so my brother could keep tipping out his coins and counting them. When he had saved up enough small change my father swapped it for a shiny Deutschmark, which my brother kept in a cardboard box under his bed. He used to take the box out every evening, kiss and stroke his Deutschmark, and then put it back in the cardboard box.

One evening, after a long, strenuous afternoon at the frogs' hospital, I came back to the room where we children slept, hung my medical bag up on the Snow White coat-rack, and saw my little brother putting his arm through the bars of his cot and fishing about for the box with his shiny coin in it. He couldn't reach it, because when she was polishing the floor my mother had pushed it right up against the wall. My brother was five, but he still slept in a barred cot. He thrashed about so much in his sleep that he would have fallen out of an ordinary bed. Now he began howling.

'My money, I want my money!' he bawled. My sister came in. The room belonged to all three of us, my sister, my brother and me. My sister got down flat on the floor, pushed off with her hands and slithered under his cot. She was wearing a red check dress that my mother had made from the same material as mine; the fabric slid well on the polished lino. When she emerged again she raised her chest off the floor and handed my brother the box. He took out his Deutschmark, stroked it, and then polished it on one corner of his pillow. My sister stayed on the floor, pushing and pulling herself forward, sliding all over the room on her stomach. 'I'm a crocodile,' she said! 'Watch out! I'm a fast, dangerous crocodile.'

She zoomed in under my bed. We slept in a bunk bed, with my sister on top and me underneath, staring up at a mattress protector with a pattern of Eskimo, Indian, African and Chinese children before I went to sleep. I heard my sister thumping about under the bed, and then she pushed herself off from the wall with her feet and shot out of the darkness again, emerging right in front of me. She was holding the shoebox where I kept my secret treasures. Before I could stop her, she opened it and took out a Matchbox car.

'Where did you get that? You stole it.'

'No, I didn't,' I said. 'Holger Deshusses gave it to me.'

Holger Deshusses was a boy who lived near us. No one could pronounce his family's surname properly, not even the grown-ups. We all said 'Dee-sus'. It had been child's play to steal that car. Easy-peasy, as we used to say. The Matchbox car was a totally inconspicuous grey Opel which Holger Deshusses kept with zillions of other toy cars in a detergent drum covered with wallpaper. When Holger had gone into the bathroom with my sister, leaving me alone in his room, I had tucked the Opel into my knickers and smoothed my dress down over it. I hadn't been silly enough to take something showy, like a police car or a fire engine, or the Batmobile with the circular saw that zapped out of the radiator grille. No one would ever have noticed that the Opel was missing.

'You're lying,' said my sister. 'I'm going to go up to Holger Deshusses with you at school tomorrow and ask him. And you just watch out if you're lying!'

I couldn't get to sleep for ages that evening, and I didn't feel good when I woke up in the morning either. I immediately remembered the confrontation threatening me. I hoped my sister would have forgotten the whole thing overnight, and I didn't look at her as I stood beside her in the bathroom, cleaning my teeth in slow motion and finally picking up the comb. The comb was oily with birch water, a lotion that my father used to stop his hair falling out. Only the larger teeth of the comb were anywhere near dry. I dawdled until my mother came in and helped me to wash, because my granny was waiting outside the door. When my parents built their house in the later years of the German economic miracle, they had fitted it out with three children and a grandmother but only one bathroom. While my mother wiped a flannel over my outstretched arms, my sister stood on a child's chair beside me, looking at herself in the mirror. She twisted and turned, and then told me: 'My bottom looks like an apple. Yours looks like a squidgy bread roll.'

I turned my head and inspected my bottom. It looked as unattractive as I'd expected. Like a squidgy bread roll. My sister got down from the chair, looked sternly at me and said: 'We'll be seeing Holger Deshusses soon.'

'I don't feel well,' I told my mother. 'Something hurts. A kind of a prickly feeling. Somewhere there.' I pointed at my stomach. 'I think I've got a temperature.'

My mother put her hand on my forehead. 'No, you haven't,' she said, removing it.

'Yes, I have!' I was almost screaming. 'Feel it again!'

She put her hand back on my forehead. I sent a wave of heat surging up from my stomach to my head.

'Good heavens, so you have! A high one, too! You're going straight back to bed.'

I dragged myself back to our room, put my nightie on again and crept under the covers, which were still warm. I watched my little brother, who was lying in his cot and rubbing the corner of his pillow over the place between his mouth and his nose. My sister and my mother came in, and my sister took a pair of red terry-towelling knickers off the table and put them on her apple-shaped bottom. My mother was holding a jar of Nivea. She sat down on the bed beside me and dipped the end of a thermometer into it.

'Turn over on your tummy!'

I had a temperature of thirty-nine degrees. I concentrated hard on keeping it up until the doctor came. When he finally arrived I was absolutely exhausted by the effort. The doctor looked inside my mouth.

'It's measles,' he said. My mother drew the curtains.

Measles meant that Holger Deshusses wouldn't be able to come into our room for days. And by then everyone would have forgotten all about the Matchbox car. From now on I was safe. Not just safe from Holger Deshusses, but safe for all time. Whenever anything went wrong I could simply be ill. Really ill, seriously, obviously ill – not just a slight temperature and a faked tummy-pain. I could catch measles, German measles, chicken-pox, scarlet fever, all solely by will-power. A wonderful life lay ahead of me. Because when I was ill I was in clover. Measles meant a new puzzle book, biscuits and Sunkist in bed, and a cowbell beside me. I had only to ring the bell to bring my mother running to fetch me anything else I wanted. Measles meant that the bird's nest with the tiny egg which Uncle Horst had given the whole family to look at was put beside my bed. Uncle Horst was my father's elder brother, a dried-up bachelor who 'lived off Social Security' in a tiny wooden house on an allotment complex. Visits to him were always boring. He had no radio or television. My father had to write out his lottery ticket for him, and every time Uncle Horst said, 'What a daft set of numbers, nobody would ever think of them!'

However, he was very glad of the cigarettes my father brought him, and he used to give me the empty packets from our previous visit. Sometimes we sat outside in the allotment garden, and Uncle Horst told us what the birdsongs were. 'Listen, that's a coal tit – twit-tweet twit-tweet. And there's a blue tit – twee-twee-too-too-too.'

He imitated the birds very badly, as if he were reading out

their cries from one of his bird books. When we left he always had a present for us: a big fir cone, the bone of a deer, a mummified toad (my mother threw that one in the garbage as soon as we were home), and the last time it had been the bird's nest, which was placed beside my sickbed.

The measles also meant that Axel, who had already had them, came visiting and brought me a bunch of parrot tulips splashed with red and yellow. Parrot tulips are the most beautiful flowers in the world, the true flowers of love. But since most people don't know anything about love they buy red roses instead. My mother put the parrot tulips in a vase and stood them on the child's chair where the nest had been. It had been taken away again because I'd tried to hatch the egg. It broke, and I'd got yolk and the tiny bird embryo all over my pyjamas. Axel sat down on the edge of my bed and took two rubber animals the size of five-pfennig pieces out of his trouser pocket. He knew I collected rubber animals.

'Oh, great – the giant squid!' I said, holding it up to the light. The giant squid was black and curiously two-dimensional, which made it look even scarier.

'And the sheep,' said Axel. I hadn't got the sheep yet either.

Axel visited me every day. He persuaded my mother to bring the radiogram up from the living-room to the children's bedroom and let us have an album full of singles. The radiogram was a rectangular wooden box on thin splayed legs. Its round loudspeaker was hidden behind a kind of woven mat, but you could feel it, and the graduated radio frequencies glowed green. One of my parents' photograph albums contains a picture of my father with a small sombrero on the back of his head, sitting in front of this radiogram holding a record in his fingertips. He's smiling at the camera, and his hair – much thicker then – was shiny with the birch water. My mother is standing behind him and slightly to one side, with her arms already held at an angle as if she were about to launch into a dance. She's wearing Capri pants and a roll-neck sweater, and she looks stunning. The strange young man with his arm round her shoulders evidently thinks so too. They're having a pretty good party, all of them relaxed and fooling around. They really seem to be having fun. The photo dates from when my parents were already married but didn't have any children yet.

Axel took six singles out of the album, stacked them on the spindle in the middle of the turntable, and held the arm of the player above them. The radiogram worked by letting one disk drop and playing it, after which the next dropped on top of the first, so we could listen to all of them one by one without interruption. Then we discussed which we liked best and played it again. Our first winner was Bill Ramsey's 'Pigalle', second time round we chose 'Banjo Boy' by Jan and Kjeld from the Netherlands, and the third time it was 'Café Oriental', with Bill Ramsey again. Bill Ramsey was the tops anyway. Sometimes my brother and sister joined us to listen to the hit parade. My mother said they might just as well catch my measles so that we could get it over with 'in one fell swoop'. But I liked it better when Axel and I were deciding on the winner by ourselves. We nearly always felt the same. When I was better we went back to spending our afternoons under the rhododendron. My father sometimes took us and my brother and sister to the nearby pool. He always warned us never to jump into 'unknown waters', and especially not to dive in head first.

'Always make sure how deep the water is before you jump in,' he said. 'The Boberg hospital is full of people who dived into shallow water. Paraplegics now, all of them.'

It was the summer when the Americans landed on the moon, and I remember the whole family sitting in the living-room with the curtains drawn, even though the sun was shining outside. Usually my brother and sister and I tried in vain to get permission to watch TV on sunny afternoons. My father was seeing the whole thing for the second time round. The television picture looked grainy. Sometimes it twitched, like when my father tried tuning in to East German TV. An astronaut climbed very slowly down a ladder in his white suit. Then the picture froze and someone explained something, and then you saw information charts that I didn't understand. I didn't think it was particularly exciting. I was only seven, so most things were new to me, even my parents' fifties records. I'd only just learned at school that there was a God who was responsible for everything. No one at home had mentioned it. I accepted God's existence as I accepted the existence of aircraft, telephones and running hot water. I think seven is an age when you can't afford to be over-impressed by new experiences. What really upset me was that our teacher said animals had no souls. I liked animals. Animals were Professor Grzimek's little friends that he brought into the TV studio with him. Funny monkeys, or thin cheetahs that never kept still, and as a special treat I was allowed to stay up after eight o'clock to watch them. I didn't see why they shouldn't have souls.

I took no interest in space flight until Shell filling stations began giving away medallions. You collected them and fitted them into sockets on a card. The card showed the rocket that had put Apollo 11 into orbit round the moon, with a caption saying: 'The Conquest of the Sky'. Every time my father filled the car up he got a little envelope with a medallion in it. He really brought the medallions home for my brother, but my brother sold them to me for ten pfennigs each, and I collected them instead. It was my first serious collection, by which I mean that I wanted the whole set. When I collected the rubber animals I was only aiming to get a lot of them, as many dangerous and unusual animals as possible. In the end I was short of only two in the medallion collection, Apollo 8 and J. Alcock. On the other hand I had three Charles A. Lindberghs. I had to buy the medallions from my brother sight unseen every time. He opened the envelopes himself in advance, but he didn't let me look inside until I'd paid. I never did get the two I still needed. The series was discontinued, and I couldn't swap with Axel, who had begun a Shell medallions collection at the same time out of loyalty to me, because by then we weren't friends any more.

As the year went on it got too cold to go swimming, the animal hospital had been obliged to close down for lack of patients, and Axel and I played indoors. Oddly enough, we almost always played at my house. It was very unusual for us to go round to Axel's, although there would have been much more space there. He was an only child. Instead, we fought so fiercely with my brother and sister for space in the room I shared with them that my mother finally told us to build Lego partitions, and we used them to divide the floor of the room into three large sections. Crossing anti-sibling ramparts a few centimetres high always caused a lot of loud shouting. But it wasn't these arguments that set my family against Axel – on the contrary. I don't remember just how it began, but at some point Axel developed the habit of flinging himself unexpectedly at people. At first he only did it to me. He would attack me at least twice a day, clinging tightly to my neck until I was breathless. It got on my nerves. But I put up with it because I was fond of him, and waited for him to let go of his own accord. Then he started rushing at my sister and my mother too, flinging his arms round their waists, hanging on tight and pressing his head against their hips, and he could be shaken off only by force. My sister in particular hated it.

'Stop it, you idiot,' she shouted, hitting him on the head with her fist, 'stop it this minute!' Which only made Axel cling tighter. Even my mother was delivered up more or less helpless to his attacks.

'If you don't stop this you can't come here any more,' she told Axel one day, after detaching his arms from her hips with difficulty. Axel opened his big eyes even wider, rushed straight at one of her legs and clutched it so fiercely that my mother almost fell over.

That evening she had a private word with me.

'Look, tell your friend Axel to stop it. It's getting to be too much. Every time I set eyes on him I'm afraid he'll rush me. I hardly dare turn my back.'

But however cautiously you broached the subject to Axel, the only result was that he silently widened his eyes and rushed at you again. By now he was hanging round my neck at least five times a day, and it was with less and less enthusiasm that I saw him turn up earlier and earlier.

One day we were just sitting down to lunch when the doorbell rang. All eyes were immediately turned reproachfully on me, and my father, who always came home from work at about one-thirty and therefore had lunch with us, said, 'Oh God, it's Saucer-Eyes! Already!'

'Let's just not open the door,' suggested my mother, serving out the chops. Her husband got a whole chop and her mother-in-law and children half a chop each. She herself ate only vegetables and potatoes. She said she didn't especially like meat. The doorbell rang again.

'It's that lad. That wild little lad's here again,' said my granny in her high-pitched voice. When Axel turned up she usually took refuge in her room in the loft, although he hadn't attacked her yet.

'Does he have to come every day?' asked my sister.

Only my little brother crowed happily: 'Saucer-Eyes! Saucer-Eyes!' and spilled his canned peas on the Formica table top.

'Ssh,' said my mother, and then turned to my father. 'Don't keep calling him Saucer-Eyes. The children will copy you.'

My granny took a damp dishcloth out of her smock pocket and swept the peas up with it. The cloth was made of greyish-brown fabric, and you didn't have to put your nose especially close to catch its revolting smell. My sister always called it 'the Plague cloth'. Anything wiped by the Plague cloth smelled as revolting as the cloth itself. My granny carefully wrapped the peas in the cloth and put it back in the pocket of her green and orange flowered smock. Axel was now ringing the bell frantically. My sister tried to swap her half chop for mine, because I had the bit with the bone, but I noticed in time and pushed my plate away from her, sending another tidal wave of peas over the table.

'Oh, for heaven's sake, what are you two doing? You'll have to go and eat your lunch in the lavatory!' cried my mother through the ringing of the doorbell. She was always making this threat, but she never put it into practice. I didn't think the idea of eating alone in the lavatory was so bad. My granny took the Plague cloth out again and gathered up more peas to rot away in her smock. Then the ringing stopped, my mother smiled with relief, and we enjoyed the silence for a moment. I stuck my feet behind the legs of my chair, and we began to eat. All of a sudden my father, who could see into the garden from where he was sitting, choked and waved his fork in that direction, coughing. We all turned our heads to the picture window. There stood Axel Vollauf, pressing his face to the glass and goggling in at us with eyes the size of mill-wheels. I quickly turned away again and pretended to be studying the canned vegetables on my plate.

'Oh, let him in before he smears the whole window up,' sighed my mother. My sister punched me on the arm and hissed, 'Go on, get up! It's you Saucer-Eyes wants to see.'

'Saucer-Eyes, Saucer-Eyes!' crowed my little brother.

Many, many years later my therapist told me about an educational ruse apparently employed by the Eskimos to teach their children to keep away from the dangerous edge of the ice. As soon as an Eskimo child is at all capable of reasoning, the whole village comes together. The child's mother or father says, 'Now then, go over to the edge of the ice where the open sea begins.' The child marches off with everyone watching, feeling flattered by this sudden attention. But no sooner does he or she reach the danger zone than all the Eskimos begin laughing. The child stops, looks round in confusion, maybe hesitates, wondering whether to laugh too or not. But then he realises that he has fallen for a trick, and all the others are laughing at his stupidity. So he stands there on the edge of the ice, crying, and the others don't stop laughing until the child has left the dangerous area again. My therapist claimed that, once humiliated in that way, an Eskimo child never willingly goes near the edge of the ice again, and said this kind of education works better than any stern prohibition. I don't know if the tale is true. It could be just another story thought up by the kind of people who believe that other races have a better fundamental grasp of the meaning of life. Perhaps the Eskimos really all just sit around playing bingo while their children chuck themselves into the Arctic Ocean by the dozen. As for the method itself, however, I haven't the slightest doubt that it works.

When Axel flung his arms round my neck that afternoon and clung tight, half strangling me in the process as usual, I couldn't take any more of it. My brother and sister were there too, watching. I immediately hit out, punched him in the stomach, kicked his shin and finally pushed him to the floor.

'Go away!' I shouted at him. 'You just go away! I hate you! I never want to see you again!'

And I meant it. Axel went all green in the face. I may have hit him in the stomach too hard. He blinked, his eyes suddenly weren't wide open and large any more, they looked quite small, with naked, soft albino lids. Then he began crying; his nose ran and he snuffled and wiped his face with his sleeve, he got up, pushed me aside, and ran out of the room and into the corridor without making the slightest attempt to cling to anyone. As his crying rose to an ever shriller screeching and bawling, he snatched his brown anorak off the coat-rack and stuffed his feet into his shoes. My mother came out of the kitchen asking what the matter was now. Axel flung the front door open and ran out, with his shoelaces untied and his anorak half on. Still screeching and bellowing. My brother and sister and I watched him go.

'I hope I never see you again!' shouted my little brother.

At first it was very nice to be rid of Axel. It was nice not to attract those reproachful looks when there was a ring at the front door, and it was nice not to be throttled. It was nice to go to school alone and play with other children at last.

Except that I wasn't nearly as good at playing with other children. We did exactly the same things as I'd done with Axel, we built Lego houses and staged road accidents with Matchbox cars, we fed Steiff teddy bears with jam or tied their arms behind their backs. But it wasn't the same. In the end I got ill every time a child from my class wanted to play with me after school. Sometimes I went to the trouble of being really ill, sometimes I just pretended. From then on I sat in my grandmother's musty-smelling attic room in the afternoons and evenings. Because my granny had brought her own TV set with her when she moved in with us, and now she needed someone to change channels for her, or adjust the aerial, or hit the set when the picture slipped. Recently she'd been finding it difficult to get out of her chair, and every time I had to hit the set or adjust the aerial I got something to put in the chewing-gum machine. I could watch TV that way without being rationed by my mother, too. Unfortunately my granny never took any interest in whether Flipper, who was caught in a fishing-net with a mine, could be freed before it hit a rock; she just watched sports programmes and feature films with a lot of singing and telephoning in them. The men telephoned in a perfectly normal way, but the women in these films always clutched the receiver with both hands. Or if they were black-haired or particularly elegant, one of their hands toyed with the cable. My grandmother liked operettas and musical comedies even better than these telephone musicals. Truly awful. Whenever it seemed as if the plot was about to get going at last, the circus princess or the czardas princess would begin to sing. And when Marika Rökk started swaying her hips back and forth, I knew: here comes the break. Then I used to leaf through the *Neue Post* or *The Best of Reader's Digest*, which were on my granny's table. I always read the *Neue Post* starting from the back. First the back page with the ads for sauna outfits and bra pads and slimming girdles and a kind of foil to stick over your black and white TV to make it into a colour set. Then I read the funnies, and then I leafed through all the boring reports until I reached the middle of the paper, where there was a double spread of miscellaneous news items, things that children had said, stories about animals and so on. My favourite section was headed: 'Parents Be On Your Guard! Seduction on the Way to School'. That danger lurked everywhere. A girl was attacked because she'd been putting on lipstick on the bus. It turned out all right, and the girl vowed never to make herself up in public again. *The Best of Reader's Digest* was full of horror stories too, the kind where someone lost his whole bottom jaw just because he was careless enough to chew a blade of grass. Because if your gums bleed, the bacteria on a blade of grass can get right into your jawbone.

When the czardas princess had finished singing there'd be a bit more of the story again, nothing like enough, and along came the next song. My granny liked the singing, but then my granny didn't have all her marbles. Sometimes she sang along in her tuneless, high-pitched voice, and when the sports programmes were on she always claimed that she could do it all just as well. Even when Pele shot his thousandth goal she said, 'I can do that too.'

Once, when I'd switched the TV on for my granny and the tube had warmed up enough for a picture to show, neither sportsmen nor singing telephonists appeared on the screen, but men with long hair down to their waists playing their guitars and almost falling over backwards. A sweaty man in an undershirt was bashing his drums.

'Oh, those stupid old Beatles – quick, change channels,'

piped my grandmother. The Beatles were the only modern band whose name even I had heard of. And now I knew what they looked like too. It always took some time for anything modern to reach Barnstedt. Officially we were part of Hamburg, but in morals, modes and music we lagged five to ten years behind. Our most important if not our only link with the present day was TV. It took me years to discover that the Beatles didn't play heavy metal.

Unfortunately my parents and brother and sister didn't seem as grateful to me for sacrificing Axel for them as I thought they should have been. My sister went on teasing me about him, only now she did it in the past tense.

'You were in love with Saucer-Eyes, you were madly in love with him,' she claimed. Holger Deshusses was standing around.

'No,' I shouted. 'I don't love anyone. I never will! Ever!'

My father wouldn't give me a dog for my birthday. He said dogs tied you down, they meant you couldn't go away whenever and wherever you liked. Although so far we'd only been away once, to Denmark. The fact was that my father had been in a trap for ages. He had these three children, and because of them he couldn't afford holidays in Italy or Spain, only rainy stays by the North Sea. He was as tied down as anyone could possibly be. I thought that if I wished for a dog hard enough my father would give me one in the end. If I promised not to invite school friends to my birthday party any more, my parents would realise that I deserved a dog.

Then my birthday came, and with it my presents. Chocolate from my brother and sister, pink woolly knickers and two half-empty packets of biscuits from my confused grandmother, dog books and a soft toy dog from my parents. I pretended to be pleased. It wasn't actually a law set in stone, but deep inside me I knew that my most important task in life was to sense what other people expected of me. So I hugged the soft toy dog enthusiastically, feeling choked with disappointment. Perhaps my parents weren't going to give me the real dog till the afternoon, when all the guests were there and could see how pleased I was. The surprise would work even better then, when I wasn't expecting it any more. In the afternoon Granny Two came, and Uncle Horst, and a woman who used to work with my mother, an old lady who always gave you sets of underwear. Granny Two gave me a book of fairy tales and Uncle Horst gave me a box of *langues de chat*. No dog. But a dog was still possible. It was possible that my father would suddenly get to his feet and go out, with a mysterious grin on his face. It was possible that he'd suddenly come back into the living-room with a little basket under his arm. And there'd be a huge bow tied to the basket, so that I couldn't see what was in it at first. Only at the last moment would I see the little dog. Or perhaps I'd suddenly hear barking and paws scrabbling. My parents would look at each other with a smile and tell me, 'Go and see what all that noise is in the cupboard.' That was another possibility. There'd be a sudden whining noise somewhere.

'Have some cream to help it down,' said my mother's old friend from work, putting a dollop of whipped cream on my slice of peach tart. All the others were already shovelling peach tart down. My grandmothers were making soft little clicking sounds as their cake forks tapped their false teeth. My father pushed his chair back and went out. I watched the door until he came back, but he'd only been to the lavatory. I stood up too, took my sweets and the book of fairy tales and retreated to the armchair in front of the TV set in the furthest corner of the living-room. I turned it so that its back was between me and the coffee table, and then I devoured the *langues de chat*, two marzipan pastries, and a bag of Haribo 2000s. While I ate I read the fairy tale about the flying trunk. Suddenly I noticed my mother's old friend from work standing beside me. She must have crept up when I wasn't looking.

'I don't believe it!' she cried, clapping her hands. 'Come over here, dear' – she meant my mother – 'and look at this little gourmet.'

My mother did come over, and the pair of them goggled at me. I had tipped the chair back so that I was reclining in it, looking up at them with my cheeks still full of liquorice. The empty packaging was heaped up beside the chair.

'A real little epicure!' crowed my mother's old friend from work again. She was wearing a heavy gold chain around her neck. It pushed her fat old flesh into a bulge.

'Yes, she likes to do that,' said my mother, laughing. I forced a grin, but I was perfectly well aware that what I was doing was better done without witnesses.

The afternoon passed too, and my mother laid the supper table. Perhaps the dog-breeder had been very busy all day, and my father couldn't fetch the dog until evening. The grannies, Uncle Horst and my mother's old friend from work stuffed themselves with Waldorf salad, and put small, dry, golden fish on their bread. My brother and sister quarrelled over the decorative toadstool, an egg with a cap made of half a tomato and dabs of mayonnaise. Then there was another schnapps for the grown-ups, and a few nuts on Chinese porcelain plates for everyone, and my father dragged the projector into the living-room to show his home movies. I hated them. There was a scene in almost every film with me crying. This time my father showed the swimming-pool scene. It had been taken three years earlier, but unfortunately you could still tell it was me. First you saw my brother and sister: athletic, cheerful, sun-tanned children in red swimsuits. They both jumped into the pool and came up like young sea-lions, spluttering and spitting out water. Then you saw me, white as a milk roll and flabby in my dark-blue swimming costume. I didn't so much jump in as drop in, and even that went wrong. I wriggled over the side of the pool on my bottom and then hung there in my swimming wings, screeching and red-faced. Disgustingly ugly and out of control. A totally repulsive child. My father had zoomed in on my face so that you got a good view of my scrunched-up eyes and my trembling, dribbling lips. The grannies and my mother's old friend from work laughed. They thought it was sweet.

'You were a rather weepy child,' said my mother. 'You get it from me. I was just the same.'

After the film show my father took Granny Two, Uncle Horst and my mother's old friend from work to the station. This was the last chance. It was only sensible not to fetch the dog until all the hustle and bustle of the birthday party was over.

But my father came back without any dog, and I put the books and chocolate and the toy dog away in the cupboard, took my old teddy bear, got into bed and held the duvet over my mouth until I fell asleep for lack of oxygen.

Of course there was still Christmas. I could pin my hopes on that. Christmas and all my birthdays to come. I was keeping an eye open for tell-tale signs now. Wasn't my mother buying an unusually large amount of meat? A couple of strangers walked down our road with a poodle. Maybe this was their way of secretly showing my parents their dog. A good trick, but of course I noticed all the same. If I managed to get all the way to school without treading on any of the cracks between the paving stones, I'd get the poodle. If I could finish all the crosswords in my puzzle magazine without leaving any blanks, if I could do my arithmetic homework within five minutes – no, make that eight – if I could manage to run this pin half-way into my arm – no, let's say two-thirds of the way – then I really would get a dog this time. But nothing that was within my control had the faintest effect on my life.

'Just a little one,' I begged, 'a tiny little Pekinese, and I'll look after it. Because I'm not playing with Axel any more.'

'No one's stopping you playing with Saucer-Eyes,' said my father.

Axel hadn't said a word to me since we parted. Or I to him. Although we sat only two desks apart at school, and were always bumping into each other at break, we sternly ignored one another. If we met on the way to school Axel quickened his pace while I slowed down, pretending that I had to tie my shoelace or wanted to look at something by the roadside. Then Axel increased his lead, until I was about twenty metres behind him. We kept this up until the end of Class 4. When he finally spoke to me again it was in PE.

I remember Physical Education in primary school as something cheerful and harmless at first. Little boys and girls ran around in a circle in dark-blue PE shorts and white shirts, while our class teacher, tall and beautiful Frau Müller – she was divorced, which was still thought worth mentioning at the time – played her tambourine. The blue and white PE outfits were school uniform; they had to be bought in a special shop and kept, with our gym shoes, in a musty-smelling black PE bag. The shoes didn't have to be any special shape or colour, but by tacit consent all the mothers bought blue trainers with white laces for their sons and black ballet shoes for their daughters. At first this distinction didn't matter. We did knee bends and bunny jumps, we played ring-a-ring-a-roses or jumping jacks, we threw balls and caught them, we skipped rope and rolled around on the floor of the gym. You could do that almost as well in ballet shoes as in proper shoes with laces. If my mother had equipped me with sensible footwear, and I was the only girl thus shod, I'd probably have complained bitterly. Things didn't get really uncomfortable until Class 3, when we started playing ball games and people were always standing on your feet. The worst was a war game called Dodge-Ball. Two teams – standing for two different nations – tried to wipe each other out by hitting their opponents with the ball. Anyone who was hit was Out and had to go to a prison camp behind the enemy lines. The boys' ambition was to land the ball on the girls in the thigh area as painfully as possible – and those were just the nice, gentle boys. The boys who were not so nice aimed to hit us 'right in the gob', as they put it. I'd have loved to pay them back, but like all the girls I wasn't strong enough. Some of us couldn't even throw far enough to hit anyone at all, even if we only aimed for other girls. If we were the target ourselves, most of us didn't even think seriously of getting away. We huddled together in a corner, waiting for the sharp pain that at the same time meant release, because then you were Out and didn't have to fear being hit any more. It was best, really, to be shot down right at the start. Except for one very athletic child called Steffi, none of us girls even tried to catch the ball. Our sole ambition was not to get hit in the face. Sometimes we screeched a bit, sometimes one of us shed tears, two pairs of glasses were broken, a girl once had to be taken to the doctor with concussion. In her innocence, Frau Müller was firmly convinced that these were just accidents which had happened 'in the heat of the moment', and before every PE lesson Margit Holst tied Jens Kleinschmidt's laces for him, because he still couldn't do it even though he was in Class 4. And then, during the game, he would aim exclusively at Margit.

One day, when I had been shot down – a direct and not very painful hit on my hip which wouldn't leave much more than a bruise – and I'd walked down the side of the playing field to the enemy's prison camp, I found a couple of girls and Axel already there. Axel and fat Helmut were the only boys who were sometimes shot down even earlier than the girls. Axel looked at me. Although the game was in progress again, he concentrated entirely on me. He watched me approaching. I felt nervous. For years he had quickly looked somewhere else if our eyes happened to meet, and I had done the same. I took care to stroll along as casually as possible, but I was painfully aware of every step, and every movement of my arms seemed wrong. Axel went on staring unblinkingly until I was right in front of him. He let his eyes wander down me, and asked in tones of revulsion, 'Why do you girls have thighs that wobble like that when you walk?'

It was like getting a medicine ball right in the gob.

Of course you don't lose your self-esteem all of a sudden just because a boy says something derogatory about the nature of connective tissue in females. You don't lose confidence in your appearance and your worth overnight. You lose it over a long period, gradually. While I was still thinking about thighs, girls' thighs in general and my own in particular, our class teacher had the idea of bringing bathroom scales to school to weigh all the pupils, write down their weights and turn the results into arithmetic exercises.

Who is the heaviest boy in the class?

What is the average weight of all the pupils?

Who is the second lightest girl?

Work out the difference between the heaviest girl and the lightest boy.

What is the average weight of the five heaviest girls?

I found out what I weighed for the first time. It was forty-two kilos, making me the second heaviest girl in the class. That was mainly because I was the second tallest. But I can't say now how tall I really was at the time. On the other hand, I still remember very precisely that I weighed forty-two kilos. And I remember that there was a girl who weighed only twenty-eight kilos.

Work out the difference between the second heaviest girl and the lightest girl in the class.

I'd have given anything to weigh twenty-eight kilos.

'If being so heavy bothers you, you'll just have to go on a diet,' said my mother, and the days when I had eaten happily, without stopping to think and without remorse, were gone for ever.

The decision to go on your first diet is an important, if not *the* most important, moment in a girl's life. At least, it's more significant than the greatly over-rated experience of losing your virginity. A kind of initiation rite, except that you don't emerge from it a mature woman, you have to keep starting from the beginning all over again. You're eleven or twelve, maybe only ten, when you realise that you simply cannot stay the way you are. From now on you'll try to be different and better – meaning thinner.

The PE lesson in which Axel made me self-conscious about my thighs was the last lesson that day. The class didn't disperse at once, but played around on a deserted building site near the school for a while. When Axel Vollauf, beaming, eager and sure of success, tried to take a pile of sand by storm, I seized my opportunity to push him so hard that he rolled all the way back down it. I didn't break his heart this time, only his collarbone.

The plane's wobbling, but we stopped climbing long ago, and we can't be coming in to land at Heathrow yet. It's just that the plane is wobbling. It would be dreadful to die now. I'd wish that I'd done more with my life, or at least that I'd had more fun. I'd wish I'd broken not just Axel Vollauf's collarbone but both his arms too. None of the passengers except for me are taking any notice of the wobble. So it can't really be so bad. The woman in front of me is offering her daughter liquorice sweets. They're eating perfectly normal Haribos. The 300-gram bag at DM 1.39 in Aldi. But this woman would never buy her Haribos at Aldi. The shop where she got them will be called something like Chocolate Heaven, and they'll have put the loose liquorice sweets into a cellophane bag with a little shovel for her. A hundred grams for DM 2.99. The woman is holding out the crackling bag. The daughter looks in the bag, and then she takes a single sweet, and after that her mother takes a single sweet, and puts the bag away in her handbag again. I'm astounded! They'll take the bag out again in half an hour's time, and then each of them will have another single liquorice sweet. If there's one thing I hate it's moderation and restraint. I hope to God I never end up like these well-disciplined cows. I'd rather be a drug addict. Or an alcoholic. I'd rather crawl in the gutter in my own vomit, drunk, than find myself opening a cellophane bag full of over-priced Haribos and taking just one liquorice out. I'd rather stay disastrously fat all my life, a total physical fiasco, the horror scenario in the mind of everyone who reads the Keep Fit For Fun pages. If only it wasn't for these legs that won't fit into any seat in a plane. I can't help it, but these legs just look so crappy.

My Walkman is at the bottom of my bag. I have to get all the tapes out first; I've brought six. They were compiled by six different men that I once went out with, and they're not all brand new. You learn more about a man by getting him to make a tape for you than by sleeping with him. This one, for instance, has a home-made cover. If you can say a tape has a cover. The man who gave it to me stuck a *Mad* magazine picture on it, showing hideous mutants with warts all over their necks. The card inside just has the names of the bands: Laibach, Sister of Mercy, Nick Cave, Lords of the New Church, Screaming Blue Messiahs, Snake Finger, Yello. The titles are missing and the names aren't in the right order either. If anyone asked the man who recorded this tape for me why they're in the wrong order, he'd say, 'It's obvious who's singing what.'

Or take this one, number two. It has 'home taping' written on it, and the cover consists of a magazine photo of Modern Talking. Of course that's supposed to show that there won't be anything by Modern Talking on it, only music that no one except the man who recorded it has ever heard of. He didn't write either the names of the bands or the titles of the songs on it. Nothing at all. I had to ask him what the fourth song on side two was, the live track with the guitar backing at the start. He said, 'What? What do you mean? I've no idea what you mean.' I had to hum him the tune before he told me. 'Oh, so that's what you're on about. It's Nation of Ulysses with "Shakedown".' And I could tell from his face that of course I'd asked about the most run-of-the-mill song of all, one he'd recorded just as a concession to my conventional taste, so I suddenly lost any wish to buy the Nation of Ulysses record.

The third tape has no home-made cover but it's beautifully written up. The left-hand side of the lined card lists the song titles in black, and the bands are on the right in red. The tape begins with 'The Belle of St Mark', by Sheila E. Dann, and then comes 'Midnight Man' by Flash and the Pan. That one isn't a song this man chose himself – I asked him to put it on the tape. He had to borrow the record from a friend to record it for me. This particular man usually listens to nothing but reggae, but he didn't tape his own favourite tracks for me. He didn't even try to impress. He chose the music he thought I'd like best. He's the man who loved me most of all. Unfortunately he's also the man who thought I'd like to listen to Mel Brooks's 'Hitler Rap'.

The fourth tape doesn't have a cover either, but it does have a title which is both a Bowie quotation and a declaration of love: 'I'm the king and you're the queen'. It consists entirely of David Bowie songs. This tape was from a man who thought he was the one who loved me most. All the tapes he ever recorded for me are of Bowie songs. Tape number five has a cover that presumably went wrong, because the man who gave it to me ended up colouring the card in completely with a black Edding pen. A black Edding pen is a favourite among men who make covers for tapes. Most of the music is recorded from the radio. Possibly because the man's record collection wasn't very up to date. Or possibly because of the super-cool presentation by the super-cool English radio station, which ended up on the tape as well rather too often. Anyway – musically it's one of my best compilations.

But the one I'm going to play now is number six, where the original card has been replaced by a piece of thick, pretty, Paisley-patterned paper. It may be off the cover of a mail-order catalogue, but you don't see the rug it could once have been, only the pattern. The words 'It's just a hell of a good time' are stuck over the paisley pattern, and under them there's a black and white photocopy the size of a postage stamp of Helmut Kohl and François Mitterrand holding hands. Inside, in tidy little letters, all the artists and the song titles are written out in full: the Mood-Mosaic: 'A Touch of Velvet – A Sting of Brass'; the Jesus and Mary Chain: 'Just like Honey'; Der Plan: 'Europa-Hymne'; Box Top 5: 'The Letter'. The change from the A side to the B side is marked by twenty-three tiny diagonal strokes. Inside, in the bend – or on the spine or whatever it's called – are the initials of the man who made me this tape: P.H. The letters are curiously broadened and intertwined. Beside it he wrote not just the year but also the month when he recorded the tape. 10/85. Another man who knew as much about music could have come upon the tape six months later and said, 'Yes, it's fine, but there's nothing really new there', until he found that date, and then he could only have drawn in his breath apprecia-tively. This tape was made by the man I love. It was a long time before I finally fell in love. I look out of the plane window again. Nothing but the blue air, and a bed of clouds below me.

When I went to secondary school I had a choice between Heddenbarg Grammar School, considered liberal and progressive or left-wing, and later renamed Carl von

Ossietzky Grammar School, and a more conservative institution, Bellhorn Grammar School, which had always been called Bellhorn and always would be. The only reason why I decided on Heddenbarg was that most of the children from my old class were going to Bellhorn. I could do without people who knew about my past. My life to date had been a labyrinth of blind alleys. This was the way out. During my interview with the headmaster he asked which of my girlfriends I'd like to stay with.

'None of them,' I said. 'I'd like to be in a class where I don't know anyone.'

He was taken aback.

'I have friends, of course,' I said, sounding deliberately cheerful, 'it's just that I'd like to make lots of new friends too.'

If I managed to get put in a class where no one knew me, I worked out that I could assume an entirely new identity. I could be anything I liked, I could re-invent myself. And this time I'd do everything properly from the start.

I was put in Class 5.4. The Heddenbarg classes weren't called by letters of the alphabet, they were numbered instead.

'I suppose it means something,' said my mother.

My plan almost worked out. Of the people I knew, only Gertrud Thode had been put in Class 5.4 as well. We had played together a couple of times because our mothers knew each other, but I wasn't her friend, and if she said I was in her own interview with the headmaster, she was lying. When we were looking for our new places on the first day of school Gertrud promptly sat down beside me. She did it so much as a matter of course that I was taken totally by surprise, and let her. There was a tall and very beautiful girl with long black hair sitting in front of me, the sort who always gets the part of

Snow White in plays. She was perfection itself, apart from a little dark down on her upper lip. Why hadn't *she* sat down next to me? Our class teacher picked up a piece of chalk and wrote her own name on the blackboard: Frau Schott. Giggling instantly broke out, and several people whispered 'Frau Shit!' Frau Schott had her hair cut short and wore a smart suit, but she was not in her first youth. She handed out slips of cardboard folded in two on which we were to write our names, and then she told us to choose someone to be class representative.

'Any suggestions?' said Frau Shit, resting her hands on the desk. A boy put up his hand.

'Anne Strelau,' he said. He was proposing me. I took a quick look at his name badge. He was called Volker Meyer. Volker Meyer had a round face, a haircut like Mecki the cartoon hedgehog, and dirt on his chin. My wonderful new life full of significance and friendship was off to a good start. And if they voted for me – oh, if only they'd vote for me! – I wouldn't let them down. I'd be the best class representative this school had ever seen. I'd rule my class gently and kindly, I'd oppose injustice and clear up any misunderstandings. They'd all be able to bring their troubles to me, and I'd have the answer to every problem. I'd organise wonderful summer parties, with yellow lanterns hanging in the trees, and after I'd made sure everything was all right, and checked that there was plenty to eat and drink, I'd step on to the dance floor exhausted but smiling. The moonlight would be reflected in my silvery mini-dress, and everyone would stop dancing to applaud me.

Apart from me, two boys were proposed, Bernhard and Till. It was a secret ballot. Frau Shit handed out scraps of paper torn from an arithmetic exercise book and wrote the names of the three candidates on the board. I wrote 'Till' on my ballot paper, and left it lying so that everyone who wanted could see the name. I folded it up only at the last minute, when Frau Shit was already coming round holding out a man's hat, a greasy old thing.

'I voted for you,' whispered Gertrud Thode to me as she put her ballot paper in the hat.

It was close. It was terribly close. I acted quite unconcerned, but as every ballot paper was unfolded and read out I trembled inwardly and hoped it would be my name. And as I said, it was very close, but in the end mine was the name with most chalk marks beside it. Frau Shit came over to congratulate me and asked if I would accept the job. I nodded. I couldn't help blushing. While she was asking Till, who had the second largest number of votes, if he would accept the job of deputy representative, I was wondering whether I should give a party right away, and if it would be appropriate for me to give presents at the party to everyone who'd voted for me, and everyone who hadn't as well to show how magnanimous I was. Then a boy whose name badge said FALKO LORENZ rose to his feet and put up his hand. He was rather good-looking, with tousled brown hair.

'Yes?' asked Frau Shit.

'We've been thinking it over,' said Falko, 'and we'd like to have the vote again.'

Again? What for? The blood was roaring in my ears. We'd already voted. For me. The class spokesperson and her deputy had accepted their posts, and by the simple, good old rules of democracy that was it. What was wrong with the election?

'I'd like to propose Kiki,' said Falko. Sure enough, there was a girl sitting behind him who had written KIKI on her

40

name badge, not Kirstin or Corinna or whatever she was really called, no surname either, just KIKI. She was small and delicate-looking and had long blonde hair. Suddenly the whole class was very keen to vote again. Apparently they were only just getting the hang of it. Frau Shit asked me and my deputy if we agreed, and what could we say but yes? At the second count I wasn't praying for every vote any more. I knew quite well how it would turn out even before Frau Shit had unfolded a single scrap of paper. The first vote had been a terrible misunderstanding. No one could be daft enough to vote for someone like me. How could I have been stupid enough to accept the job? They'd taken me for a ride. I was an idiot! I ought never to have agreed to stand! Of course Kiki won. Kikis always do. That's the way the world goes round. I was chosen to be deputy. I had no intention of ever lifting my little finger for this horrible lot, but all the same I accepted, so it wouldn't look as if my feelings were hurt. It was only because I didn't care that I'd agreed to be class representative after the first vote. Well, someone had to do the job. And now that I was just the deputy that was all the same to me too.

I didn't make any friends in my new class. I didn't try. It was safer not to. Gertrud Thode went on sitting beside me. Every time she tried to fix to meet me after school I turned away and pretended I hadn't heard her. I could amuse myself, I didn't need anyone else, and I didn't mind that no one else liked me either. Only that wasn't true. For a while it looked as if Tanja Kehlmann, the girl with the Snow White hair, would be my friend. She asked me home to her place, and we did our homework together and played board games. It was just the way I'd wanted it. Except that I was on edge the whole time. Tanja's home looked distressingly odd. It had abstract pictures hanging in half-empty rooms, and even the lunch that Tanja's mother cooked us one day was peculiar: potatoes and curd cheese, no meat. And nothing canned either. I felt really glad my parents were normal! What was more, I wanted Tanja to like me, but how was she going to like me when nothing about me was right? I had the wrong figure and the wrong jeans, I laughed in the wrong way and said the wrong things; even my bicycle wasn't a proper bicycle but a folding bike. It would be pointless to list all my failings – I was just one big mistake. Once I'd said goodbye to Tanja and was riding home on my folding bike I immediately felt better. After a while I started making up excuses so as not to have to visit her. It was a miserable time. I still wanted her to be my friend, but I found her friendship even more difficult to cope with than my own loneliness. Then she suddenly started making dates with Gertrud Thode. Perhaps she was picking the ugliest girls on purpose, so that she'd look all the more radiant beside them. It was a good thing I'd backed out in time.

It wasn't so bad being alone. Being alone was okay in itself. I just didn't want anyone to know how lonely I was, so I made out I was busy all the time. While the others were still chatting before the next lesson began, I was doing homework from the last one or reading a book. Then it wasn't so obvious that no one talked to me. During lessons I could relax to some extent. Before long I was Frau Shit's favourite. She liked me because I was so attentive and would always do what she wanted. She probably thought I enjoyed her German lessons, but only the fact that they kept me away from the others for forty-five minutes at a time interested me. And I liked the stern old teachers better anyway. The young ones were always telling us to push our desks together into a circle and making us work as a group. Probably because then they could go out of the classroom to smoke a cigarette. Long break was the most difficult time. I would hang around in the classroom until the teacher on duty caught me and threw me out. The teachers thought their pupils badly needed fresh air. So I would dawdle downstairs as slowly as possible. Another fourteen minutes to go. Out in the playground I took care to avoid the rest of my class, and steered a course over to a place where I didn't know anyone. I pretended I had something important to do, and walked all round the school yard with a purposeful expression on my face, but of course it was still obvious to everyone that I just didn't have anyone to keep me company. It was a dreadful strain. Finally I thought of going into the girls' toilets during break. After that I spent a lot of time in toilets. It was a good thing I'd stopped trying to be popular or join in. That spared me the worst. Well, no, of course it didn't really spare me the worst. Because the worst was PE, now called sports. I was in a class full of sinewy, muscular sporting fanatics, the girls as well as the boys. They flung the ball at each other in Dodge-Ball with enthusiasm and actually enjoyed being shot down, groaning with delight and trying to catch it. They didn't mind a bit if they sprained a finger. They loved pain and exertion and the smell of the gym. The girls now all wore black or dark-blue gym trousers, in an elasticated fabric that held your legs in a light but firm grip. Of course you sweated horribly in them. They slipped about too, and it wasn't easy to pull them up without looking silly. But they kept wobbly flesh under control, and my legs looked as black, smooth and firm in them as if they were made of plastic.

I still hated Dodge-Ball, but as long as we were playing it at least we didn't have to use the apparatus. Using the apparatus was hell, was torture, was incompatible with human dignity. After only the second week our sports teacher divided the class into three groups according to our proficiency. The first was the 'Youth Trains for the Olympics' group. It consisted of eight girls who were doing just that. Every year they went to West Berlin for a big competition, and if it rained they took silly little capes out of their bags with the words YOUTH TRAINS FOR THE OLYMPICS on them, and put them over their rain jackets. These girls didn't have to join in ordinary sports lessons. They had a corner of the gym all to themselves where they did incredible things with their bodies, leaped into the air without any apparatus to help them up, and twisted and turned somersaults before coming down. The second group was most of the rest of the class, who could get over the boxes and the vaulting horse with a simple handspring, even if they couldn't do double somersaults in the air. The third group was the hopeless rabbits. It consisted of just three people. I was one of them, of course, and then there were fat Helga Steinhorst and Ines Dubberke. Ines Dubberke wore the kind of glasses that God gives only to people who are going to be beaten up anyway – lenses like jellyfish, with a strength of about 28 dioptres. When I remember that time I see myself dangling from the knotted end of a climbing rope like a wet sack. I see myself unable to jump over even the lowest horse. I see myself making my way up the asymmetric bars with difficulty, I feel the nausea when I hit one of the bars with my tummy without gathering any impetus at all, I feel the humiliation again, the helplessness, pain and shame – oh, the terrible shame of having to move my body around in front of everyone, feeling its weight pull me mercilessly down. I didn't see why I was being made to do all these things. Why were sports lessons on a par with maths or English? Unless you wanted to be a sports teacher, there wasn't a single profession in which you had to jump over a horse. Even fire-fighters didn't have to be able to do handsprings. Why didn't they just let the idiots who loved sport train for the Olympics and leave me alone?

When I came home from school I ate lunch, did my homework, and then went to bed and opened one of the books I borrowed in large quantities from the school library. I didn't go to see my granny any more, because these days she had to wear nappies, and it smelled like it. My mother was glad I never brought friends home. She saw me as an uncomplicated child, wonderfully good at keeping myself amused. And in a way she was right. My bed was an island in the shark-infested ocean of life. If I put so much as a foot out of it, horrible things might happen to me, but among these pillows I was safe. I wouldn't have minded spending the rest of my life in bed. When my brother and sister weren't there I drew the curtains too. I read mainly girls' books these days. Hanni and Nanni Go To Boarding School. Dolly went to boarding school too, and as the youngest girl she had to do chores for the older ones. She rebelled, but in the end they broke her resistance, and suddenly Dolly was mad keen to be a servant to the other girls. This book made me feel quite ill. I couldn't believe the things you were supposed to sympathise with. Deliah was rather better off. Deliah was trekking through the Wild West in a covered wagon. The party was attacked by Indians and everyone except Deliah was killed. All the same, the Indians had spared her life only to torture her to death at the stake. Britta, Billie and Gundula lived in a perfect world where there were a few difficulties to be overcome at first, but the horse they longed for was there at the end of the book, a present waiting for them. Then all their parents decided to give up their city flats and go to live in an ivy-covered farmhouse in the country. During the move they saw a poor lost dog beside the road, and the dog came to live with them. A kindly deity watched over Britta, Billie and Gundula, ensuring that they won first prize at the gymkhana in spite of making a bad start.

A steady intake of chocolate and wine gums helped to carry me away into oblivion. Just reading wasn't enough. I felt the same about the sweets as about the books – quantity mattered more than quality. I needed enough to get me safely through the afternoon. What I could really have done with was alcohol, but the idea of turning to the hard stuff didn't even enter my head. Anyway, my mother would probably have objected if she'd found me drunk in bed every day.

I often thought I ought to give up chocolate and eat nothing at all. I wasn't really fat, not fat enough to be teased for it. Helga Steinhorst got the teasing. She wasn't so very much fatter than me, but she had a round, full moon of a face, and that was my salvation when the others were looking for a victim.

Once a really fat girl from an older class came into our English lesson with a note for the teacher. While she was standing up in front with Mrs Meyer-Hansen some people began giggling, and the fat girl blushed. When she'd gone out again Mrs Meyer-Hansen told us off. She was slender and pretty and could afford to.

'Can you please tell me why you were laughing just now?' she asked, sounding cross.

Silence.

Then Kiki said, 'Because she was so slim,' and everyone giggled even more.

'I don't call that fair,' said Mrs Meyer-Hansen. 'There are people who have something wrong with their glands. They're ill, they can't help being fat.'

Illness! Illness was the only excuse. If you'd just been over-eating you were fair game. And only thin girls were really safe. If I'd been slim I might have looked elegant even when I couldn't get over the horizontal bar or I was left hanging over the horse. It was just that it would have taken me weeks to get really thin. It was just that I needed something to help me deal with the terrible fear I always felt of the next day. Because the next day I'd be faced with either the apparatus, or working in a group, or something else horrible. And even if there was nothing in particular I still had to get through long break. Perhaps 'fear' is rather too strong for what I felt, perhaps it was more like depression. But it was a dreadful feeling anyway, and I could escape it only by lying in bed and stuffing my mouth with something so penetratingly sweet that all other sensations palled beside it.

'Just the same as me,' my mother said when she came into my room. 'I always used to like lying around too.'

She was always saying that I was just the same as her. 'You're like me. You're exactly like me, and your sister is exactly like Aunt Magda.'

Aunt Magda sometimes came to family birthday parties, but not very often. She was my mother's elder sister. When they'd been children, Aunt Magda used to put one hand up beside her face at lunchtime so that she wouldn't have to look at my mother, she hated her so much.

I didn't want to be like my mother. She was lacklustre, anxious, and tired all the time. When my sister and I came home we just dropped our anoraks on the floor and left them there with our dirty shoes, and my mother picked them up.

She was nothing. Even her own name wasn't on many of the letters that came for her. They were addressed to Frau Robert Strelau. And I was like her. I was so like her that I always knew exactly how she was feeling.

I'd rather have been like my sister. She wasn't just older and prettier than me, she was also far superior to me in every other way. The mere fact that my mother was always objecting to something about her was a plus point. There was nothing to object to in me. The legs of my only pair of jeans didn't even flare much. My sister went around in tall white boots and a red artificial-leather mini-skirt, and she wore a pair of Jackie O sunglasses. In spite of her sensitivity to noise, she and a girlfriend watched the TV hit parade on ZDF every week. Once the singer Danyel Gérard couldn't whistle his tune because something made him laugh, and my sister and her friend squealed with delight and moved closer to the screen.

'Isn't he just cute?' cried my sister. Danyel Gérard had a beard and was wearing a black slouch hat. I didn't see what was so cute about him. I had no idea what had come over my sister and her friend, but they seemed very sophisticated. It was as if they had an intimate relationship with Gérard that let them feel all maternal when he made a mistake.

When my sister met her first boyfriend, her record collection was extended by the addition of Franz Josef Degenhardt's 'Don't Play with the Sloppy Kids' and a Leonard Cohen LP. I couldn't stand my sister's boyfriend. He was already twenty, he was studying psychology, and he claimed that the only reason I couldn't stand him was because I was secretly in love with him myself. When my sister wasn't at home, and my father didn't happen to be asleep in the living-room, I listened to her records on the radiogram. I played some of the songs ten times running. Ten replays of 'Dear Rudi Dutschke, Daddy used to say'. Wow, what a song! It showed me how backward I was. The only two records I owned were Bruce Low's 'Noah', and 'I Wish I had a Pussy-Cat' sung by Wum, the animated cartoon dog with the pear-shaped head from the 'Three Times Nine' TV programme.

Not only did my sister have better taste in music, she had also managed to wangle herself a room of her own where she could shut herself in with her boyfriend. She had nagged our parents until they gave her their bedroom and put a folding bed in the living-room for themselves.

'Having three children in a house like this is downright irresponsible,' my sister had said. 'It isn't big enough for six people. You ought to have stopped at one child.'

My parents' old bedroom was almost twice the size of the room where the three of us had slept up till then. They had let my sister decide how to furnish it herself. The walls were covered with white-painted woodchip paper. There was a white built-in wardrobe along the wall, a white bookcase, a white flokati rug, a white desk, a white chair, a white bed and – wait for it – a bright-red bean-bag to sit on, like the one the cartoon dog Wum had. Little white polystyrene globules trickled from its zip fastener. The children's room where my brother and I still slept had new wallpaper too, but chosen by my father, with a pattern of huge, childish orange and yellow poppies.

'Nice cheerful colours,' said my father.

We put a set of shelves in the middle of the room to divide it up, but otherwise everything was still the same. You had only to look at those two rooms, and they told you everything you needed to know about my sister and me.

* * *

I skipped school as often as possible. I really did feel ill every time my mother woke me in the morning. Leaden-footed, with vague and muted hatred in my heart, I would stagger to the bathroom. Usually it was already occupied. I leaned against the wall by the bathroom door, closed my eyes and tried to go on sleeping standing up. I cursed my mother. Why couldn't she wait until the bathroom was free before waking me? Some time or other my granny or my father would come out, and I'd stagger over to the loo, pee in it and then stay sitting there for a few minutes with my eyes closed, while my sister and my little brother were already hammering on the locked door. I didn't know how I was ever going to get my eyes open again to stand up and wash, but somehow I managed to put my face under the tap and run the comb, already smeary with birch water, though my hair. It just wasn't worth the effort. When I imagined this going on for years and years, at least until the end of my schooldays – and what reason did I have to think that things would improve then? – human mortality seemed a very sensible arrangement. Anyway I no longer believed I could ever be like the other kids at school and share their sort of life.

Sometimes I felt so awful in the morning that I didn't get up at all and just turned my face to the wall, groaning. I got ill on those days. For instance, when there was a sports day at school. Of course the simplest thing would have been to be permanently bedridden, but I somehow couldn't manage to waste away in the grand style. I recovered from rubella and mumps. I'd have liked to go blind. Then I'd finally have got a dog. A guide-dog. Or paralysis wouldn't have been so bad, I could still have read books, and my father would probably have given me a dog all the same. If you're as ill as that people don't refuse you anything. In fact something seriously, visibly wrong with me would have made everything much simpler. Of course I'd be let off sports lessons if I was blind or paralysed, but I wouldn't take advantage of that. I'd insist on joining in. I'd wander around during Dodge-Ball, blind, and no one would dare to shoot me down. But I'd take my bearings from the sound of the ball flying through the air, I'd stand in its path, and to everyone's surprise I'd catch it. I'd be one of the best players, a kind of miracle, and *The Best of Reader's Digest* would publish a story about me and how bravely I'd risen above my fate. I'd have myself pushed to the asymmetric bars in my wheelchair and insist on being lifted up to the top bar. No one would expect anything marvellous of me, but no one would dare refuse the poor cripple what she wanted either. And with the muscular upper arms of a wheelchair user, and my wasted, thin legs underneath, scarcely weighing me down at all, I'd move from bar to bar so lightly and elegantly that everyone would burst into spontaneous applause. I was quite sure that if no one expected me to be normal any more, I'd be in a position to achieve extraordinary things.

As far as paraplegia was concerned, I got no further than a pair of supports in my shoes for weak ankles. In my attempt to go blind by pure will-power, I did at least have some partial success: my eyes were found to be minus four dioptres. At first I was glad to have glasses. They not only brought me closer to my aim, they'd change me too, and change appeared to me desirable in principle. In addition I was the only one in my family who needed glasses. At least I didn't resemble my mother there. But I was glad only until the glasses actually arrived: cheap frames made of transparent, brownish-pink plastic. This was not the kind of change that got you anywhere.

'Luckily it isn't the way it used to be; you can get really nice glasses on health insurance these days,' said my mother.

The glasses were not dramatic enough for people to do me any favours because of them. They were just the reason why there are no photos of me from that period.

The only kind of physical activity that didn't make me feel ill was going riding with Susi Klaffke. If there was anyone I was friends with in the real sense at this time it was Susi. We hadn't got on particularly well at primary school. Susi Klaffke and another girl had once waited beside the road to school to tip the contents out of my satchel. But first I didn't carry a satchel any more, I had an artificial leather briefcase, and second Susi Klaffke, besides her many other advantages, had two horses – a big chestnut gelding with white feet called Caliban, and a fat, bad-tempered Shetland pony. Occasionally, very occasionally, I had a chance to ride the chestnut. When I sat on Caliban I was a different person – taller, stronger, better-looking. The inadequacies of my own body no longer mattered. It was . . . well, kind of sublime. No, I don't think 'sublime' is too strong a word. Usually, of course, I rode the black Shetland pony. His name was Prince and he kicked and snapped at everything that came within his reach: people, dogs, other horses, chickens. Prince hated the whole world, which I could well understand. But of course he had no chance. We would corner him in the paddock, grab his halter and tie him to a post while we groomed him on such a short rope that he snarled and bit the wood in his rage. The pony didn't have a proper saddle, just a Shetland one, a piece of leather with hardly any padding and two stirrups. It slipped about a lot on his round back. If you didn't distribute your weight properly between the stirrups you were soon underneath his belly.

Of course it was nice being carried by a live, warm creature through the woods and meadows, but what I really liked, what I always looked forward to, was the race-track: a four-hundred-metre stretch in an old gravel pit. The pony felt the same. The closer we came to it, the more idiotically he behaved. It was probably the only thing that linked us: our longing for that one wild minute when he snorted and galloped off, his short legs drumming over the ground so fast that, up on his back, I scarcely felt we were moving at all. I stood in the stirrups as if I'd turned to concrete, while his speed blurred the grass beneath my feet. I leaned far forward, let the reins follow the rhythm of that nodding head, and gave myself up to his tempo. If the pony stumbled, or stopped abruptly out of malice, I was done for. And he often liked to do exactly that, suddenly ramming his front hooves into the ground and kicking out with his back legs. I always described the same flight through the air, first diagonally upwards, then doing a half somersault as I reached my zenith, and then, with the fleeing sky the last image before my eyes, falling vertically to the ground, where I landed on my back. The impact pressed all the air out of my lungs. When Susi Klaffke finally found me in the tall grass, looked down from her horse and asked if I was all right, I could only make strange croaking sounds. It hurt so incredibly much that I was always convinced all my ribs had pierced my lungs. I could have prevented these falls by leaning back and shortening the reins, but that would have acted like a brake. If I really wanted to enjoy the race I had to lean forward and give myself up to it, trusting the pony, even though experience had taught me that he was not necessarily to be trusted at all. But if – for whatever reason – he decided to put up with me for once, the speed left me positively intoxicated with happiness. I stopped existing as solid material and turned into movement, I *was* movement. The possibility of breaking my neck any moment only made it better. What did being ugly and unpopular matter? This sensation was beauty itself.

Getting a horse was an even more hopeless prospect than getting a dog. I know that words like 'hopeless' don't really have any comparative, but it really was more hopeless.

'Boberg is full of paraplegics, all of them victims of riding accidents,' said my father. He seemed to assume that you didn't fall off a horse until it belonged to you. The other argument, of course, was money. If I could have worked to pay for the horse myself that's what I would have done. But I was too young, I couldn't even deliver the *Hamburger Abendblatt*. A few roads away from our house there was a piece of land lying fallow. I stopped going to bed in the afternoons after school, and instead cleared the site and laid it out as a paddock. I worked really hard, scratching my arms and legs as I cut down birch trees and dug out tree stumps until my hands were all over blisters – the work had to have some kind of effect, and bring me closer, if only a very little closer, to having a horse of my own. I showed my father the land I had cleared. He shrugged his shoulders. There was nothing I could do. Nothing at all.

At first I'd accompanied my father on his walks just to pester him to buy me a horse, and demonstrate how much I knew about them by enumerating the fifty different possible marks on a horse's face: star, blaze, stripe, snip, stripe and snip combined, bald, streak, spot . . . But although my father was as hard and indifferent as a coconut where my wishes were concerned, I realised at some point that I really enjoyed walking in the woods with him, and I liked him. Of course I had liked him before. It was easy to like him. My mother was always around: by contrast with her life, his seemed exciting and mysterious. I still had no clear idea what he really did for a living. While he was away driving round the country in his Opel, parcels would arrive, sometimes twenty large ones all at once. No one else was allowed to open them, and my little brother and I used to look over his shoulder in awe as he did so. Mostly they just contained papers, or tubes of something, or sometimes there were more interesting things, like rubber hippopotamuses, panels with Roman and Egyptian reliefs, or a hundred and fifty bright-red life-size plaster feet. By now I had realised that my father was unhappy, perhaps in much the same way as me. At the time I sometimes imagined I knew what he was feeling. When I saw him curled up on the sofa, wrapped in his llama-hair rug, my throat tightened. In fact my father soon thawed out when we had visitors. He just felt wretched alone with his family; with visitors, he was always cracking jokes and telling everyone that in theory he had three Ferraris in the garage. He'd read in the paper that from birth to the end of a child's education it cost the parents on average 100,000 marks – exactly the price of a Ferrari. After that he kept making this joke. But I knew that in a way he meant it seriously, and the life he led was not what he had once dreamed of. I decided to stop begging him for a horse. My father had a hard enough time already. I could at least spare him that. But as until then I had been telling him exclusively about the relative merits of different horse breeds, and how you could keep a horse quite cheaply, I now had to find some new subject of conversation. Of course we couldn't talk about unhappiness. We discussed nature and technology, physics and chemistry. Since my brother and sister and I had been old enough to think, my father had been in the habit of asking us what the chemical formula for water was, so by now we immediately shouted, 'Aitch – two – oh!' like a water pistol going off. Even the bedtime stories he used to tell us were physics homework in disguise. In every story a king asked his three sons a riddle, and only the youngest prince could solve it. For instance a ball had rolled into a narrow U-shaped underground pipe. The prince who could get it out again would inherit the kingdom. The two older princes failed, as they always do. The youngest prince just held a garden hose in the pipe, and when enough water had flowed in the ball was washed up to the surface.

I told my father that at school we had connected a bicycle lamp and a battery with wires and made the bicycle lamp glow. To my relief he jumped at the subject. I was never sure how much longer my father would put up with my company on his walks, but now he lectured me in animated tones about closed circuits. I asked him how the energy got into the battery, and he told me that no one had ever managed to make a *perpetuum mobile*, although in principle it was easy enough.

'You have to imagine a watermill,' he said, 'placed in the middle of a closed container. The right-hand side of the container is full of air and the left-hand side is full of water. The paddles are made of a material that is lighter than water. They fall on the right, because of course they are heavier than air. Then the buoyancy of the water raises them again on the left. The problem is to fit a seal allowing the paddles to move from the air-filled side of the container to the water-filled side without letting any water into the air on the right.'

I was bowled over by my father's cleverness. It was a brilliant idea. Perhaps I'd study physics later and solve the problem of the seal. My father would show me the way to an exciting, heroic world if I could only persuade him to go on talking to me. I racked my brains for subjects which might interest him so much that he'd forget it was only me he was talking to. My mother, of course, always wanted to talk to me. She asked how school had been, or what I'd like for lunch, or she told me what some boring neighbour had said to her. She had a small mind and would never invent a *perpetuum mobile*. And I hated her wet kisses. Of course I realised how pathetic it was that I needed my father's company because hardly anyone else wanted anything to do with me. On the other hand, I didn't believe that any of the others in my class could have said such clever, interesting things as he did. I liked my father's enthusiasm for peculiar problems. Would a closed cube with two hundred budgies inside it weigh less if you clapped your hands and made all the budgies fly up in the air? Could you survive if you were in a lift dropping out of control and you jumped up in the air at the very moment when the lift hit the bottom of the shaft? When he asked me questions like these I felt close to him. He really enjoyed knowing so much. But sometimes he would stop in the middle of what he was saying, look at me with a frown and fall silent, as if he couldn't make out why he had just been expounding his brilliant ideas to someone like me.

One Sunday morning, when the whole family was sitting round the breakfast table in the garden, I tried to grab my father's attention by telling him about a chemistry experiment at school. Just as I was describing, with some slight exaggeration, the size of a purple cloud we'd produced, my father suddenly stood up, collected the eggshells from the table without a word, and crossed the garden to the compost heap. I stared at him. He couldn't be serious. He'd probably just forgotten to tell me to come with him. I followed. When I had caught up with him my father walked faster, and I almost had to run to keep up. Now I could sense what he was thinking.

When is this going to stop? he was thinking. When is it finally going to stop? Is it never going to stop?

I realised I'd be better off going back to the breakfast table. At once! Instead, I talked breathlessly to my father, as if my life depended on it, trying to fend off his distaste and my shame with a torrent of words. When he reached the compost heap my father stopped and turned to me. His face was distorted.

'Why do you keep following me around?' he snapped. 'Can't you leave me alone? Do you have an Oedipus complex or what?'

At that moment my world exploded. I knew what an Oedipus complex was. Something to do with sex. I felt unwell. It was as if I were falling and falling and falling. And when I thought I'd reached the bottom of my shame there was still no ground under my feet, and I fell on down into a second cellar full of self-disgust. I'd made advances to my own father. Oh God, how revolting I was! I don't remember how I got away from the compost heap, whether I ran off to fling myself on my bed in tears, or whether I made some ludicrous attempt to preserve my composure, turned calmly, walked back, sat down at the breakfast table again and acted as if nothing had happened. That seems to me the most likely. I probably spread myself a piece of toast and jam while my heart broke and broke and broke. And perhaps I spooned my yoghurt down – one spoonful for humiliation, one spoonful for disappointment, one spoonful for self-disgust and a big spoonful for hatred. Okay, so I was pushy, ugly and embarrassing – but what had I ever done to make my father suppose I wanted to go to bed with him? That was probably what he'd been thinking all this time. All the weeks we'd gone for walks together he'd been telling himself that no normal girl of twelve voluntarily went for walks with her father, so that meant I must have the hots for him. What an arsehole! What a stupid arsehole! And I'd admired him so much. He was my clever, my dearest Daddy. Dearest? Oh, I was so horrible! My father was quite right. If only someone like me had never existed! I ought to kill myself, I ought to cut my veins with nail scissors. But I was too pathetic even for that, and I hated myself for it, I was ashamed of that too.

One day, when I went to the girls' toilets, there were two boys from Class 9 leaning against the tiled wall opposite the plywood cubicles, smoking. The Class 9 toilets were a floor higher, and the teachers checked them, so they came down to our floor to smoke.

'Listen to that,' said one of the boys, pointing to a closed cubicle. 'There's someone sitting in there peeing. Listen!'

In the silence I heard a soft splashing. Soon afterwards the door of the cubicle opened and out came Ines Dubberke, the girl with the jellyfish glasses. The boys laughed and threw their cigarettes on the floor. I pressed close to the wash-basin and let them pass. Then I went into one of the loos, tore off half a metre of paper and let it hang from the toilet seat into the bowl. If you peed right on the paper your pee ran down it and trickled into the water without making any noise. When I came out, Ines was still standing by the wash-basin.

'They're holding the door closed,' she said.

I could see she was glad not to be shut in there on her own.

There was giggling outside. I looked through the keyhole. I could see Kiki, a girl called Barbara, and fat Helga. Then the keyhole went dark, and there was an eye staring straight into mine.

They did that quite often, shutting a girl into the toilets. There was nothing personal about it. It could happen to anyone. Not Kiki and Tanja, of course, but everyone else. I leaned on the wash-basin with my arms folded and waited. When the maths teacher came upstairs, at the latest, they'd let go and take refuge in the classroom. Ines was pulling frantically at the door. She was stupid. There were probably about ten of them hanging on to the handle out there. But Ines was too stupid even to pee silently. I heard the girls giggling and moving about again. They were crowding around the keyhole to take a look at us, the girl with the thick glasses and the girl who couldn't even jump over the lowest horse in the gym. It was hilarious that two idiots like us couldn't get out of the toilets.

'If they go on staring in here I shall stuff soap in their eyes,' I said.

'Ooh, will you really?' whispered Ines, and her eyes sparkled. Or perhaps it was just the light in the toilets reflecting off her prismatic lenses. I took a handful of soap granules out of the dispenser, and when the keyhole went dark again I squeezed the whole lot through it.

'Come on,' I shouted. Ines and I pulled at the door to the toilets together. It gave way and we stumbled back. When we came out no one tried to stop us. The girls were surrounding Doris Pöhlmann, the smallest girl in our class. Everyone called her Little Doris, because there was a bigger girl whose name was Doris too. Little Doris was sitting on the floor with her eyes tight shut. One of the girls went to the wash-basin, wetted her handkerchief and wiped Doris's eyes with it. Ines moved away, and all the girls looked at me, horrified. Gradually I began to feel scared. Suppose I'd done Little Doris serious harm? I still thought she deserved it. She'd wanted to see me shut in there, not knowing what to do. Now she was weeping soap lather. The girls didn't even look reproachful – just horrified. Some boys stopped and asked what was up, and then the maths teacher came along and we all automatically moved into the classroom after her, Little Doris still surrounded by the other girls. I sat down in my place. I didn't think it was appropriate for me to help her. I was ostracised. The others had just been playing a harmless little schoolgirl prank, but I was vicious, I'd hurt someone. At last the teacher herself realised that something was wrong, went over to Little Doris and asked what the matter was.

'Someone put soap in her eyes,' said Kiki. I drew squiggles in my exercise book. The maths teacher examined Doris's eyes.

'One of you will have to take Doris home,' she said. 'Will you do it, Tanja?'

Tanja was getting the lesson off. She owed it all to me.

'Who did it?'

There was whispering, and the maths teacher looked angrily my way.

'. . . But she's sorry she did it,' I heard Kiki say. 'I'm sure she didn't hurt Doris on purpose.'

Kiki seemed to take her job as class representative very seriously. So much blood shot into my head that I thought one of my ears would burst any moment. The maths teacher turned to me.

'Did you do it on purpose, Anne? Did you mean to hurt Doris?'

What a stupid cow! Of course I meant to hurt her. That's

the only reason you'd put soap in someone's eyes, to hurt her. Why else?

'No,' I said quietly, 'I didn't mean to. I'm sorry.' The idea that Little Doris might go blind made me feel very bad. Then I'd stay with her for the rest of my life, and be her slave, and do everything for her that she couldn't do for herself. And still my guilt would never be any less. But for some reason they were all convinced that I could only have done it unintentionally, and it was better to leave them thinking that.

I packed my briefcase up before the end of the lesson, and when the bell rang I ran out of the classroom ahead of everyone else.

At school next day the first thing I did was to go up to Little Doris. I'd decided on this move during a long and sleepless night. Her eyes looked perfectly normal.

'I want to apologise,' I told her. 'I'm sorry for what I did. Does it still hurt?'

'No, I've forgotten all about it,' she said in a friendly voice.

'I really am very sorry,' I repeated. I wasn't sorry in the least. I suddenly felt that with overwhelming clarity.

'It's all right,' she replied. 'Honestly! Let's drop the subject.'

'No,' I said, 'it was really awful. I'm so sorry. I really didn't mean to.'

I squeezed her hand, and then I went home again instead of going into the classroom. When I got home I was running a temperature. I told my mother and went to bed. I imagined Little Doris having an accident on her way home that day, an accident that was nothing at all to do with me. A tanker truck would skid, hit Doris on her bike and fling her into a bush. Then the tanker would crash into the wall of a building.

Poisonous, caustic acid would run out of it and all the way to where Doris was lying in the bushes. The acid would eat away her face, disfigure her for life and destroy her eyesight. I prayed to God for a tanker truck. Then I took a new book off the pile, one I'd borrowed from the library two days earlier. Dolly was still at that boarding school. By now she was one of the older girls and could get the younger ones to do everything for her. She was so nice that all the younger pupils competed to light the fire in her study or make her tea. It was another of those books that made me feel like throwing up. Luckily I was sick anyway, and I stayed sick for a week.

Little Doris became my friend. Even in Class 8 she still looked as if she belonged in primary school – Class 4 at the most. She had a narrow, pinched mouth, and short, thin, pale-blonde baby hair. Little Doris not only looked like a child, she dressed like a child too. She wore a little girl's dress of big red and blue checks, and she carried a satchel instead of a briefcase. The satchel was made of fine, expensive pigskin, and was probably better for the posture, but of course it looked silly all the same. During lessons she drew pictures with a sharp pencil, pictures of villages full of millions of details, hundreds of little houses with curtains in their windows, and not only did the curtains have all kinds of different patterns, you could even see a tiny little cat looking out from behind one curtain, and behind another there was a vase of flowers that had fallen over, hardly any bigger than the blob you could squeeze out of a fountain pen cartridge. A little church had a tiny church clock saying twenty to eleven, and above the church door were the words 'God Bless You' and the date 1872. There were ships called *Heini* and *Seagull* in the harbour, and rowing boats with oars as fine as hairs. There were loaves the size of grains of rice in the baker's window, and alarm clocks like pinheads in the watchmaker's, and ant-sized trumpets hanging from the ceiling of the music shop. I had to look at all this because Little Doris sat next to me. Our classroom at that time was in a blue annexe to the school, and was torn down a few years later because of asbestos contamination. Frau Schott had retired, and we had a new class teacher. He taught sports too, and that was my salvation. Herr Koopmann usually ignored working with the apparatus and all other kinds of gymnastics in favour of football. I don't know if football was supposed to be on the curriculum at all, but I'm sure it wasn't meant to be played as often as we played it. The 'Youth Trains for the Olympics' people could go on training in the gym – Koopmann considered girls no loss – but everyone else had to go out on the field. Karlo Dose was the only one in the class who was really keen on football. Till Hinsberg and Volker Meyer played as well as Karlo did, but they didn't think much of all the fuss about it. Neither of them had joined a club. Dose had. He'd have been lost without football. He had personally drawn up two Federal League tables and pinned them to the classroom wall. One gave the actual rankings in the Federal German Football League, and he kept it up to date, the other showed the rankings that Dose would have chosen himself. When we left the gym for the football field, Koopmann gathered the best footballers around him and jogged ahead with them. Evolutionary failures trotted along behind. I was glad to be only one among many rabbits all of a sudden. On the football field I was below average, but the people who were average were pretty bad too. When I kicked with the tip of my toes I aimed well and shot hard. I was really good with the toe of my shoe. But Koopmann always noticed, and then he shouted, 'Not that way!'

If I tried using my instep, the ball either flew off completely out of control, or I missed it entirely. Missing it was the most embarrassing thing. I usually missed it when I thought that this time I had the run-up right and it could be a really good shot. So a point came when I stopped trying. It was better to shoot the ball feebly on purpose, approach it half-heartedly knowing in advance it wouldn't be a good shot, and make a fool of yourself only a little bit rather than entirely.

'Put more zing into it! The ball won't bite you!' shouted Koopmann. It still wasn't fair that when people were picking teams I was always one of the last chosen. Hinsberg, Meyer, Lorenz and so on were the first to be picked, of course, but after that it wasn't even clear what the criteria were. There were girls who obviously played worse than me, girls who would reduce any ambitious team to despair, and yet they were picked before I was. While I waited for one of the team captains to take pity on me at last, I was always imagining how one day I'd show them what I was worth. The whole thing would go like this:

Our class has a big football match coming up against the hated team of an enemy school. (Of course there wasn't any enemy school, but you kept finding that sort of thing in Erich Kästner books.) *Anyway, this match is terribly important. If we win we can go up into the next group or league or whatever. Falko Lorenz picks his team: Karlo Dose, Till Hinsberg, Hoffi Hoffmann . . . he doesn't want me in his team at all, but over half the class is off sick with Japanese flu, and if he doesn't pick me he'll have to pick Ines Dubberke with her prismatic glasses, and Ines is a total disaster. So he reluctantly decides on me and tells me I'm to stay at the back and always pass the ball on as soon as it comes my way. He'd like to put me in goal, but Karlo Dose is there already, because just to make matters even worse he sprained his ankle getting out of the school bus. Karlo Dose fails and lets a ball through in the seventh minute. Our team is demoralised and plays worse and worse. But for my own intervention we'd have conceded two more goals. I see several chances that the others fumble, and when I get the ball in the penalty area and I'm all by myself, I can't stand it any more. I run forward with it, I run and run almost the whole length of the pitch, and in spite of allegedly being so weak with the ball, I dribble it around five of the opposing defenders. But just before I can finish my energetic solo run with a shot at goal Falko Lorenz, who has been running with me, shouts, 'Pass – here!' and I grind my teeth and pass him the ball. But Falko botches it, he shoots several metres wide of the goal, the chance is gone, and we go into the second half with a psychologically fatal score of 0–1. Falko Lorenz has taken me out of defence now and put me with the forwards. I make no comment. The opposing team is in great form. I have to keep going back to the defenders to prevent us giving away another goal. In the eightieth minute it's still 0–1 and all seems lost. But then I get the ball again and race forward, Falko Lorenz is with me on the other side, two opposing defenders coming towards me, their legs reaching for the ball, I swerve left, keep on running, and the ball is positively sticking to my foot, it's my ball, it does what I want. I hear my name, at first only a few voices, then lots of them, then it's a shout, a great roar from the collective throat of the spectators.*

'Anne! Anne!!'

Falko Lorenz is still level with me.

'*Well done!*' *he shouts.* '*Now, pass!*'

But I'm not crazy. Without slowing down, I lever my right leg sideways from my body, I get the ball with my toe, I turn in the air and send it into the net as the goalie's fingers reach for it in vain. A roar of applause. The whole school has come to watch this important away game. Even Koopmann can't sit still any more. The boys in my team all come staggering up to clap me on the back, and I trot a little way down the side of the field to get away from them. Looks like it's going to be a draw. The last minute of play begins. The opposing team race forward. My brilliant reactions prevent them from scoring another goal. I'm still standing far back, but since there are only a few seconds left, and there's no other chance, I take the risk: I coolly manoeuvre the ball into position with my lower leg, and then it thunders like a cannonball through the air, it travels half the length of the playing field, the opposing goalie dives for it, he touches it, but he can't hold on to it and – 'Yeees . . . Gooooal!' I've given Heddenbarg the lead. The final whistle goes. We've won. And they all come running, the whole team, they want to lift me up on their shoulders, and the spectators surge on to the pitch, Koopmann in the lead, they run towards me . . . and suddenly they daren't come any closer. Because my glance is so cold and withering. I look calmly at them. They stop a few metres away from me, shuffling their feet. And I turn, and put my hands in my trouser pockets, and walk away across the football field, all on my own. That was the end of many of my fantasies. I ended up walking away over a wide, empty space all on my own.

When I was fourteen I began to suspect that I'd never have a boyfriend. Although I had no intention of falling in love, getting a boyfriend was important. Grown-ups always acted as if you had everything going for you at that age. But to the boys in my class my youth meant nothing. They were fourteen and fifteen themselves. Youth was not an advantage, just a basic condition. Luckily it was the same for most of the girls. They might keep talking about the boys they liked, but only Kiki and Tanja had actually kissed anyone. Those two had something going for them that girls like Gertrud Thode, Ines Dubberke, Little Doris and me just didn't. Our fate was now sealed. We would always be standing on the sidelines, sharing our home-made cakes and watching as the smart girls led their real, rewarding lives. We'd listen to their stories with bated breath, and comfort ourselves by knowing that we did better at school. For even if Kiki and Tanja knew much more than we did, they were a little bit worse in all academic subjects. Typically, we mousy grey girls never looked beyond the boys in our own class. Our imagination stretched no further. It was all the same to me who kissed me, I just wanted it to be one of the boys who had as many as possible of the other girls in love with them: Falko Lorenz, Till Hinsberg or Kai Hoffmann, known as Hoffi. But none of these admirable beings, who alone were in a position to bring me esteem and respect, ever took any notice of me. Strange boys sometimes called after me in the street, that was all, especially if there were several of them. They shouted, 'Look at that bum! Look at the arse on her!' and remarks of that nature. I never understood why. (Okay, so I was ugly as sin, but couldn't they just leave it at that?) My mother said I was the only woman in our family with narrow hips, which of course was totally ridiculous. I didn't have narrow hips. If boys called things after me they were almost always to do with my bum. And suddenly grown men began doing it too. I kept being stupid enough to stop when someone spoke to me in the street. Sometimes they really did just want to ask the way. I couldn't be sure that everyone was going to talk dirty. They said the most peculiar things, words I'd never heard in my life, but all the same I always knew just what they meant. 'Ready for a good screw yet?' a man called after me from his garden as I cycled past. I rode past this garden every day. It was my way to school. What made that man so sure that I wouldn't tell on him? Or that no one would help me? After that, whenever I saw him pottering about in his garden I crossed to the other side of the road, and he would give a triumphant laugh. By now I felt sick when I merely set eyes on a building site, even from a distance. The closer I came to it the worse I felt; I became an insect, a beetle watching the sole of a boot advancing. I looked down at the ground and pretended to be deaf while sweating, sun-tanned workers in vests told each other what they could do to me. What was wrong with me to make people say such things and laugh at me? If I didn't keep eating, if I'd only been thinner, then the bastards wouldn't have noticed me, and the boys in my class would finally have woken up and seen how beautiful I really was. Because sometimes I was beautiful.

Whenever my parents went to one of their slide-showing evenings I stayed up late, and I was still watching TV long after my brother and sister were asleep. There was a point around ten when I felt really tired, but once I'd overcome that it was as if I'd never have to sleep again. After closedown I put on the Beatles record I'd bought myself after we analysed 'Eleanor Rigby' in music at school. I opened the living-room curtains. In the nocturnal reflection in the window-pane I suddenly looked like the girl I could have been. At this enchanted hour I was pretty. Even with my glasses on. I stared at myself, held my hair up with one hand, touched the cold glass reverently with the other, and could hardly realise that this was me. I danced to my reflection a little. Sometimes I dashed out into the corridor, where there was a real mirror. I didn't look quite as good in it as in the black window-pane. I took my glasses off and leaned far enough forward to see my face without them. Without glasses, perhaps I could even be beautiful. There was something not quite right about me, it was hard to say what, but if that went, and then I lost ten pounds, I could look really good one day. At that moment I already looked much prettier than I ever did in daylight. Why didn't one of those boys ring my front-door bell now? Maybe Till Hinsberg, because he happened to be cycling down the street where I lived at one in the morning and had a flat tyre outside our door. Maybe Volker Meyer, because he was secretly in love with me and couldn't stand it any more. If I opened the door to him now, he'd be stunned by my beauty. I opened the front door, quietly so as not to wake my brother and sister, switched on the outside light and stood in its glow. Anyone passing our house could see how incredibly beautiful I was. But at this time of night you could wait for hours for a car to drive past. People who didn't live here didn't pass through. I used to stand in the light for a little while, and then switch it off again and go to bed.

Surprisingly, my father said he would buy me contact lenses. They cost an enormous amount of money. It was the first time I'd actually got something big that I badly wanted. Perhaps my father thought my glasses were as awful as I did. Without glasses, my face looked to me unusually naked and soft at first. I drew round my eyes with a black kohl pencil to give them an outline again. And I painted metallic blue eye shadow over them. Now I only had to get thin.

My mother, my sister and I went on the Mayo diet. My mother had copied down the recipes in a neighbour's house. It was dead easy to lose weight. I ate half a grapefruit and three hard-boiled eggs for breakfast, half a grapefruit and three hard-boiled eggs for lunch, and three hard-boiled eggs and a green salad dressed with lemon juice for supper. Next day I already weighed two kilos less, and my trousers were loose at the waist. On the second day I ate three hard-boiled eggs and half a grapefruit for breakfast, three hard-boiled eggs and half a grapefruit for lunch, and half a chicken with the skin removed for supper. After all those eggs the chicken tasted wonderful, you even felt almost full. Next morning I'd lost three kilos. And so it went on every day, with vast quantities of eggs, and it was only at supper that you could eat cooked meat or fish and a horrible grilled tomato. Apparently you could lose up to eight pounds a week. I lost twelve. Of course you felt dizzy all the time. When I was going up the two flights of steps to the language laboratory at school I sometime had to stop and cling to the banisters, because everything was going black in front of my eyes. And after the third day you began to smell of phosphorus. But what did that matter now that I finally weighed fifty-five kilos again? I had weighed over sixty kilos – indeed, I'd weighed sixty-one. Now I was looking good at last. I kept running to the toilets at break to look at myself in the mirror. If I could see myself I felt good. If I couldn't, I still felt ugly.

Sad to say, I put on two kilos in the first two days after finishing the Mayo diet. So I started the diet from the beginning again until I was back to fifty-five kilos. The whites of my eyes turned yellow. When I couldn't stand the sight of another egg, I went on the *Brigitte* magazine diet. Fifty-five kilos was the threshold. If I weighed more I felt guilty. Either guilty or hungry. But I felt guilty when I weighed fifty-five kilos too, because I ought really to have weighed forty-nine. Forty-nine kilos would have been an acceptable weight. Or forty-seven.

When I weighed fifty-four kilos, Hoffi Hoffmann spoke to me. It was on the way back from a class outing, in the disco on the ferry home from England. Hoffi came over to me and said, 'Hi.'

'Hi,' I said, and clutched his shoulder, because at that moment the *Prince Hamlet* was rolling from one side to another. Life was very simple. He asked if I'd like to go up on deck with him, and offered me a cigarette. I took it – it gave us something to do. We walked along the deck, smoking, not sure what to talk about. The wind blew our hair in our faces and made our skin damp and sticky. It got colder and colder, I was shivering and shaking, probably because I hadn't eaten for two days, and had only drunk water. That always made me freeze very quickly. We went back in again, and Hoffi rubbed my arms and shoulders, allegedly to warm me up. I could feel his awkwardness and uncertainty, and it made me even more awkward and uncertain myself. He rubbed my arms more slowly and came closer. It was bright in this corridor. This was the second-class section of the ship, and men in business suits walked past and looked at us, grinning. I would have liked to stop now, but then he was kissing me. His tongue thrust far into my mouth, ran along my teeth and felt my gums.

Then he said, 'Come on, let's sit down here,' and we slid

our backs down the wall and sat on the floor. We didn't talk much, and now and then Hoffi kissed me. I felt his skin getting warmer and his breath coming faster. The blood in his throat was pulsing against the palm of my hand. Later Hoffi went to sleep with his head on my shoulder. I was perfectly calm, only slightly disgusted, and very proud that Hoffi was mine.

Next morning we were all sitting in the cafeteria having breakfast. There wasn't a spare seat for me, so I sat on Hoffi's knee along with the interesting boys. Falko Lorenz was talking the whole time. All the others were too tired. The girls looked at us and envied me. I was still wearing my satin disco outfit from the night before, and I knew my hair was untidy and my eye make-up smeared. Little Doris was wearing red dungarees, a flowered blouse, and had three tin slides in her fair hair. There was no helping her. Doris didn't eat any breakfast, she was starting a diet. She had always been thinner than me anyway, and now she was eating even less to increase the difference. I realised what her intentions were and I didn't eat anything either.

The reflected glory of being a couple with Hoffi surrounded me like a halo. It was nice when he kissed my cheek during break at school while the other girls were there; it was flattering to turn up with him at parties which I'd never have been invited to otherwise. I liked the way Hoffi lit his cigarette from mine. But what meant most was just being with him, sitting in his room with no idea what to talk about. He expected something from me, I could clearly feel that, but he himself probably wasn't sure what he expected. When we had said nothing for long enough he kissed me. That was even worse.

We were together for eleven weeks, until the beginning of the summer holidays. On the last day of term Hoffi was late for lessons, and when he came into the classroom he was wearing a sombrero. Everyone roared. Little Doris nudged me with her elbow.

'Take a look at Hoffi!' she said with glee. I was trembling with indignation. Why had I put up with it all – the kisses, his damp, questing hands, those incredibly dreary afternoons – if he could play about so easily with my reputation when it depended directly on his? He smiled at me. How I hated him! How could he do this to me? Getting hold of Hoffi had been important; having him was a nuisance and an incalculable risk. I hurried home that day without exchanging a single word with him. When he rang, I got my mother to say I was out. She happily obliged. And when the holidays were over, Hoffi and I were no longer an item, without anyone having to say so straight out.

Soon after that Falko Lorenz gave a party, and although I wasn't with Hoffi any more he invited me. By now I'd kissed a couple of other boys, but this was the first time I'd been invited by one of the interesting ones. It meant nothing at all if an interesting *girl* invited you to a party. Now that Kiki, Big Doris and Ines Dubberke had had to stay down a year, there were so few girls in the class that never mind who gave a party we were all invited, even Little Doris. The interesting boys didn't have to take such considerations into account. If one of them gave a party he would invite at most four of us, and get the other girls from the other classes in our year. Some of the girls at Falko's party even came from the older classes. The girls from the older classes were a little alarming, as if they knew something that we didn't know yet, something that could be used against us at any time. I was relieved when someone put an Otto record on, because now that we were all listening to it we didn't have to talk to each other any more.

Falko had put up an orange tent in the garden for the party. When the Otto record was over we all stood around the barbecue smoking. Falko's mother came out of the house and put a dish of pasta salad on the camping table. Falko's mother wasn't at all like mine. She had long, straight hair and wore jeans, and although she was in a bad temper for some reason, and took no trouble to hide it, she stayed with us for at least an hour. In that time she smoked more than all of us put together. She got a different boy to give her a light each time, looked at him through the flame as he did so, and then blew smoke in his face. When darkness fell she kicked the barbecue for no obvious reason, and went indoors without a word. Falko was not in the least annoyed. He picked up the sausages that had fallen off the barbecue, wiped them on the tablecloth, and put them back on the grill. The girls from the older classes passed a cigarette packet around. They had a special method of smoking, which they taught me. You took your first drag, inhaled deeply, kept the smoke in your lungs as long as possible and then expelled it. Everything normal so far. But now came the point: you took another drag without a breath in between. Your lungs were crying out for oxygen now, and all they got was more smoke. There was nothing they could do but suck that smoke into their fine little alveoli and lobes, and hope there might be a bit of oxygen in it somewhere. You were soon feeling pleasantly woozy. You let the smoke out again, and instead of finally breathing in the air you so urgently needed, you drew deep on the cigarette for the third time. If you were standing up – and of course we were standing up so as to enjoy the effects to the full – your legs gave way at this point, you lost consciousness for half a second, slumped to the ground, and when you came back to your senses you felt all soft and peaceful. The boys watched us. They thought it was 'cute' when we collapsed.

'Sooo cute! It's just so cute!' squealed Dirk Buchwald, a boy from another class, and then he put his arm round my waist, draped my right arm round his shoulder, and helped me up, and the other boys made sure they picked up a girl who'd collapsed too. Like Red Cross orderlies removing the walking wounded from a battlefield, the boys led us into the party tent and laid us down on the mattresses there. It was nice to lie there for a moment looking up at the string of coloured lights. Not just because I was feeling dizzy. When I stood up my back soon hurt, and I wasn't in any condition to spend long sitting down either. I'd shot up like a weed this year. I'd grown at least twelve centimetres. My mother's eyes clouded over when she looked at me. She was mad about China, she'd read everything that Pearl S. Buck ever wrote, and was always praising the delicate grace of Asian women. Only the year before she'd been delighted because she said I was so small and delicate – the first delicate-looking woman in the family, which of course was totally nuts. I was still, and always had been, one of the biggest girls in my age group. But my mother had heroically refused to take that in, and instead compared me with my sister. Who of course was taller than I was; after all, she was two years older. But this year I even overtook my sister, I was taller than all the other girls in my class anyway, and only four of the boys outstripped me. When I measured one metre eighty, my mother dragged me off to an orthopaedic surgeon to find out where it was all going to end, and to have me prescribed the pill if necessary.

The orthopaedic surgeon X-rayed the joints of my hand and said I wouldn't grow any more. I was not relieved. I felt it was already too late. My height was horribly conspicuous, and gave rise to hundreds of comments. As if people felt personally insulted by my body and wanted to take it out on me. 'You'll soon be drinking from the roof gutters,' even Uncle Horst had said.

Dirk Buchwald lay down beside me and nuzzled my neck. He was wearing a denim waistcoat and short-sleeved blue check shirt. The pockets of his waistcoat were bulging. The one on the right had a square bulge because of the Marlboros in it, and the red plastic handle of a brush stuck out of the other. On the left of his waistcoat he had drawn the head of the Pillhuhn cartoon character in ballpoint. On the right shoulder it said AC/DC. With a zigzag arrow between them. He had hair in long strands, a bony face, and attractive tanned forearms. There was a silver bracelet round his right wrist, with a little plate engraved with his first name.

'Like to come round behind the tent with me?' he asked. I couldn't see why he wanted to go somewhere else. All the others were smooching on the mattresses. That's what they were there for. It was pitch dark behind the tent. Dirk Buchwald took my head in his hands and started kissing me. A boy had never held my head in his hands to kiss me before. I thought Dirk Buchwald was simply marvellous, although he kissed so hard that he bit my lips. I thought he was doing it by accident, so I let him and didn't resist, so as not to make him feel ashamed. Then he positively rammed his teeth into my mouth. I tasted blood. I tried to twist away from his hands, but he held me tight and drew his incisors back and forth over my lips until there was blood running down my chin. When he finally let go of me I was more confused than scared. I wasn't sure if I might not even have liked it, and if I should let him kiss me a second time to find out. While I was thinking about that and searching for a tissue in my trouser pockets, Dirk Buchwald suddenly let out a loud fart. Once again I thought at first that perhaps he'd done it by accident, and now he must be feeling terribly embarrassed, even more embarrassed than I felt on his behalf, but then I sensed through the darkness that he was grinning at me, very pleased with himself. I couldn't see anything, zilch, just inky blackness, but I could sense that grin as clearly as if I'd put my fingers on his mouth, and then I knew that he'd done it on purpose. That was a thousand times worse than the blood I had to wipe off my mouth. It revolted me so much that I ran off, fetched my denim jacket, got on my moped and rode home. My moped was a blue and white Puch. If you let in the clutch fast enough you could ride for a way on the back wheel. I considered myself an unusually good moped rider, far better than everyone else. On the other hand, some things that my fellow pupils could do easily were way beyond me. For instance, I was unable to travel by bus or train except to the main rail station, which didn't involve changing. I couldn't understand the timetables. I just couldn't manage to read timetables. Until then, if I absolutely had to go into the city centre, I'd always gone the twenty kilometres by bike. When I bought the second-hand moped, of course my father started on about paraplegics again.

'Boberg is full of wheelchair users – all of them moped accident victims.'

As I rode home I wondered whether Dirk Buchwald always did that, just farted after kissing someone, or only with me. Only with me, I guessed. It was raining slightly. I held my face up to the fine pinpricks of the drops and rode faster, letting my hair fly free at 38 k.p.h. I'd wedged my helmet on the carrier. I forgot about Dirk Buchwald. I hummed 'Kiss You All Over' to myself, '. . . need you . . .' Suddenly the cobblestones I was riding over slid away from under my back tyre. There was nothing, absolutely nothing for the tread to get a grip on. I leaned over sideways and skidded along the road with the moped. When I finally stopped skidding I just lay there shedding tears. Not because I'd hurt myself, but because I was such a failure. I ought to have bought myself a slow, tame, girlie moped, like a Velo Solex, or I ought to have gone on riding my push-bike. Why couldn't I finally accept that I was useless, totally useless, a complete idiot? I stayed lying in the rain for a while, I didn't even haul my leg out from under the fuel tank. I made out I was badly injured and unconscious. I hoped a car would run over me. But of course there wasn't anyone out on the streets after midnight in this dump.

Two weeks after the accident I sold the Puch to Yogi Rühmann, a boy in my class. My left knee still hurt. Not that I was entirely sure about that. I'd pretended to be ill so often that by now I couldn't tell if something really hurt or if I just wanted it to hurt.

At the next party Yogi told me accusingly that the moped – *that* moped, he said emphatically – had collapsed under him, and when I refused to give him his money back he asked if I'd like to go out with him. Like most boys, Yogi Rühmann was shorter than me. If he stood beside me I had to fold myself up, bend my back, hold one leg at an angle and brace the other diagonally. He was thin as a weasel, with narrow eyes, he smoked two packets of Rothhändle cigarettes a day and looked shifty. You could see black behind the enamel of his mossy little teeth. All the same, I couldn't say no when he asked if I'd like to go out with him. Three girls in my class were in love with him. They said Yogi Rühmann was cute. He did have a baby snub nose pointing skyward, and if that's enough to make someone cute, then he was cute. In addition, when he came up behind me in the language laboratory once, Yogi had whispered, 'You've got a lovely fat bum.'

So it was not to be taken for granted that he liked me, far from it. Perhaps no one would ever like me again. My weight had increased along with my height. It now swung between sixty-five and sixty-eight kilos. If I could manage not to eat or drink for several days running I weighed sixty-four kilos, but I just couldn't get below the magic sixty kilo mark. Fifty-nine, or even better fifty-seven kilos would have been my ideal weight. Every morning I got on the scales, every morning I was too fat. Sometimes I weighed myself in the afternoon or evening too. Then I was *really* too fat. And too tall as well. Perhaps I had a tumour in my spine pushing my vertebrae apart. One day they'd find it and remove it. The anaesthetist would make a mistake and I'd fall into a coma, and when I finally woke up two months later I'd suddenly be eight centimetres shorter and also pitifully thin. Then my life would begin. You could already see my ribs, and my hipbones stuck out as well. Lying in bed in the evening, I looked with satisfaction at my flat stomach and those hipbones, which stood out even more distinctly and were even bonier when I lay down. Once a boy had stroked my hips and said, 'Wow, you're so skinny!'

Except unfortunately he was wrong. My legs weren't thin enough to match those bones, and my bum was so fat that a lot of men just had to touch it, and Yogi couldn't look at it without passing remarks. There were some boys who wore jeans size 26. I wore Wranglers size 31. Size 29 would have been acceptable. 29 or 28. The jeans fitted very closely, and the fabric stretched from hipbone to hipbone without touching my tummy. When I walked the jeans slipped about on my bones and rubbed the skin that covered them. I liked that feeling. It reminded me how thin I was there. Another pleasant pain was the constant slight pang when my stomach turned over. I never ate enough for that pain to go away.

'Tummy pains are good,' Little Doris agreed. 'If you're hungry, so hungry that your stomach hurts . . . well, when it hurts is when you're losing weight.'

If that was right I should have been losing weight the whole time. But suddenly my weight shot up to sixty-seven kilos again. Little Doris, on the other hand, was getting thinner week by week. Never taller, just thinner. She was still as small as she had been when I'd stuffed soap in her eyes. All her bones stood out, and her arms and legs were beginning to grow yellow down on them, like a bee. No one would ever whisper to *her* outside the language laboratory that her bum was too fat. On the other hand Yogi would never ask someone like her if she wanted to go out with him. Doris thought I had a fat bum too, but in her opinion I'd have to resign myself to it. It was just my natural disposition, the way it was her natural disposition to stay small.

'I'll never look really good,' she said. 'I'll just have to make the most of being the cute type.'

I was astonished. Little Doris was indeed relatively small, but I would never have thought of her as cute. Narrow lips, big chin . . . and she was far too grumpy to be cute, anyway. Now I realised why she bought all her clothes in expensive children's boutiques.

'Jesus, Doris,' I said, 'you're making a big mistake. How are you ever going to get a boyfriend if you go about in little-girl check smocks and yellow playsuits? With your figure, I'd wear the sharpest mini-skirt of all time.'

'*I* have very good taste,' said Doris. 'Those dungarees are from Oshkosh. Because I save up my money and I buy something new only every six months, but then it's good quality. As for you, you have no sense of style at all! You wear cheap, totally tasteless stuff.'

She was right. I always looked horrible. I either wore jeans with a dark-blue sweatshirt that did nothing for me, and a crumpled Indian scarf round my neck, or mechanic's blue overalls with the collar turned up to make them look a bit like a Mao uniform.

All the same, I had more success than Doris – with boys, I mean. At school, on the other hand, I was getting worse and worse. I let Little Doris swot away for class tests on her own now. She was studying all the time. She just didn't understand that good marks weren't going to be any use to her.

When I agreed to go out with Yogi, he told me, 'It's just as well that you didn't meet me in the dark when that moped collapsed under me.'

We didn't get on particularly well in the light either. When we met at his place his friends were usually there too, and Yogi talked solely to them, while I sat in silence. His friends were Falko, Hoffi Hoffmann, and a boy called Natz from a class above ours. Sometimes Locke was there too, and then I had someone to talk to. Locke had the worst reputation of any girl in school. The boys used to twist her breasts like the knobs of a radio set by way of greeting, saying, 'Hey, want me to turn you on?' They invited Locke to all their parties because she looked quite good and went along with everything, but at the same time they looked down on her for it and made disparaging remarks about her. Yogi had a whole series of barely credible stories about Locke. How she'd had three boys at once. How she managed to get a Four in physics. How she sat behind Falko on his moped and jerked him off while they were riding. I admired Locke. I think all the girls secretly admired her. She was what we didn't dare to be. Most of us acted as if we couldn't stand her, but when she walked past you couldn't help looking. I imagined that Locke was very lonely and despised us all. She was the only girl who played football well. Her mother appeared in shows with snakes – pythons, they were. I wished Locke would be my friend, but then she left school and went to work in a perfumery. Also she couldn't tolerate the pill, and she got fat. Really fat. Not just like me, but brimming-over, bulging out of her clothes, X-size fat. In effect she withdrew herself from circulation, because of course boys didn't ask her out any more.

When Locke and the boys had gone again, Yogi and I lay on his mattress until it was perfectly dark. There were posters on the walls above the mattress, one showing an ashtray shaped like a mouth, with 'Who wants to kiss an ashtray?' under it, and another mouth with yellow teeth and a caption saying 'Nicotine makes kissing so sexy'. You always found posters like this hanging in the rooms of people who smoked like chimneys. Yogi put his hand briefly under my shirt and let it slip down to the zip of my jeans. He pushed his hand down the front of them without undoing the button, and though the jeans fitted very tightly he managed to grope between my legs with his hand. Letting him do that was the inevitable next step if I was going to be like Locke some day.

Yogi's fingers scraped my dry mucous membrane. It hurt so much that I twisted back and forth to get away from those fingers, or at least have them scraping some other part of me, somewhere not so sore. It was torture. But I couldn't say so. Because when Yogi had been torturing me for a while it was as if someone had thrown switches inside me and my whole body began humming like a power station. The pain was still there, but it suddenly meant something quite different, and then there was a kind of wave rolling unstoppably through me, and pain, shame and despair dissolved into a terrific feeling. Hot and soft, better than anything I'd ever felt before, even better than eating. I tried not to let it show, but something in my body was shooting from side to side like a pinball, even when the terrific feeling was over and the pain was just pain again. I wanted Yogi to stop. We had a proper wrestling match. A point came when it hurt so much that I grabbed his hand and did say something after all.

'Stop it! Please!' I said, and when I said that it was as if someone had turned the light on and was pointing at me. But at least Yogi finally stopped. He was pleased that I asked him. He thought I wanted him to stop just because it was *too* good.

Yogi had already slept with girls. I knew that. Everyone knew it. So I would have to sleep with him too. When his mother was going away for the weekend and he asked if I'd like to spend the night with him I said yes at once. I bought some Patentex Ovals in the pharmacy. All the girls who I knew had already slept with boys used them as a contraceptive. At first the woman in the pharmacy wanted to know how old I was, but then she let me have the packet even though I didn't have my ID on me. Next I asked my mother. I didn't bother to lie to her. I assumed she'd let me stay out overnight without kicking up any fuss. Normally she didn't interfere in my life. But this time, surprisingly, she began telling me off. Would I kindly remember that I was too young, that was the gist of her remarks, and she might be taken to court for procuring. Total nonsense. I was fifteen and I knew girls who'd had their first abortion at fourteen. And my sister's boyfriend had stayed the night with us before she was sixteen too.

'That's the very reason,' said my mother. 'And that's the last I want to hear about it. This is not a brothel!'

I didn't reply, but ran upstairs. At the time I was occupying my granny's little attic room. She had gone into a home when she couldn't manage to climb the stairs any more, but her granny smell still hung about the room even after it had been redecorated. My father was furious because I'd painted the room dark brown, including the ceiling.

'Like being in a shoebox,' he'd said. If he'd had his way, it would have had amusing poppies stuck all over it again.

So I stood in my shoebox and kicked the brown wall. Once. Twice. The second time I did something to my ankle. I lay down on my bed and clasped my hands behind my head. I would have liked to put a record on. By now I owned four LPs and eight singles. Johnny Wakelin's 'In Zaire' would have been the right track to play now, but I didn't have a record player. So I just listened to the blood roaring in my ears. After a while my mother came in. There was no key to my room, so she could walk in whenever she liked, and she did, often.

'I've been thinking,' my mother began. 'You're right, really. You're not so young any more. It was different in my time. So as far as I'm concerned, well, as far as I'm concerned it's all right. If you really love this boy then sleeping together is lovely.'

I listened to her in amazement. She had never set eyes on Yogi, and I had never said I loved him either. But now there was no stopping my mother, she was talking herself into a frenzy. Finally she sat down on the side of my bed and mopped the tears from her eyes with the hem of her apron. I knew that my mother knew hardly anything about me except where I lived, but only now did I realise that she thought she was completely in the picture and had invented a happy little life for me. She was probably still sure I was just like her. I thought it better not to contradict her.

My mother wanted me to ask my father too. I'd hoped she would do it for me. I had barely spoken to my father for over three years.

By now I was really fed up to the back teeth. Why did I have to let half the world know about it before I could go to bed with Yogi?

My father was in the garden. He wasn't lying on the recliner, he was tramping around among the flowerbeds with his arms folded.

'Dad?'

'Yes?'

'Mum says I'm to ask you if it's all right for me to spend the night at Yogi's, and then she'll let me too.'

What utter shit you had to talk with your parents! What idiotic things they forced you to say!

'You must be out of your mind!' said my father. Then he slumped back in on himself again and turned away. I stayed beside him. It felt horrible being so close to him.

'Why not?' I shouted.

My father made a dismissive gesture. 'You all do what you want anyway,' he muttered, and he shrugged, folded his arms over his chest again, and went on checking his flowerbeds.

I took that as permission, showered, washed my hair with apple shampoo and packed my toothbrush, the packet of Patentex Ovals, my best nightie, a pair of panties and a towel in a sports bag. Then I got on my bike and rode away. It was hot. I tried not to sweat. I might not be able to shower again at Yogi's. I had used an intimate feminine lotion which was blue, like Domestos, but I was still afraid I might disgust Yogi. I had heard all kinds of horror stories from Locke about what the first time had been like for other girls, stories where you were practically swimming in blood afterwards and the idiotic boy had the nerve to ask if he had been good. But it said in *Bravo* how lovely the first time could be if a boy and a girl wanted the same thing, and how it was a very significant occasion for girls. Yogi had experience, so it was his responsibility. Perhaps he'd be kind and thoughtful with me if I told him it was my first time. Perhaps we would suddenly feel really close and know what to talk about. I thought of what I liked about him. There had to be something about him I could like.

When I arrived Yogi's mother had already left. There wasn't a father around at his place. I'd never met his mother either. We had always gone straight to Yogi's room. I was perfectly happy with that. I didn't want to meet any parents, and I wasn't keen for anyone to meet my parents either. What point would there be in it? This time Yogi showed me all over the house. When we got to his little brother's room he said, 'I was just passing this morning, and the door was open, and my little brother was standing there stark naked looking down at his prick in surprise. He had a hard-on. I think it was his first ever. It was really cute the way he was looking at his prick. I went away quickly so he wouldn't notice I'd seen him like that. It was his first time, see?'

I wasn't sure what had moved him so much about this scene, but his eyes had gone all dark as he told me about it, and I didn't want to upset his feelings by asking questions. So I just nodded. His little brother had gone away with his mother. We went into Yogi's room and lit cigarettes. Yogi put a record on. The sleeve showed a bearded man wearing a stupid cap. He was leading two stout horses, Shires or Clydesdales. The music was full of throaty piping.

'Do you like horses?' I asked.

'Only the Holsten horses that bring the beer,' said Yogi.

We lay down, smoked, listened to the horse music and watched the room get darker. Now and then Yogi cleared his throat, once he stood up and turned the record over, and once he stood up and lit a candle. When he lay down beside me again he put one hand on my shoulder and pulled me close to him. He kissed me. I liked that. Usually I only liked kissing at first. As soon as I'd been going out with a boy for a couple of days his kisses began to disgust me. The better I knew him, the more disgusted I felt by whatever his kisses tasted of. Yogi's kisses always tasted of cigarettes. That was kind of neutral. The advertising people who'd written the words for the poster with the yellow teeth and the ashtray mouth simply hadn't thought it out to the end. Yogi put his cheek against mine – a trick to avoid having to look at me – and felt for the zip of my trousers.

'Just a moment,' I said, standing up and reaching for my sports bag.

'Hey, wait,' said Yogi. 'Stay here! Stay here, will you?'

'No,' I said, 'do you think I'm totally crazy?'

I went to the bathroom, closed the door behind me, undressed and got under the shower. When I'd showered I put my nightie on and opened the box of Patentex Ovals. The suppositories were welded into foil that you could only open with your teeth. I immediately got a soapy flavour in my mouth. Locke had once told me how she threw a Patentex Oval capsule in the loo at a party and the water instantly began foaming. She'd flushed and flushed, but finally the foam even spilled out of the toilet bowl.

When I got back to Yogi's room, he said, 'You didn't have to go away.'

I lay down. You have to lie down when you've put in a Patentex Oval or it runs out of you again.

'There's something I have to tell you,' said Yogi. 'It's like this . . . well, I can't always quite make it when I'm sleeping with a girl. I mean, the last girl I went out with . . . it didn't work with her, for instance. And I don't know if I'll manage it now.'

'It doesn't matter,' I said. 'It's not all that important.'

That was what the girls in the photo-love stories in *Bravo* said. They also said 'What matters is that we like each other,' but I couldn't bring myself to say that.

'You must help me a bit,' said Yogi. 'Then I can do it!'

'Sure,' I muttered. I imagined Yogi being very unhappy because he couldn't get it up for the second time. *When a boy can't get an erection for the second time he probably thinks it's his fault*, they said in *Bravo*. *But all he needs is a loving partner.*

'Maybe if you touch it . . .' said Yogi.

I'd expected that it might hurt, and Yogi might be horrible and say nasty things about me afterwards. But I hadn't expected to have to do something myself. Why had he asked me here if he couldn't get it up?

'You have to touch it like this,' said Yogi, 'and then run your fingers up and down.'

Warm, dissolving foam was running down the inside of my thighs, leaving a greasy film behind.

'Sorry,' I said, 'I have to go to the loo again.'

The foam ran over my knees, calves and feet. I got into the bathtub. Nothing but cold water came out of the shower head. I laid my forehead against the tiles. I wished I was one of those good, boring girls who never got invited to the exciting parties, but baked yeast cakes instead, the kind that take days to rise, and could go on dreaming about cute boys without having to touch their musty pricks.

From now on my dates with Yogi were always the same. When his friends had gone we lay down on the mattress, Yogi lit a candle, and I had to take his prick in my hand and rub it till it went hard. Then Yogi would roll over on me, but when he wanted to start he couldn't. Then there would be another vain attempt, a third and a fourth, and finally I had to bring him off with my hand, and sometimes even that didn't work. It was as strenuous as running up a sand dune.

'I once had a girlfriend who made it easy,' said Yogi. 'She just sat on me while I lay on my back. It was dead easy then.'

When I had a date with him I always lay in my room beforehand as if paralysed, hoping a car would knock Yogi down in the next half hour. I didn't want to go to his place and have to touch his soft prick. It was just revolting. But I couldn't leave him either, or Yogi would think it was because he couldn't get a hard-on. At that moment he really did need understanding.

And then he was the one who ended it. He told me on the day the dog came. My brother had said he wanted a dog. My father was still very much in favour of being free to travel –

particularly in the winter months, when he flew to some Canary Island *to cut the cold season short*, as he always put it. He still didn't want a dog. But this time my mother had simply gone off with my brother to see a Rottweiler breeder and buy a puppy. It would be my brother's dog, he was allowed to choose the puppy, and the dog would sleep in his room and not mine, but still there'd be a dog in the house. So when Yogi called I wanted to go round to his place even less than usual, but Yogi said it was tremendously urgent and he had to talk to me. I went to my room and cried. Everyone except me would be there to welcome the puppy and play with him, while I had to rub Yogi's prick. Before I set off I weighed myself again. The scales stopped on sixty-five kilos, quivering. I'd lost weight quite naturally in the last few weeks. I was going the right way. In the movie *Bilitis* there was a scene where a man was talking to Bilitis about a beautiful woman living in the castle. He said she wouldn't be half as beautiful if she was even a little bit happy. Her unhappiness was what made her perfect. I got on my bicycle.

This time his friends weren't there. We sat in his room on our own, and Yogi made no move to light a candle. He stayed very cool the whole time, said even less than usual, and kept looking out of the window, or he picked up a record and looked at the sleeve. This could go on for ever. I wanted to go home. I wanted to see the dog.

'What's the matter?' I asked.

'How do you mean? Why would anything be the matter?'

'You're acting so oddly.'

'Me? No, I'm not!'

'What did you want to talk to me about?'

'Oh . . . nothing.'

'You've stopped taking me to the Tomtom with you

recently. You don't want me there with you any more. Do you want to call it a day?'

Oh yes, please, I thought. Call it a day! Say you've fallen in love with another girl. He shrugged and went on staring intently out of the window. It was over. I'd never have to touch his prick again.

'Why?' I asked. He shrugged again, narrowed his eyes and concentrated on something that must be in the far distance. Suddenly it felt bad to be left after all.

'You're embarrassed to be seen with me, aren't you?' I said. 'Is that it?'

He shrugged for the third time.

'Well, you know yourself you're nothing special to look at,' he said. I got up, put my jacket on and left. The dog – I tried to think about the dog.

When I got home my parents and my brother and sister were on the living-room carpet crawling around the Rottweiler. Even my father. The puppy was jumping up at all of them. He came over to me on his wobbly legs too. I knelt down, and he climbed on my lap and licked my face. I picked him up, rose to my feet with him and turned slowly in a circle. The little Rottweiler licked my throat and barked out loud, and then he pushed his muzzle into my face and snapped at my nose. It happened very fast. By the time I screamed he'd already bitten my nostril. Blood was dripping on the dog, and he was licking it off his muzzle with his tongue. My sister was the first to laugh. Then my brother laughed, and then my parents laughed too. They laughed and laughed. It was so funny that the dog had bitten my nose.

'Why did you pick him up? Serves you right!' said my brother. When I went into the bathroom they were still laughing. They just couldn't control themselves. I put my head over the wash-basin and watched the red blood dripping into it.

I don't think I ever really wanted to kill myself. In reality, I clung to my life like a burr. If I kept cutting my wrists all the same, it was just because I had such a strong feeling that someone like me ought not to exist. I ought to be eliminated. And then, when the first blood was flowing, I immediately felt better and stopped.

This time it was something completely ridiculous that set it off. It was because I had to move out of my room. We were expecting two French schoolgirls on an exchange visit. My sister had already been to stay with them in Bordeaux, and now they were coming to us in return. I was to sleep on a mattress in my brother's room, but he refused to share it with me.

'Can't you move right out of the house?' said my sister. 'Why not go and stay with a girlfriend while Valérie and Brigitte are here?'

Her tone of voice was within the perfectly normal range, so I don't know why this time I went into the kitchen, opened the larder and took the wicker basket off the top shelf. Behind the cough syrup and a box of camomile tea there were several tubes of Sedapon, pale blue tranquilliser tablets that helped my mother cope with everything. I filled a glass with water. Perhaps I simply meant to take one or two tablets at this point, as I sometimes did, but after I'd swallowed two I took a third and a fourth, and finally I'd taken twenty and the tube was empty. Now they could have my room. That was what they'd wanted. I reached for the second tube of tablets, but at the same moment my despair vanished again. Instead, I began feeling worried. I was going to die. Perhaps. Or perhaps not. I put the basket and the tablets back in the larder. I didn't want to die any more. But anyway it was only tranquillisers I'd swallowed, not sleeping tablets. I probably hadn't taken enough. On the other hand, you never knew. It was just that I'd have felt stupid telling my mother. With the small amount of Sedapon I'd taken, it was obvious from the outset that I hadn't really meant it seriously. Perhaps I ought to take a few sleeping tablets too, and then confess? I walked around for an hour, thinking it over, and although I should really have been calming down, I felt more and more anxious. That was a good sign, anyway. If you still felt anxious with twenty Sedapons inside you, the tablets couldn't be all that strong. I went to my room, while it was still my room. I wanted to find a book to take my mind off things, and as I was standing in front of the bookshelf my legs gave way and I found myself on the floor. Suddenly I desperately wanted to live, however ugly I was. And however embarrassing it was, now I'd go and tell my mother what I'd done.

So I went downstairs, brimful of tranquillisers, and looked for my mother. Benno, my brother's dog, was lying in his basket in the corridor, whining quietly to himself. I didn't have to look for long. My mother was standing in the kitchen shouting at my sister. I could tell at once that this was a bad moment.

'You spoil everything!' my sister was nagging back at her. 'Other parents give their children really nice things! They send them to America on holiday! And you make all this fuss just because two French girls are coming here for a week.'

'Can't you see that this house is too small? You're always making so much trouble here. It's always you! Your brother and sister never do it,' shouted my mother. Now it was my sister's turn again, and she shouted back that it was completely antisocial to bring up three children in these conditions, and my parents ought to have stopped to think for a moment before bringing child after child into the world, and the French girls had been invited and they were coming, so my mother had better stop making unnecessary trouble.

'Then I won't make any trouble! I won't be making any more trouble for any of you at all!' shouted my mother. 'I'll shoot myself, and then you'll all have more room! I'll shoot myself with your father's rifle, and then I'll finally get some peace. I just hope people don't have to work in Heaven. With my luck I'll still be having to clean the clouds up there!'

My father had inherited a gun from his father, and hid it in the house because he didn't have a gun licence for it.

'Who says you won't be making any trouble?' said my sister. 'Have you any idea how much mess it makes when people shoot themselves in the head? No trouble my foot! It spurts right up to the ceiling.'

'I'll shoot myself in the garden!' shouted my mother. 'I won't leave a mess for anyone! It will be perfectly tidy – everything will be neat and clean.'

I was quite calm now. The tablets finally seemed to be taking effect. 'You can put a cushion on your head,' I said. 'Then it won't spurt so much.' I'd read that somewhere in a book. Where was it? Presumably Arthur Schnitzler. Or had it been in a film? Anyway, in the nineteenth century lieutenants used to hold a cushion to the other side of their heads when they shot themselves. 'Get out of here! Both of you! Go away!' screeched my mother. I went back to my room. I felt almost cheerful. There were no more decisions to make, I just had to continue along my path to the very end. This house wasn't my home any more, it was a transition stage, an unimportant stop between two infinites, Not Alive Yet and Never Alive Again.

I think I undressed and lay down to sleep. I can't remember. I woke up in the middle of the night. I was wearing a nightie and lying with my face in a pool of vomit. I didn't mind. I was even tempted just to lie there in my vomit and go on sleeping. Then it occurred to me that I absolutely had to clean the pillow. So I trudged downstairs, holding the pillow out in front of me on the way to the bathroom. Like a ghost covered with sick. Of course my mother woke up. She arrived as I was stuffing the pillow into the wash-basin, and was just in time to stop me getting the feathers soaked.

'What's going on here?'

'I took some tablets,' I mumbled. I didn't feel like a ghost any more, I just felt as if I were under water. God, how embarrassing – I'd taken tablets and I still wasn't dead. But the embarrassment was floating like a cork on top of the peace and calm in which I was hovering like floating seaweed, and it didn't get to me.

My mother woke my father.

'Dad! Dad! Wake up! Anne's taken some tablets!'

He asked what tablets and how many.

'Forty,' I said. I didn't want to admit that I'd taken no more than twenty.

'It's only Sedapon. They're harmless. She's brought them all up again anyway,' said my father. 'Let her go on sleeping.'

Thirty hours later I woke up just before the French girls arrived. We solved the space problem by having me sleep in the living-room with my parents, on the couch. 'Did you stop to think for a moment how shocked those little French girls would have been if they'd arrived to find there had just been a suicide in the house?' asked my mother. When she mentioned our exchange visitors she always called them 'those little French girls'. The little French girls were indeed smaller than we were, one metre sixty-five tall at the most, and they spoke neither English nor German. If my sister wasn't around they could communicate only in gestures. But they were very good at that. They bubbled over with charm and danced rock 'n' roll for us, and once they cooked us a five-course meal, full of highly seasoned dishes that stung your throat, and it was three hours before we got to the fifth course. And then there was still a *tarte* to come.

'They seem to have all the time in the world,' said my mother crossly through clenched teeth when the little French girls had disappeared into the kitchen again. 'A *tarte* still to come! What's the idea, a *tarte* still to come? Can't they see I have a household to run? I can't spend four hours eating. Maybe they can in France. And you can bet I'll have to wash the dishes.'

The little French girls did indeed leave washing the dishes to my mother, and danced more rock 'n' roll for us instead. My father smiled at the sight of them. Ah, the daughters other men had, such little whirlwinds, bubbling over with charm! Surreptitiously he glanced at those great big sour-pusses, his own daughters.

The plane's coming in to land. We have to fasten our seatbelts again. Any moment now. Any moment now I'll have landed and survived yet again. We plunge into the cloud cover, the aircraft noses around in it for a little while, and then we drop lower and lower, you can see houses now, with little gardens attached, and a castle surrounded by a park, with flags flying, and with every metre that we drop my chance of survival increases. That's probably not true. It probably makes no difference if you crash from a height of ten thousand metres or fifty metres. But given the choice I'd rather fall from fifty metres, even if that means less time for the whole of your life to pass before your mind's eye. However, I know I've messed everything up anyway. The only thing to be said for me is that I never told my therapist about Peter Hemstedt. I didn't want to see his raised eyebrows or that alert, understanding nod. I didn't want to hear his therapeutic opinion, which doesn't know anything about love, only about chilly fathers and the compulsion to repeat negative childhood experiences over and over again. I didn't want to hear him say I deserved a better man, I ought to find myself someone who would *do me good*. As if love depended on making sure your investments were good value, the way my horrible financial broker of a brother does. He recently tried palming a risky investment off on me over the phone. He said he'd get me the credit I'd need for it. I hate the idea of loving someone just because he might *do me good*. It's like advising a football fan who backs, say, St Pauli to start cheering for Bayern Munich instead because they win much more often. How do you explain to a therapist that there are some injuries you don't actually want cured?

Although that's probably exactly what will happen. Meeting Hemstedt will cure me. Everyone knows how these reunions turn out. Disappointment is inevitable. He doesn't have a chance. Even if he were a paragon of virtue, beauty and good taste, he'll never come up to the ideal image my undisciplined heart has made of him. I last saw him five years ago, and when I called him the other day I put on a ridiculous pretence, making out I wanted to stay with him just to save money. I've never been able to express the love I feel for him in a way that people would normally understand.

Hemstedt has asked me to go to his office so that he can give me the key to his flat. The taxi stops outside a building which is glass from top to bottom. I get out, look up and down the green-tinged wall of windows, see my reflection, suffer the usual shock and ask myself what I think I'm doing here. He didn't love me when I was young and beautiful, and I haven't exactly improved my chances. Perhaps Hemstedt won't even recognise me. There are forty-two kilos between our last meeting and today. And I look rather unbalanced too, fatter below than above. It used to be the same when I was still dieting. When I starved myself I lost weight from my face and breasts. Pretty soon you could count my ribs. Then, when I started eating again, the weight went straight to my bottom and my legs. These days I look like a troll, or as if someone had carved me out of a tree trunk and hadn't got around to the details yet. I'm practically disfigured. I'll be facing him any minute now and his glance will tear me to shreds. He'll see how fat I am. So what? Let him. Let him see! Is it any big deal, me being so fat? Whose fault is it anyway?

I noticed Jost Merseburger, Richard Buck, Stefan Dorms and Peter Hemstedt right at the beginning of the new school year, because they were the only boys who had picked Gymnastic Dance as their individual sport. After the tenth year of school we had tutors instead of class teachers, and the subjects we took were divided into compulsory, compulsory with options, and optional. Anyone who opted for Gymnastic Dance had to be either a girl or a complete rabbit at other sports. I, for instance, qualified on both counts. Jost and his friends didn't look particularly fit either, more the sort who wouldn't be considered for active service in the army, tall and lanky. But even if a choice between light athletics, working with the apparatus and gymnastic dancing seemed like choosing between the rack, the thumbscrews and the Spanish boot, male rabbits at sport usually preferred fooling about on the cinder track to dancing with girls. I didn't know much about the quartet, except that they were always carrying plastic bags from record shops around the school yard, and holding the bags open to show each other what was inside. Jost was regarded as the most sensitive boy in our school and was treated that way. If he leaped to his feet in the middle of a lesson, looked wildly around him, and then ran out of the room, slamming the door behind him, the teacher would always say soothingly, 'Never mind Jost. Jost is *sensitive.*'

What a load of rubbish. We were all sensitive at that age. Probably even the editors of the *Survey* were sensitive. The *Survey* was an alternative school magazine that had suddenly appeared at Heddenbarg. It regularly included an ad for the Young Christian Democrats, and its editors wore pullovers with diamond patterns and Burlington socks and put empty Mumm champagne bottles on the common-room shelves. What distinguished Jost from the rest of us was his total lack of restraint. Perhaps he was unrestrainedly sensitive too. Of course Jost, Peter, Richard and Stefan often skipped sports lessons, getting out of them whenever possible. They would take ages doing up their shoes, or they made out they'd forgotten something in the changing room. But once they were there, they saw the thing through without turning a hair. The lesson always began with a folk-style dance where you ran round in a circle, joining hands in the middle so that your arms formed the spokes of a living wheel. And Jost, Richard, Peter and Stefan, stony-faced, their eyes expressionless, would reach their hands out too. They never fooled around. They seemed almost autistic, moving only as much as they absolutely had to. When we were supposed to hop they would stretch one leg slightly and let a foot drag over the floor. If we were to raise our arms in the air, they would half-raise them with their elbows bent – as if someone were holding a pistol to their backs. I couldn't help looking at them all the time, although of course they were not among the most desirable boys, those the other girls envied you for. I decided to make a pass at Peter Hemstedt. He was the most insignificant-looking of the four, thin, but without the elegant lankiness of his friends. His bone structure was made for a short, sturdy person. As far as I knew he'd never had a girlfriend. I marked him down as someone who would probably be glad to be allowed to kiss me. This Peter Hemstedt, this nonentity of a boy with his big nose, his nonentity's haircut and his nonentity's name was someone I could still venture to approach in my condition at that time. My weight had risen to sixty-nine kilos. I very seldom got it down to sixty-seven. Even keeping it at sixty-nine kilos wasn't easy. It was such a strain being hungry all the time. My whole life was a strain. Not being invited to parties. Being invited and having to go home without kissing anyone. Getting boys to kiss me. Kissing boys who really disgusted me. Passing building workers in the street. Not letting it show in lessons that I had no idea what the teachers were going on about. Nothing in my life went easily or of its own accord. Except eating.

By now even the good, plain girls almost all had steady boyfriends. Good boyfriends, of course, but they must do *something* with them. When they crossed the school yard I watched them, and tried to imagine them jerking their boyfriends off. But I really couldn't believe that anyone except me did a thing like that. Although of course I knew it did happen. Gertrud Thode did it, and Petra Behrmann, and plump Rulla and her boring pasty-faced boyfriend did it too, and Henriette with the fat pigtail, and Gabi and Sabine. I couldn't imagine it! How could they walk over the school yard afterwards behaving as if nothing had happened? Only Little Doris, of course, had no boyfriend. In this she was a reassuring factor in my life. She still hadn't grown any taller, and she was still as thin as a rake. Her mother had taken to packing up thick cheese or Nutella sandwiches for her for break, but if she thought she could lead her well-disciplined daughter into temptation that way she must have been amazingly naïve. Doris unwrapped the sandwiches during lessons and looked at them. She just looked at them and then put them under her desk. It sent me crazy. For some time now I'd been trying not to eat at all except at lunch, so when Doris put those big fat cheese or Nutella sandwiches under her desk I hadn't eaten for at least twenty hours. And of course Doris always offered them to me.

'Would you like these? I hate that chocolate stuff,' she said. First I refused. I asked myself: which is more important, having boys chase you or stuffing yourself with that sandwich? But after four or five days I reached the point where eating the Nutella sandwich was clearly more important. I wanted it now, too! At once! After a while I was regularly eating Doris's sandwiches. After a while I was asking her for them. Then she suddenly wanted to eat them again.

'No, I'm hungry myself today,' said Doris, taking a tiny mouthful and chewing it for hours. She would put the sandwich with the bite taken out of it under her desk, where I had to look at it the whole time. She wanted me to beg for it, and sometimes I actually did.

'Come on, hand it over,' I growled. 'You know you don't want it!'

'How can anyone be such a pig?' Little Doris would say, handing me the sandwich with her bony, down-covered arms. She got a kick out of it, she really loved watching me eat her sandwich. What she didn't know was that I brought it up again afterwards. I always spent a great deal of time in toilets, but I still stuck at that sixty-nine kilos. Doris now weighed forty kilos, and had an average mark of 0.9 for her school work, almost as good as you could get. She wanted to improve even on that.

'What for?' I said when she started on yet again about how she must study harder and get better marks. 'What on earth for? It makes no difference to anything. It's all crap anyway!'

Personally I was getting worse at school work every week. I just couldn't concentrate any more. Even when lessons were really interesting, I was always overcome by the idea that there was something even more important and urgent that called for my whole attention, only I couldn't think what this more urgent thing was. Instead I watched movies in my mind. I did want to listen, I tried hard, but while the teachers were talking to me someone switched on a tiny projector in my head, and I had to watch the same movie over and over again. I was the only person in it, and the single take showed me sitting on my chair in the classroom. All the desks in front of me or beside me were empty. Suddenly I stood up, I began to run, and then I jumped out of the window. That was all. Less than five seconds all told. I jumped sideways, one leg stretched out, the other under me, with one arm bent and held in front of my face, the way I'd seen someone jump in a Kung Fu series. The movie stopped at the moment when the glass broke. There was no impact. It was worst in chemistry. Our chemistry teacher would mention a term, a formula that sounded terribly complicated although it turned out to mean just iron or copper, and the cinema show in my head started up again. I saw myself standing up, taking a run-up, making for the window, and then came the sound of breaking glass. I replayed it twenty times in some lessons. Not that I wanted to jump out of the window, or summoned up this vision on purpose. The scene was more like a banal tune: you're tired of it but you can't get it out of your head. It really bored me. It got a little better after six months, and I didn't drift away so often. Then, during a maths lesson, a new spool was suddenly played by the projector in my head. This time I was in a building which looked the way Hollywood props people would probably imagine an ancient Egyptian or Aztec temple, tall columns painted red, yellow and blue, dust-motes dancing in beams of light. I was more or less naked, wearing just a kind of long apron, and my brown, oiled legs showed at the sides. I was holding a large silver dish in my hands. A high priest in a blue and gold robe was standing in front of the altar. I walked devoutly up to him, knelt down on the stone floor, and raised the dish to below my chin. Then all I saw was the flash of a sword, and my head fell on the peat in the dish. I hadn't noticed that there was peat in the dish before. This film too lasted no more than ten seconds, and then I was back in the maths lesson again. I'd missed at most a sentence of what the teacher was saying. Concentrate, I thought, concentrate, you have to concentrate! You mustn't slip away again! As I was thinking this I missed the next sentence too. At last I could hear the maths teacher once more, but I didn't know what she was talking about, and I stared at her, feeling more confused and desperate than ever. You're stupid, I told myself, you really are quite extraordinarily stupid.

'. . . and consequently, in this case, the third binomial formula applies,' said the maths teacher, and there I was kneeling in the temple again, seeing the flash of the sword, with my head dropping softly into a dish full of peat.

The third time I got a six for chemistry, my father refused to give me any more money for school books. Someone who kept getting a six for chemistry was a hopeless failure in his eyes. Luckily we got most of our books for free anyway. Our chemistry teacher Dr Kirch had given me a four minus in my report for oral work in class. That was a joke really, because I never said a word in class. Once Kirch tried asking me questions. I stared at him in panic. I'd spent the last fifty chemistry lessons either jumping repeatedly out of the window or having my head repeatedly chopped off. Kirch was very nice. He had dark hair that he combed back all smooth and wet, like someone out of an American movie of the forties. He started explaining something, and I listened to him, and for once there was no film show in my head, but all the same I had no chance of even beginning to understand what he was talking about. He asked me question after question in a quiet, friendly voice, until I couldn't stand having him take so much trouble with me any more, and I said, 'I don't know! I don't know anything about it. You needn't go on explaining. I'll never understand it.'

And I was to be perfectly right about that.

'Do you have a laundry basket in your bathroom at home?' asked Kirch. That was the first question I was able to answer. I nodded.

'Where I suppose you're ready to throw in the towel?'

That was one of those typical laboured teachers' jokes, but still it was nice of him, because the other pupils, who had been listening ever more intently to the depths of my stupidity, now giggled in a muted way. He asked something else, probably a tremendously easy question, but I knew nothing, nothing, nothing, and then he asked what you would have to add to get the reaction you wanted. I was on the verge of tears.

'What would you *add*?' he said.

'Water?'

I think he was even more relieved than I was.

'That's right!' he said. 'Now, what's the chemical formula for water?'

I even knew that one. I slumped over my desk again. If Kirch had any sense he wouldn't ask me anything else in this lesson. I wondered what it would be like going to bed with him, and I had no difficulty at all in imagining it. He would be very nice. If I did something stupid he'd make a joke, a nice, unoriginal, harmless chemistry teacher's joke, and then he'd take me in his arms and everything would be all right. I tried to imagine what he looked like naked, and sized up his body. He was sturdy, a little thick-set. I liked that. I was probably staring at Kirch so hard that he was bound to think I'd been following his explanations, and he thought it would be a good idea to ask me another question. He was beaming as if he hadn't the faintest doubt that I'd know the answer. That film started up again inside me: there was the Egyptian temple, and the rays of light falling in through narrow openings high up in the wall, I was wearing my apron and holding the dish in my hands. The high priest appeared, looking like Kirch. Kirch had put on the high priest's blue and gold robe. I knelt down and held the dish out to him, and Kirch poured a clear liquid into it.

'Water?' I asked cautiously.

'You've got it!' rejoiced the real Kirch.

*   *   *

One day my sister called and asked if I'd like to go to the disco with her and her boyfriend that evening. We'd been getting on better since she moved out of our house, even if she still couldn't spend more than half an hour alone in a room with me without falling into a fit of frenzied rage. At five in the afternoon I dragged all the dresses, trousers and T-shirts that seemed even remotely suitable for a disco into my brother's room and spread them out on the floor. Benno the dog was sitting on the bed. I kissed the top of his head and put hair-slides between his paws. My brother now had a compact stereo system. I put my Hit Fever LP on. 'And when we talk it seems like paradise.' I spent the next three hours changing my clothes over and over again, trying all possible combinations. Now and then I went out to check the results in the mirror in the corridor. 'Why won't you free me, free me from your spell?' I smiled at my reflection and put my hair up. I hoped my mother wouldn't come creeping out of the room that had been my sister's; my father had turned it back into the parental bedroom again. My mother was ill. Unlike me, she was usually never really ill. Now yesterday's dishes were stacked up in the kitchen and there hadn't been anything to eat all day. My father was in the living-room, in a bad temper, my brother had gone off with his friends. I decided to let my hair fall loose over my shoulders again. 'Everyone's a winner, baby, that's the truth.' Before I started doing my face, I put my brother's Kraftwerk LP on. I'd been keeping it for this moment. I only ever listened to the second song on the A side. It was a thousand times better than the others. I played it again and again as I put on lipstick, first very pale, then dark, then I decided on very pale again, and I drew round my eyes with black kohl. I looked as if I were beautiful. It wasn't just make-up, it was the Kraftwerk music making me more and more beautiful. Luckily, when my brother came into the room I'd put the record back in its sleeve and was listening to the Hit Fever LP again.

'Hey, are you crazy?'

'Pogo dancing!' I shouted at him.

He snatched the needle off the record. The dog jumped off the bed, scurried and whined around my brother, and tried in vain to attract his attention. The worse my brother behaved the more his dog loved him. He couldn't help it.

'Oh, piss off! Who said you could touch my stereo? Buy one yourself! Then you can listen to your crappy music every day.'

I took my LP and went out into the corridor. My brother flung my clothes after me. As I was picking them up I heard my mother call me quietly. I dropped the clothes again and went into the bedroom. My mother's face was pale and covered with beads of sweat. There was a bucket with sick in it beside her bed. She must somehow have managed to get up and find herself that bucket. I took its handle. I told myself that my mother had wiped my bottom when I wasn't in any state to do it yet myself, and no one else would have wanted to. I owed her practically everything. So I went into the bathroom with the bucket of sick and emptied it down the loo. I rinsed it out, let a little water run into it, and took it back to the bedroom. My mother's humble gratitude turned my stomach. I looked at the floor. It wasn't right to feel like this; she was my mother, after all. But she didn't exactly make things easy for me. Although she should have known better by now, she still believed that if she was a good little girl, made no demands and sacrificed herself all the time, everyone would be touched by her simple virtue and love her madly for it. The only problem was that to us children my mother was just someone who cleaned, cooked, washed and cleared up after us. As soon as she stopped racing round the house armed with a mop she ceased by definition to exist, and we were put off and turned away from her.

I sat down on the edge of her bed with my guilty conscience. After all, someone had to give her love – or whatever you call it. I wanted at least to stroke her forehead, but I couldn't manage even that. I stood up again. I'd emptied the bucket, anyway, and the room didn't smell so revolting.

When my sister and her boyfriend called for me I was wearing a blue-grey knee-length dress with a V-neck, fitting very close around the waist and with a skirt that would fly around me while I was dancing. First we drove to the Madhouse. My sister's boyfriend Uwe was sitting at the wheel of the car with his friend Karsten beside him. My sister and I sat in the back. The stereo in the BMW was much better than my brother's, and the tape now playing was much better than the music I usually listened to. But I didn't ask what it was they'd recorded. I didn't want to talk. I just wanted to sit listening to that song for ever, watching the street lights glide past me in time to it. Everything was exactly right. I leaned my face against the side window and hoped we'd have a serious accident and I would die. I didn't want the car to arrive anywhere. I didn't want us to have to get out. But of course we ended up getting out and going down the low, badly lit walkway outside the Madhouse. Every time someone opened the steel door at the end of this tunnel a scrap of music wafted out to meet us. When the door had closed again you only heard the bass line. There were boys leaning against the walls, and older men too, men over thirty, standing beside each other right and left of the door. They wore suede cowboy boots and black leather jackets and had mastered the art of looking at you in a way that was both hungry and scornful. Inside people were pushing past each other in a crowd, you became part of a flowing soup of humanity, with heads and outstretched arms holding glasses sticking out above it. My sister and I stayed in the wake of Uwe and Karsten because people made way for them. There were niches with tables and chairs at the side of the dance floor. Half a VW Beetle was mounted on the wall. More boys were lounging around in front of the niches. In fact the place was full of boys. There weren't half as many girls. These boys had the slave-trader look in their eyes too. If you looked back at them, most would smile and suddenly seem quite friendly, but some just went on staring as if a girl like me was in no position to return their gaze. One boy leaned forward and said, 'Hey, you,' but I was already past him. Uwe went to say hi to the DJ, and they talked, not that talking was actually possible in all this noise. My sister stood on the steps beside me, looked into space and yawned. A wave of humanity washed me away with it. I didn't resist or get out of the way, I let it cast me up on the dance floor and tried to catch the rhythm. I was afraid everyone would see how badly I danced now. But there was no real danger of that, the place was too full. And then it was like driving along in the car; I didn't decide how to move for myself, I let the music decide for me. Two men picked a woman up and put her down on the overhanging top of a column. The woman held on tight there and went on dancing above our heads. All the boys had their eyes glued to her. She wore transparent plastic jeans with what looked like leopardskin tights under them. She was considerably older than me, she was a grown woman, and she looked beautiful and infinitely superior. In a completely different league. I went on drifting with the crowd, dancing, dancing, crossing the dance floor on purpose and by accident, and finally I bumped into Karsten. He pointed to the woman in the plastic jeans. 'Uschi Obermeier,' he yelled in my ear, and I nodded. Whoever that might be. Then I saw him yelling the same into my sister's boyfriend's ear, but Uwe shook his head and tapped his forehead. So perhaps she wasn't Uschi Obermeier after all. As I danced I let my eyes stray around the room. They met the glance of a blond boy wearing dark brown leather trousers and a white shirt, leaning against a column with one knee bent, his cowboy boot propped on the edge of a table. He scarcely blinked, just looked at me very seriously. I looked back. Surprisingly, I didn't feel at all awkward, although he was much older than any boy I'd ever been involved with yet. He was at least twenty-four, and he looked much too good for me: strange, blond, tall, smooth and radiant and . . . and grown up. Yes, virile, that was it. He wasn't one of those school-kids I was used to necking with. I went on dancing, turning to look at him again and again, and our eyes met every time and we looked at each other long and hard, until I turned a little way aside, dancing in another direction, and when I looked back his eyes were already waiting for me. It was all just right, but it was also as if I wasn't really there, because if I'd really been there he would have intimidated me dreadfully. My sister's boyfriend touched my shoulder.

'We're off,' he said, and I moved away behind him, walking, gliding, dancing towards the exit, and when I was almost outside there stood that good-looking boy again, his foot propped on another table this time, and he pushed off from the table and made his way through the crowd, walked beside me for a little way, put a pencil and a waiter's pad in my hand, I wrote my phone number on the pad and he smiled and fell behind us. And then we were in the car again, and the street lights were drawing their bright tracks through my brain. The boys were discussing where to go next. Uwe wanted to go to the After Eight. But Karsten said the pizza gang would be taking the After Eight apart right now, and my sister complained that she wanted to go home. My heart faltered for fear it might be all over, but finally we dropped my sister off at her place and the three of us drove to the Sitrone. I showed my sister's ID at the cash desk, paid, took my drink voucher, a door opened in front of me, and I was in. The music positively flew to meet me, it enveloped me, it hummed inside me and at the same time in the dancers moving to it. I became a part of the music myself, dissolved into it, merged with the room and the sounds and the other people. I couldn't understand my sister. How could she bear to miss all this? I'd never tire of it. Never. This was life. Three marks at the cash desk and a rubber stamp on your hand. It was a thousand times better than the Madhouse. The music was better, the room was bigger, the dance floor was better – you had to climb up to it as if you were going on stage – even the boys were better. They didn't stare so aggressively. I placed myself beside the dance floor and looked up. The back wall was lined with mirrors. Up there it was full too, but not as bad as in the Madhouse, you could move without mopping the sweat from other dancers' faces at the same time. Suddenly I saw Jost Merseburger, Stefan Dorms, Richard Buck and Peter Hemstedt. What were they doing here? None of them could be over eighteen. They were dancing really close to the mirror, without either looking into it or turning their backs to it. They moved the way they did in Gymnastic Dance lessons at school. Their feet dragged over the floor, their movements broke off wearily halfway, as if they were unintentional, yet it was completely different. It was so casual. As if they weren't expecting anything to come of this world, and didn't mind either. Like melancholy skaters who had been skating for hours already.

For the next song the dance floor noticeably filled up.

'What's this?' I asked Karsten.

'Don't tell me you don't know David Bowie.'

I stared up at Jost. Jost was singing along to the words of the song, his lips pouting. He sang the entire song from beginning to end, reached out his arm and pointed to other surprised dancers as if he were an archangel flinging them out of paradise. His friends went on shuffling around him. On the whole Peter was rather more sharp-edged, disciplined, thoughtful about it. Kind of mathematical in his movements. I hid in the shadow of the scaffolding where the DJ sat enthroned, and went on looking at them. The boys I'd kissed recently had been good at sport, one of them had had a convertible, others had been popular for some other reason: as a leftie who talked big, or a class representative, or at least a near-criminal and a druggie. Now I realised that none of that counted. What counted was being casual like that, standing aloof from it all. Suddenly I saw how boring the sportsmen were, how pompous the lefties, how feeble the druggies, how ridiculous the big cars. I looked more closely at Peter Hemstedt. He didn't look average at all. He had a wonderful profile, perfectly straight eyebrows, and the back of his neck was neatly shaved. He had the softest, most beautiful mouth in the world. It had been my own mediocrity that stopped me seeing how good he looked. I was by no means still sure I could have him so easily.

*   *   *

The boy from the Madhouse didn't call. I'd have liked to go to the Sitrone again, but I didn't dare on my own. At the end of the week Yogi called. He hadn't made it into the sixth form. His report said he could have compensated for his marks in written work if he had made a much greater oral contribution in class, but presumably he was taking the wrong drugs for that. For a moment I contemplated asking if he'd go to the Sitrone with me. I didn't. Next time I went there I'd leave my previous life behind. I'd begin a new, brilliant, casual life, and no one would guess what a miserable failure I'd been to date. Yogi was asking me to a party. Another of those barbecues. Dreary long-haired boys would play dreary records with fat horses on their sleeves. Still, perhaps there'd be the chance to make a play for one of them, kiss him, maybe even sleep with a boy and arm myself against Peter Hemstedt that way.

'Have you ever told anyone about it?' asked Yogi.

'No . . . about what? Well, no . . . what do you mean?'

'Oh, you know . . . Are you sure you haven't said anything to anyone?'

For God's sake, no, I had not. Why would I?

I didn't get to Yogi's party until nearly midnight. How stupid they all looked. The boys wore flared jeans and the girls wore those long flowered dresses. So did I. Peter and his friends always wore trousers with narrow legs. They looked a hundred times better. I went straight over to Natz, Yogi's friend who was putting on the music, stood beside him and looked through the stack of records. It was pointless, I didn't know any of them. No title, no group, no singer. I was condemned always to hear what the boy on whose mattress I happened to be lying was listening to. I simply couldn't make myself go into the Membran store and look through the records. I could only just manage to enter the bookshop in the shopping centre, and I never bought anything but paperbacks there because they were on the shelves directly to the left of the door. I dared not go any further in. I was afraid the bookshop manageress might speak to me and ask what I was looking for. And no way did I want to be spoken to.

'Looking for anything in particular?' asked Natz.

I shrugged my shoulders.

'You don't have anything by David Bowie, do you?'

Yes, he did.

At two in the morning I kissed Natz, and he asked if I'd like to go on with him and a few people to another party, where there was said to be a swimming pool. There were seven of us, but Natz had a huge and ancient Mercedes, and we could all fit into it. Three of the boys squeezed into the front, we girls in the back were pressed as close together as golden hamsters in the pet shop, smoking grass and giggling. Natz took a short cut through the woods. It was still warm, and he opened the sunroof. The trees rustled past above us, and the boys yowled like dogs, and the right kind of music came out of the tape player and then out of the sunroof, rising to the sky and getting caught in the treetops. I got my knees up on the back of the driving seat and then on to Natz's shoulders. I stood with my torso above the sliding roof and laid my outstretched arms on the metal.

'What's that song?' I shouted.

'You like it? Shall I put it on a tape for you some time?'

I nodded down to him.

But I still didn't know what the music was called. Even if I did venture into Membran some day I wouldn't know what I was looking for. I was going to ask about the song again, but the next one had already begun, so I just bent down to Natz, let my hair hang in front of his face and gave him a long kiss on the mouth to make him drive into a tree. Then I'd be paralysed, a quadriplegic, and finally there would be a good reason why I didn't function like a normal person in so many ways, and my parents would be full of remorse and let me have a dog of my own after all, and I'd give Jost and Peter Hemstedt money to go and buy me the right records, they could hardly refuse to do that little favour for a poor cripple who couldn't get up the escalator herself. But one of the boys in the passenger seat just took over the wheel while Natz couldn't see. Natz laughed.

'You're crazy,' he said, 'you are totally crazy.'

He seemed to like that.

There really was a swimming pool at the other party, but no one had used it for years. The little bit of water at the bottom was covered with duckweed.

'Looks more like a breeding-ground for leeches,' said Natz.

I acted the teenager stoned on drugs, took a run-up and jumped in, landing more or less on my feet and then rolling forward. While the others sat around the edge of the pool and went on smoking, I splashed through the knee-deep water, draped in duckweed and climbing plants. I thought if I only kept going long enough I was sure to get a nice attack of pneumonia and waste away, and by the time I finally got better after all, I'd be nothing but skin and bone, and Little Doris would be absolutely furious, and Peter Hemstedt would fall hopelessly in love with me out of pure sympathy. Natz kept murmuring that I was totally crazy, and then he laughed, high on grass, and let himself fall over backwards. I was freezing.

'Natz,' I wailed, 'Natz, I'm so cold.'

We left the others behind at the party. They'd have to make their own way home. All through the drive I didn't make a sound. I just looked out of the window and shivered. Natz closed the sunroof. Outside our house he kissed me, undid two buttons of my dress and put a pleasantly warm hand on my ribs. I couldn't stop shivering, and he held me close and said, 'I'll warm you up. Just wait, you'll be warm in a minute.'

But I shivered and shook more and more, and finally Natz himself said it would probably be best if I went indoors and took a hot shower. He asked for my phone number, and I wrote it on the inside of a chewing-gum wrapper for him.

To my surprise, Natz really did call the next day. He asked if I'd caught a bad chill. But as I had been extremely keen for years to fall ill, by now I was very well hardened and as healthy as a cocker spaniel. Natz was a quiet, friendly boy, three years older than me. I had no objection if he was going to be the first person I slept with.

As soon as we were officially together, Yogi called me again. 'Don't tell Natz we never slept together, will you? I told him we did it all the time.' I promised to keep my mouth shut. I thought his problem was just as bad as he did, and I felt a glow of importance in keeping his secret.

The first time with Natz was on the floor of my room. It went badly from the start. Natz wanted to do it, and I wanted to do it – but it soon turned out that neither of us had much experience, and we didn't love each other either, which might have helped us over our awkwardness. This time I didn't wait for Natz to ask me, I brought him off at once. I didn't want to have to hear him asking me. And I wanted to get it over with as quickly as possible. Afterwards Natz lay beside me stroking my hair. I'd have liked to wash my hands, but my brother had locked himself in the bathroom downstairs. It was almost an hour before I could finally go to the loo. Natz asked me to bring a flannel back for him. Before he went home he gave me the tape he'd recorded for me. I still didn't have a tape player of my own.

When my parents flew to Tenerife to cut the cold season short, I seized the opportunity to run away from home. I couldn't see any alternative. I had to sacrifice myself, give myself to the first man who came along so that Natz wouldn't realise I'd never slept with a boy before and Yogi wouldn't lose face. In fact it wasn't as conclusive as all that, because by now I had two more attempts to sleep with Natz behind me, and in the process had at least tacitly revealed Yogi's secret. Natz was deeply upset. Perhaps I was running away to spare myself the fourth attempt. Perhaps I was running away because it was my last chance ever to run away from home. I would be eighteen in six months' time anyway. I had told Natz and Yogi what I was going to do, but I left them in the dark about my reasons.

'I have to get away, understand? I just have to get away.'

In a rather lukewarm way, they tried to persuade me not to.

'You're crazy, totally crazy,' Natz repeated admiringly several times, but no sooner had I made off than he gave me away to the police.

I still remember leaving the Elbe bridge behind. I was in a white BMW, hitch-hiking for the first time in my life. It was much easier than travelling by train. The clean asphalt ribbon of the motorway stretched ahead of me, all the way to a blue sky full of fleecy little clouds and possibilities. The car radio was playing 'Sailing', not exactly the song I'd have chosen as the soundtrack for my flight from home, but all the same I realised with every fibre of my body that I was free, free for the first time in my life, and well on the way to losing my virginity, forgetting Peter Hemstedt, and making my fortune. Far, far away in a hot, foreign land I'd wash glasses in a bar on the beach, and every time the handsome young pianist played I'd dry my cracked red hands on my blue check apron, lean against the piano and hum along quietly. 'Sing it properly,' the pianist would say one day, 'I can tell when someone has a good voice. I can tell by looking at people. And yours is unusually good.' At first I'd be shy about it, and sing very quietly, but my voice really was as clear as a bell, and so beautiful that the guests would fall silent at once. The sea would shimmer in the moonlight, and a fish would leap into the air in a spray of silvery water. The man from the record company who just happened to have been sitting in the bar would say, 'Sign here,' and six months later my first record would come out, with a synthesiser instead of the piano. I'd be famous overnight, but once a month I'd still perform in the little bar on the beach with my friends the bar owner and the pianist.

Did it turn out that way? No, it didn't. I was one of the 70 or 80 per cent of all young runaways who come home of their own accord within three weeks. My parents hugged me. I felt uncomfortable about that, because my father had never before in his entire life thought of hugging me – or at least, not since I was five – and my mother hadn't really dared to for the last three years. But just then I couldn't very well stop her.

My favourite green dress had been stolen, along with a pair of Wranglers. Terrorists had taken my passport and were now bumping off innocent family men in my name. As expected, the statement in *Bravo* that losing her virginity was a significant moment in every girl's life turned out to be a romantic fantasy. I went straight back to the old routine. In addition, my flight had turned out to be completely unnecessary. Natz had found a new girlfriend a week after I ran away. Yogi and he had talked things over, confessed to their shared problem and discussed its possible causes, and now they were both doing fine. No one needed me to make any sacrifices. Yogi had a new girlfriend too. It always worked with her, he said. Spring had broken out everywhere. Even Peter Hemstedt had finally found a girl-friend, a plain little hippy girl.

All of a sudden I had difficulty in moving. It was more than my usual apathy. Even raising an arm or a leg was a big deal. Perhaps I'd had to break into my last reserves of will-power when I made the decision to run away, and now there simply wasn't enough left. If I moved too quickly it made me cry. Sometimes I was already crying when I got up in the morn-ing. I cried as I cleaned my teeth and I cried as I tied my shoes. Riding to school – I still cycled there – I felt whole streams of water running from my eyes. I always waited behind a bush for my face to dry off before pushing the bike into the school yard. If I made for the classrooms in slow motion it was all right, except that I was late for almost every lesson. Luckily that sort of thing didn't upset the teachers so much now. I simply opened the door, shuffled to my place and let my briefcase slip to the floor beside me. No one demanded an apology. If the lesson was German, civics, history or philo-sophy, the others would already be in mid-discussion. Some pompous idiot would always speak up at the beginning of the lesson and suggest a debate on the subject of the exclusion of people with extremist opinions from employment in the civil service, or the banning of the Say No to Nuclear Power badge, or punks and mods. Then there'd be a vote on it. Every time almost everyone was in favour of debate, even those who never joined in. A debate was better than lessons any day. It was all the same to me. I just wanted not to have to move for the next thirty or forty minutes. After I'd got through three or four lessons like this I cycled home again with the tears pouring from my eyes. I dragged myself upstairs to my room, steered my way round the table and the chair, made it to my bed somehow, lay on my back and stared at the brown ceiling. My bed was the only place in the world where I couldn't fail and couldn't be hurt, or at least not while I was alone there. I was so tired. I didn't read any more, and I didn't want to eat either. I just couldn't summon up enough interest or concentration. For anything at all. If someone addressed me directly I found it a terrible strain to keep the conversation going and not simply stare through them. I had no idea what day of the week it was. Time didn't pass any more, it just swelled up. After one or two weeks or months my father came into my room. He was carrying a brown bottle of what looked like cough syrup. He wanted me to take the stuff. He'd brought a spoon too.

'I don't want it,' I said rebelliously, never taking my eyes off the ceiling. Ever since I'd known him my father had spent every afternoon in a state of depression on the garden recliner or the sofa. So I supposed I had a right to stare at the brown ceiling a bit.

'You'll take it!' shouted my father. 'You'll get it down you this minute.'

He almost never shouted at my brother and sister and me, in fact only at Christmas. So when he did let fly for once, it was all the more effective. I immediately opened my beak and licked the stuff off the spoon. The fact that my father was feeding me said nothing at all about the degree of our intimacy. He left the bottle there. A psychotropic drug. He'd probably swapped it with a colleague. 'Listen, my daughter suffers from depression, got anything for that? I'll swap you five tubes of athlete's-foot cream and two rubber hippopotamuses for it.'

From now on I poured a sizeable dose of the stuff out of the window morning and evening. I had no interest in getting livelier. I *wanted* to spend all afternoon lying on my bed, looking at the ceiling and feeling nothing.

When I met my father I tried to pull myself together, to pass him looking reasonably upright and animated, and not burst into tears until I'd turned the corner. My father was not at all surprised to see his medicine working so quickly. He believed in such things.

Perhaps I acted the part of a lively child so convincingly for my father's benefit that in time my pretended liveliness became real – at least, I had enough energy to go looking for a job at the beginning of the summer holidays. Or perhaps I'd simply spent long enough lying on my bed staring at the ceiling. Or I'd lost so much weight by starving myself that it put me in a good mood. In fact I don't know now what I weighed at the time. My God, I really must have been in a bad way if I don't even know that.

The 'German Supermarket' was in the basement of the Alstertal shopping centre. It took me only a day to find out that the job wasn't worth it. Not for all the money in the world, and certainly not for DM 5.80 an hour. I worked eight hours a day, but what with breaks and the journey and putting on my overall and so on, I was out and about for eleven hours in all. I was on my feet the whole damn day. Sheer monotony, and afterwards all I could do was sleep. I might as well have been dead. In addition, my backache immediately got worse. The manager was called Meyer and was always pawing me in a horrible paternal sort of way, but he wouldn't let me sit on the pallets while I was sorting the cans because it looked too casual. I'd have thought it was good enough if I stacked the cans of mixed peas and carrots on the shelves the right way round. However, it seemed that not only my father but the whole world, including old Frau Scharteken who did her shopping in the German Supermarket, had a right to see me looking perky. I bit my lower lip and lived for the lunch break. In the lunch break I took the escalator up to the ground floor and slumped on a bench there, beside the pensioners with their sticks. I sat there for an hour, staring dully at the window of 'One Two Three', a shop full of useless novelties. They'd put a stuffed white chicken in the display. I always looked at that.

After I'd been working in the supermarket for a week Molly, a girl I knew slightly, came in. Molly said she was assembling retractable dog leads in a small factory. Several students from Heddenbarg Grammar School were working there. It was piecework, but even the slowest workers were earning more than twice as much as me.

'I think they still need more people,' said Molly.

The dog-lead factory was in a small detached house near our school. Four rooms with twelve tables. The owner's name was Pörksen. He hired me at once. The work suited me: easy, repetitive actions, and even I couldn't get much wrong. And you never knew in advance just how many leads you would assemble in a day and or how much you could earn. There were good days and bad days, to make it more exciting. Molly and I worked at tables next to each other. We made friends. We were both struggling with our weight. I weighed seventy kilos now. Seventy! Even sixty would have been too much. On Molly's scales I actually weighed seventy-one kilos – if I subtracted two kilos for my clothes and shoes – and Molly claimed that her scales weighed light. If that was the case I might as well go out and hang myself. Molly was a little smaller than me. As a child she had been really fat, so fat that she was sent off to take a cure. 'Big fat Molly's always eating cakes and lollies,' her brother used to chant. It wasn't until two years earlier that she got slim, or not really slim, more like me. The fear of putting on weight again still haunted her.

'How did you manage to lose so much?' I asked, putting a piece of card on the plastic casing for the lead and going on to the next one. Molly's stack was five pieces of card high by now, and she was already having to stand up to work on it.

'I fell in love with this boy,' said Molly, using a kitchen baster to squirt some grease into the casing for the springs that retracted the lead. 'He was older than me, and of course he never looked at me. I wanted him to notice me, so I went on a diet and ate just a lettuce leaf or a tomato on a slice of bread. I lost an enormous amount, twenty kilos – no, more – if I start out from my absolute heaviest, I lost twenty-four kilos. And then the boy finally did notice me. He'd known me for ages, but that was the first time he really looked at me. And guess what he said? He said, 'Lose another five kilos and you'll be a really cute girl.' So then I put on five and I haven't got rid of them yet.'

In the afternoon we took our break together. Molly smoked, and sometimes we went to the bakery to buy cakes. Our eating habits resembled those of the python. Often we ate nothing at all for two days, then we'd eat so much cake and chocolate within a very short time that it stoked us up for the next four days. We were always sorry we'd done it immediately afterwards. Every heroin addict or alcoholic at least gets a good high. But people like us, addicted to sweet things, had our enjoyment only for the few seconds or minutes while we were stuffing them in. I dared not throw up in the thin-walled factory toilets. The unfortunate part of it was that Molly and I didn't starve and binge in time with each other, and when one of us was on a binge she would sweep the other away with her. Before we met, we used to put on a kilo at most and then lose it again. But now we were steadily gaining weight. In the end I weighed seventy-three kilos. On my own scales. Molly and I decided that this couldn't go on. In our next break we went to the pharmacy instead of the bakery and bought appetite suppressants, a packet of Recatol each. To make sure it worked properly Molly immediately took two tablets and I took three. And we actually didn't feel hungry any more. I would still have liked something to eat, but I wasn't hungry. We lost weight again. And not only that: now that we were taking Recatol we worked faster too. We worked like mad, and as we were paid by piecework we earned really well. I was saving for a car. My father had said he would pay for all his children to learn to drive. He had bought an old Beetle as a second car, and we'd be allowed to drive it when we'd passed the test. But I didn't want his Beetle, I wanted a sports car, or at least something vaguely resembling a sports car. I was saving for a Karmann Ghia. Meanwhile school had begun again and I couldn't work all day any more, but if I swallowed half a packet of Recatol at all once I could spend five hours assembling almost the same amount of dog leads. Only afterwards I couldn't sleep. I lay in bed with my heart beating as if the invisible little engineer inside it was freewheeling full speed ahead. So after work I often got on my bike again and rode around until midnight. Since I'd run away from home my parents didn't forbid me to do anything. I could come and go as I liked. Somehow I was always passing the Sitrone on my bicycle rides, and then I would stop on the opposite side of the road to see who was going in and out. One day I summoned up all my courage, parked my bike and went in. After that I spent almost every evening in the Sitrone. I placed myself in a dark corner and watched the dancers, and if there was no one I knew there I danced myself. I always danced right in front of the wall of mirrors, half turned away from it, but of course I was looking the whole time. It wasn't so bad, the way I moved. Dancing in front of the mirror was the natural next step after dancing in front of the living-room window. I was always quite surprised to see how good I looked. When I studied my reflection, I pretended to be watching one of the boys in the mirror. I learned how to make a boy fall in love with you just by glancing at him, and how to make yourself fall in love with someone just by glancing at him too. At ten everyone under eighteen was thrown out. Then I went up to the castle ruins behind the Sitrone, sat down on a wall and looked at the darkness. I started smoking again, because it made you thin and because it was so nice smoking up in the ruins. Sometimes a boy climbed up after me and we necked for a while. I was in bed at midnight, but I still woke up at four in the morning. I persuaded Pörksen to give me a key to the factory so that I could start work early. The place didn't usually open until seven or eight. Of course he didn't know that I was starting at four-thirty, but even if he had he might not have minded. He was expanding fast, and couldn't keep up with the demand for his retractable leads. Even Princess Caroline of Monaco had one. I went to the dog-lead factory at four-thirty and worked there until seven, eight or nine, depending how many lessons I planned to skip, and then I went to school and afterwards I carried on assembling the leads I'd begun earlier. After that I went to the Sitrone again. Surprisingly, I was even doing better at school now. I was suddenly all there in class. I just couldn't keep my mouth shut. When I'd taken half a packet or a whole packet of Recatol, and I couldn't work it off by dancing or assembling plastic parts, I had to talk. Like a loo constantly flushing. Now I was the one who stood up at the beginning of lessons and suggested subjects for a debate, any subjects, about the Red Army Faction or women's lib or anything you liked. I didn't let anyone else get a word in edgeways, I just delivered twenty-minute monologues, marching up and down, claiming that I could concentrate better that way. It's a marvel that no one thought of packing me off to hospital. I'd always had itchy eyelids, but now it was so obvious that people kept mentioning it. I always blamed it on my contact lenses, and maybe that was true, because now that I was hardly sleeping at all, I wore them for twenty hours at a time.

I still sat next to Little Doris in lessons, but she didn't really interest me any more. She'd recently taken to offering me her sandwiches in break again. I just gave a condescending smile and shook my head. If I felt hungry I simply took another Recatol.

*   *   *

In the autumn holidays Molly and I went to Paris by train. I was relying on Molly to fix the tickets and the timetable, and just followed her lead. We were staying with two French girls we didn't know, but they were friends of a friend of Molly's. They lived in a futuristic suburb. The buildings looked like multi-storey car parks, and on the sites of the real car parks huge ventilation shafts rose from the ground, opening their diamond-shaped mouths. Bare walls lined the paths. The place was like a maze for experimental rats. In the afternoons the French girls watched *Angélique* films on TV. I liked Angélique myself. She was beautiful as the sun and totally faithful, but all the same she kept ending up in bed with new men. Either her husbands and lovers died like flies, or Angélique was being raped by pirates or pestered by Louis XIV. Generally she was rescued at the last moment, or maybe it turned out that things weren't so bad after all. Okay, so she had to marry ugly Joffrey against her will, the man with the stiff leg and the terrible scar on his face. But the scar wasn't so very ugly, in fact Joffrey really looked quite good with it. Girls like us had made very different compromises.

Soon before we left it had turned out that Richard Buck and Peter Hemstedt were going to be in Paris at the same time, and my faith in Providence revived. We met at an agreed place, the entrance to the city's underground sewage system. We went down some steps and got into a boat with a group of tourists. The boat swayed as you got in, and we quickly sat down on the seats lining both sides of it. Then we went along the stinking, foaming sewer into the darkness. I was sitting next to Hemstedt. I always just called him by his surname now. It was pitch dark. The people in the boat giggled. The boatman switched on a torch and shone it on the damp walls, or let its beam wander over the brown water and all the nasty things floating there. He punted the boat forward with a metal pole, and when it knocked against the wall it set off a long, clanging echo. And all the time I felt Hemstedt sitting beside me. That was it; I remember perfectly clearly. But when I came back to Paris some years later, and out of nostalgia went down to the sewers again, I found out that you couldn't go on them in a boat. I asked the man at the cash desk, and he said there'd never been any boat trips here. I walked down resounding corridors, I trudged through a large puddle, and I didn't recognise any of it. But I did see a boat in a hundred-year-old photo like the one in which I'd been sitting next to Hemstedt. I didn't know if I'd just been dreaming then or if I was dreaming now. I remembered it all so exactly.

When we came back up into daylight again, Richard and Hemstedt said they were hungry. We went into a café with blue check curtains. The boys ate lavishly, digging into their meat with a hearty appetite, while Molly and I toyed with our salads. Afterwards we found ourselves out in the street again, hungry, but accompanied by two replete young men. We hadn't brought any Recatol with us – after all, we were on holiday – and now we regretted it. Minus tablets and minus chocolate, we were in withdrawal. In fact we were in withdrawal throughout the trip except when we were actually eating. If we passed a bakery and saw cake in the window, we wanted a piece and we wanted it now, and we wanted another in the next bakery, and in the shop after that we wanted a Mars Bar, because what did that matter after two pieces of cake? But of course I controlled myself in front of Hemstedt and Richard Buck. Which do you want more, Hemstedt or cake? That was all I had to ask myself, and the answer was obvious: Hemstedt. But I also knew it probably just meant that I wouldn't get anything, neither Hemstedt nor anything to eat. I only got boys I didn't really want, and if I grew any fatter I wouldn't even get them.

Molly stuck it out until we reached the second sweetshop. Then she bought a Milky Way, and in the next shop she bought some kind of English chocolate bar, and when we passed a bakery she wanted to go into that too.

'How come you have to go into absolutely every shop to buy yourself something to eat?' Richard asked her.

I was so glad I'd controlled myself!

'What business is it of yours? What does it matter to you how much I eat?' asked Molly, going red in the face. Then we walked along side by side, all four of us, saying nothing. Molly didn't go into any more shops.

'I'm sorry, honestly,' said Richard lamely at some point, but there was still a bad feeling in the air. An hour later we were sitting on the little concrete wall round a flowerbed, still silent. At last Richard went over to Molly, pinched both her cheeks and pulled her face out sideways.

'You're the sweetest little frog-face I ever saw,' he said. Molly laughed, and the boys felt all right again, and Molly and I felt almost all right.

I think we were on the way to the Arc de Triomphe when Hemstedt suddenly came up beside me and took my hand. I didn't know why. There was no special reason. I looked at him, and then we began to run. We put a good distance between ourselves and the other two, so that they didn't quite lose sight of us but wouldn't be able to catch up in a hurry. They needed a chance to talk in peace. Hemstedt and I didn't talk. There was nothing to say. We were still holding hands. I wasn't used to being happy, and my eyes stung a bit.

At the underpass leading to the Arc de Triomphe we

waited for Richard and Molly to catch up with us, and then we bought our tickets together and ran up the spiral stairs, higher and higher, until we were standing, hearts thudding fast, at the very top, where the wind blew our hair in all directions. Not the boys' hair, of course; they were wearing dockers' woolly caps. We looked down at the traffic on the roundabout, and Richard told the story of the tourist who got his car on to the roundabout and couldn't manage to weave his way out of the traffic again, so he had to drive round and round the Arc de Triomphe until he ran out of petrol. Hemstedt stood at the very edge, in front of the long steel spikes that made it difficult but not impossible for suicides to thrown themselves off. I said I wanted to take a photo of him there. He turned to face me, wrapped his dark blue trench coat closely around him like a straitjacket, the side with the badge showing, and closed his eyes. I pressed the shutter release. When we had climbed back down, Hemstedt didn't take my hand again, and when we passed a porn cinema I suggested going in. I thought I might shock him that way, but to my surprise Hemstedt said it was a good idea. Molly definitely didn't want to, and Richard didn't want to either. Hemstedt and I simply bought tickets so quickly that the other two couldn't do anything but buy tickets too and follow us in. None of us could translate the title of the film. It had something to do with a harem, so it immediately reminded me of the Angélique movies. There were nine men sitting in the cinema, scattered about the rows of seats at regular intervals. We looked for seats as far as possible from all of them. Molly sat so far back in hers that she was practically lying down. Richard propped his hand on his forehead with a long-suffering expression. The film had begun some time earlier, but that didn't matter, because it was made in such a way that you could catch on to the plot within ten minutes, never mind where you joined it. There was a detective busily searching files and looking very confident. But he could never get any real work done because his girl assistant was hell-bent on sleeping with him. Then you saw a man taking a girl home with him. They had sex, and then a whole lot of men suddenly jumped out of the cupboard and up from behind the sofa like something in a Punch and Judy show. They grabbed the girl, injected something into her arm, and put her in a coffin-like box. They stuck a label with Arabic lettering on the box, and off it went by post. Then there was a scene with the abducted girl caressing another naked woman on stage in an Arab brothel. You could tell it was an Arab brothel because the men watching wore burnouses. Afterwards the women were rewarded with heroin injections. Then you saw the detective again, driving around in his car with his assistant, presumably on the trail of the men who were trafficking in girls. Not understanding the language didn't matter.

'Oh, for God's sake let's go,' whispered Molly.

'Yes, let's go!' hissed Richard.

Hemstedt laid a finger on his lips.

One of the traffickers dropped a bag of apples in the street right in front of the woman he had his eye on. She promptly fell for it and helped him pick them up, and since he acted clumsy on purpose and kept dropping the apples again she helped him to carry them home. Once they were inside the house of course the rest of the gang were there. The men clustered around their new victim and pushed her from one to another of them, while each of the men who got to touch her tore a garment off her. The woman was crying the whole time. She had sagging breasts and bad skin and looked generally ugly and flabby. Even though she was slim. She seemed to be there solely to be treated like that.

Molly covered her eyes with her hand. She annoyed me. It was only a movie, she didn't have to make such a big deal of it.

The woman was still crying and yelling and trying to cover her breasts. Two of the men came up behind her, took her arms and pulled them apart. There was a scene just like it in one of the Angélique movies, where Angélique is sold in the slave market. She folds her arms over her breasts too, her arms are bent back, and when the hundred or so men staring at her see how beautiful she is there's a devout whisper, a kind of respectful, impressed murmur, something like what must have been heard in the lecture room where Albert Einstein first presented his theory of relativity. But the traffickers in this film laughed and shouted and pinched the woman until she was screaming with pain. And of course the porn actress didn't look like Angélique, she had these sagging breasts. You weren't safe unless you were beautiful, as beautiful as Angélique. Then all the malice and unpleasantness in the world couldn't touch you.

'I'm off,' said Richard, standing up. Molly stood up too. This time Hemstedt and I raised no objection, but meekly followed them. The daylight dazzled us.

'Why do porn actors always have pimples on their bums?' asked Richard. We discussed the appearance of porn actors, coming to the conclusion that they were all too ugly for their job.

Two days later Hemstedt, Molly and I went home. Richard was staying on a little longer in Paris because he wanted to visit his sister, who was in the city working as an au pair. We had a compartment to ourselves. Molly and I sat on the outside seats of a row of three, while Hemstedt sat opposite us in the middle seat of another row, so that we could all put our feet up. At some point we started dozing, and Molly finally dropped off to sleep. The rhythm of the wheels on the rails sent me into a kind of trance. I sat there with my eyes open, but not seeing anything, just sensing Hemstedt sitting close to me more and more clearly. Finally it felt as if the whole compartment was full of Hemstedt, but I felt it most intensely in the leg I had put up on the seat beside him. I didn't know if my leg was moving towards him or he was shifting closer to me; it was a movement that went on for hours, slow as a flower opening. When at last there was no more doubt about it, when I could distinctly feel the warmth of his skin against mine through the fabric of two pairs of trousers, and I knew our legs were pressing together, he very gently put his hand on my knee. The touch was so soft and natural that I wasn't at all startled, and just hoped he wouldn't do anything that went further, like moving over to my side to kiss me, which would break the enchanted spell that had been cast over this compartment. But Hemstedt contented himself with slowly stroking my knee. During that train journey I realised that there's no such thing as a harmless touch. I looked into his eyes and put my hand on his leg too, and we went on to Hamburg like that. Once Molly woke up, gave us a searching look, turned over on her side again and put her jacket over her face. I was trying not to feel happy. If you're happy, you have something to lose, and only those with nothing to lose can face the world. When we parted at Hamburg Central station, I already felt that big black hole above my diaphragm. Of course I was hoping that Hemstedt would phone me. But at the same time I was anticipating the pain when he didn't. And of course he didn't phone.

It was nearly Christmas before Hemstedt kissed me.

Meanwhile I'd reached the age of eighteen and bought myself a pale-blue Karmann Ghia. That was all I wanted for my birthday. My parents gave me money, and my brother gave me a photo he'd taken of me throwing up in the loo. By now I could easily earn as much money in a single day working at the dog-lead factory as my parents had given me. I used some of my money to buy Hemstedt's black leather jacket from him, the one he used to wear until he got his trench coat. Now that I had a leather jacket I also got my hair cut. I wanted it like David Bowie's on the cover of one of his records, short and sticking out everywhere except at the nape of the neck, where it was long. It looked terrible. I went around with this haircut for a day, and then used my mother's dressmaking scissors to cut off the long strands at the nape of my neck. I searched her sewing box again, took the biggest safety pin I could find there, and stuck it through my earlobe. Next morning my ear was all swollen, but I left the safety pin in place all the same. By way of retaliation, my parents suggested that I might like to move out. My mother wanted my attic bedroom for an ironing and sewing room, and she'd already bought curtain material for it.

She called my sister and said, 'I've had a great idea. Anne can move in with you.'

My sister threw a furious fit that was to last two years, but of course the whole thing had been settled long before.

On the day Hemstedt kissed me for the first time there were three of us sitting in my new room in my sister's flat. I was sitting on the bed, Hemstedt was sitting beside the bed, and Stefan Dorms was sitting on the floor a little further away. We were going to watch the movie *Chapeau Claque* on TV. I don't remember how we'd decided to meet here. But anyway we had, and now we were sitting in my room. It had been dark for quite some time outside, and it was dark in the room too. The only light came from my granny's old black and white TV set. On screen, Ulrich Schamoni was going through the alphabet and demonstrating the decimal system using his fingers, and that's about all I saw of *Chapeau Claque*, because then Hemstedt got on the bed and sat there next to me. It wasn't the same feeling as on the train. Hemstedt's hand was round my neck and his thumb was stroking my throat. He bent over my face and kissed me.

I thought: it's happened – Hemstedt has kissed me.

I thought: I'm going to be his girlfriend.

I thought: Stefan Dorms is sitting there all alone on the floor.

I thought: I'm definitely not going to sleep with Hemstedt until I weigh less than sixty kilos.

Hemstedt kissed me again, and this time I managed to concentrate on it better. His kiss was too wet and too soft – as if he were licking out a jam-jar with his tongue. But a kiss was more than the touch of a leg, all the same. A kiss, however uncomfortable, gave you a right to certain expectations. Stefan Dorms was sitting in the middle of the dark room, bathed in blue light and staring at the screen.

I thought: poor guy! Why doesn't he get up and go away?

But Stefan Dorms didn't go away until the film was over. At some point Hemstedt said he had to go home too.

'I'll call you,' he said.

'Tomorrow?' I asked.

'Yes, tomorrow afternoon.'

At four o'clock I realised he wasn't going to call, so I didn't need to wait until it was time for the TV news and the afternoon was over. I realised that I absolutely ought not to ring him now, I realised that I was showing dreadful vulnerability. But if I knew myself, I'd wait all Sunday if I didn't, slowly turning myself into a piece of dirt. I'd rather hear it now. Then I could spend all Sunday crying.

His father answered the phone. He said, 'Peter's broken his arm. He fell off the ladder trying to hang the lights on the Christmas tree. We're just back from the hospital.'

I asked, 'Is he well enough for me to visit him? I'll be right over,' I said. 'Right over.'

I flung myself into the Karmann and raced to the flower stall at the station. They didn't have any parrot tulips. Wrong time of year. I bought a bunch of white roses, but as I was parking outside the Hemstedts' door and unwrapping the roses I suddenly felt embarrassed about them and left them in the car.

Hemstedt was wearing a dark-blue towelling dressing-gown with red stripes and sitting on his bed in a bad temper, leaning back against the wall. The left arm of the dressing-gown had been cut off, and Hemstedt was picking at the opening of the plaster with the forefinger of his right hand.

'This is just so disgusting,' he growled. 'It'll begin to stink in no time, and the skin under it will go all soft and white, like it's decayed.'

I gave him a kiss on the cheek and sat down beside him. 'Talk about an idiotic accident,' said Hemstedt, looking into the void. 'Typical. Falling off the ladder while I was hanging that stupid string of lights on the Christmas tree for my old folks. Not a thing you can tell people.'

He wasn't going to talk about us, and he didn't look pleased to see me. More annoyed. Or perhaps he was simply in pain. I'd have liked to be in the clear about that, but I could hardly ask someone who'd just been discharged from hospital. Then Jost and Richard arrived, and he talked to them. The answer was obvious, really: I ought never to have come barging in! I ought not to have bought those silly roses! I ought not to have kissed him on the cheek in that stupidly intimate way! I ought not to exist!

'I have to go,' I said, and I went out, got in the Karmann and drove back. I was crying. I hated myself for crying, and I hit myself in the face as hard as I could, twice. That helped. I took the bunch of roses off the passenger seat, wound down the side window and chucked the roses out.

Next week at school I started a letter. 'Dear Peter,' I wrote, 'it's just before ten. We're having a three-hour German test on *The Sorrows of Young Werther*. The first two hours are over. And if there was any more need for evidence, which there certainly isn't, if there was any more need for evidence that Goethe didn't write his book for people like my classmates this is it. They bent over their exercise books and started straight off without hesitation, without feeling anything. Doris is sitting beside me tracing her round, childish writing in her book, Volker Meyer is eating an apple, and they're both so many miles away from love and suffering that Doris is sure to get a one and Volker will get a three. They're probably saying that the author is criticising society, that always goes down well. But Goethe isn't criticising society. Goethe thinks he's wonderful, that's his problem. His

Werther is always being moved by himself and the intensity of his feelings and the nobility of his actions, getting on well with children, talking kindly and naturally to people beneath his own station in life. Well, perhaps you can make that into criticism of society if you work on it. Werther gets his biggest kicks out of his sensitivity. Every time his feelings have been so wonderfully profound, or he's shown what a kind, sensitive person he is, he has to write and tell his beloved friend Wilhelm all about it, hot off the press. He calls this friend "darling" in his letters, and once he writes something about "lips lisping of love". I ask you! Of course Beimer will say that's just the style of the period, it was how people talked then. But I think his sensitive whining is all Goethe's responsibility. If a period is horrible you have to face it down. The most revolting part is where those wannabe lovers are standing in the terrace doorway, watching "the wonderful rain beating down on the land", and then she just says "Klopstock" and he knows what she means at once. Honestly, Werther – what a priggish, conceited idiot! But all the same, when he started on about his love and his unhappiness I felt as if I were looking into my own heart. It's so clear and true and sad. I know exactly what Goethe means. And I know what I ought to write to keep Beimer happy. It's just that those two things are incompatible. So I'm writing you this letter instead. It's utterly hopeless, because what kind of arguments could I produce that would change your feelings for me? Arguments never do that sort of thing. Nothing more ridiculous than my love for you has ever been invented, but it often makes me cry . . .'

I broke off my letter at this point and tore it into tiny pieces under cover of my desk-top. I couldn't help feeling like an idiot, but that didn't mean I had to act like one too. My ear hurt. I had taken out the safety pin now and replaced it with a normal earring with a screw to keep it in place, but the swelling on my earlobe still hadn't entirely gone down. I cooled it with my fingertips. Since I'd taken to smoking a packet of cigarettes a day I always had nice cool hands. At the end of the test I wrote my name in the top right-hand corner of a blank sheet of paper, and handed it in. But I wasn't very hopeful that Beimer would understand that a blank sheet of paper was more appropriate to the subject than any interpretation, however clever.

I was having trouble with the way I felt about Hemstedt. But I was still in control of it. I could cope with rejection. One of my easier exercises. Look at it closely, and love was just an illness that you willingly brought on yourself. And it could be prevented by avoiding the source of infection. For several weeks I didn't go to the Sitrone and I skipped sports lessons. I'm sure I would have got over it if I hadn't happened to be standing right beside them when Hemstedt gave Tanja a tape.

'Let's have a look,' I said. 'What's on it?'

And Hemstedt asked, 'Shall I make you one too?'

I almost said no. What would I do with a tape when I didn't have a tape player to listen to it on? But for some reason I said yes.

'It would be nice if you could give me the money for the tape in advance,' said Hemstedt.

The very next morning he handed me a dark-blue Memorex 90 chromium dioxide tape. He had written something I couldn't read on one side in pencil, and on the other side 'Kebabträume'. I carried the cassette about all day in the inside pocket of my leather jacket, and kept feeling it. That evening I called my mother and asked if my brother was at home. He wasn't. So I drove to Barnstedt, went into my brother's room and put the tape into his stereo system. I lay on the floor and linked my arms behind my head. All the pieces lasted just a minute. Distorted sounds and distorted voices. After the fourth track it began to dawn on me that this was the most loveless tape a boy had ever recorded for a girl. Hemstedt had simply let an LP run right through from beginning to end. Whatever record it might be, I hated it. It was all crap. It was shit! Only one song about a girl on a red bicycle, sort of Asiatic-sounding, was really nice. I couldn't hate that one, because it was perfect. I turned the tape over. Hemstedt had recorded various groups on the B side, English and German groups all mixed up. The English songs sounded more relaxed, more melodious, more positive about life, while the German songs dragged, dawdled, were full of echoes and dissonances, and told you that life was boring and sex was no fun. It was as if Hemstedt were setting out his whole soul in front of me, or at least the entire range of his taste, which I couldn't follow to the outer extremes, but it enchanted me at the centre. Love songs, and melancholy music, and intellectual songs, and raucous songs. Songs that just asked questions without giving the answers, because they knew that no answer could ever be *the* answer. And songs that even refused to put the question, and claimed that was the answer. And then – near the end, after a track in which someone was yelling about flying away in a big balloon, to the land of fantasy, to the Federal Republic of Germany, and ended up screeching into the microphone with such lack of restraint that I could positively see him rolling about on the floor – then came the song, the one incomparable song that broke down all my resistance. An English song. As dark as only German songs usually are, but much softer at the same time, although there was a driving, stomping, native American type of rhythm underneath it. I closed my eyes for a moment, and when I opened them again everything around me was much clearer, much brighter, and my brother's globe money-box was shining. It must be like that to stand in the lightning flash of a nuclear bomb just before the mushroom cloud rises and everything burns out. At that moment, the notes were incredibly lovely, a wonderful compensation for all the silent years behinds me. It was like getting a glass of water when you've resigned yourself to dying of thirst. The music penetrated me, was inside me, pervaded me, filled my whole being. And the unpleasant, revolting person I'd been until then finally left my own self. There was nothing in me but the beauty of it. The wonder of it.

And then the wonder of it was gone again. The next singer started up, and a new rhythm overwrote what I'd been feeling. I jumped up, wound the tape back, tried it, wound it back and forth until I'd found the beginning of the song, and then ran it again. I didn't know what or who I was listening to. Peter hadn't gone to the trouble of writing the titles or the names of the singers on the cassette. But whatever it was, it showed me that my life had been all wrong from the very start. I listened to the tape right to the end. Afterwards I felt as if I'd come to the end of my life too. I wound the B side all the way back and began my life all over again. The songs seemed even better than the first time around. Not all of them, of course. A song where a girl got her hand caught in a bread-slicing machine and kept shrieking, 'Ow, ow, ow, ow, ow,' was no better at all on a second hearing, but most of them were, even the songs about feeling high that were delivered at top volume. But really I was just waiting for that one song all the time. I didn't wind the tape forward, I relished my wait. The excitement grew with every new song until it was hardly bearable. And when that song finally came I played it over and over from the beginning. I was just listening to it for the eighth time when my brother pushed the door open with his combat boots. The dog came in with him, panting. When Benno tried to jump up and say hello to me, my brother hauled him back by the collar.

'Hey, what's the idea? Piss off! Who said you could touch my stereo? Piss off, I said. If you want to listen to music you can buy the stereo yourself.'

'How much?' I asked. I couldn't stop now. I didn't know how I was going to last the night out if I didn't go on listening to the tape. He wanted five hundred marks. I just about had that amount. My brother was so pleased and surprised that he even helped me to take the stereo out to the Karmann, drove to my sister's flat with me, and stuck the plug in the wall. I gave my brother his money and turned the tape recorder on. There was the song again!

'What kind of garbage is that?' said my brother.

'Piss off,' I told him. 'That stereo's not yours any more.'

'Five hundred marks! Oh wow, you gave me five hundred marks!' said my brother. 'That's almost what it cost new. How can anyone be so dim? I'll die laughing, I really will die laughing.'

When he'd left I played the song again. I lay down on my bed and looked at the ceiling. That music made me remember joys I'd never had but definitely ought to have known. How could such records exist and I'd never heard of them? How had Peter Hemstedt heard about them? I wanted him to be lying beside me with his arm round me. I wanted to touch what I'd just heard. And because I couldn't, I wound the tape back yet again, listened to the song for the eleventh time, and then at last I went to sleep.

The woman at the reception desk has her hair in a chignon, despite her youth, and wears a red and black check top with a white ruffle at the neck. She puts the receiver down again, points her ballpoint in the direction of the glass swing door at the end of the lobby and says Mr Hemstedt will be down in a moment. I take a few steps in that direction, the rubber soles of my shoes squelching and squeaking on the marble floor. Both halves of the door have brass fittings, and the outsize handles are brass too. It's much darker on the other side of the door than in the lobby, and the reflection in the glass makes it impossible to see through it. My heart is pumping cold blood up through my throat to my temples. I try not to think of anything, just breathe slowly and deliberately to calm myself, and divide my weight equally between both feet, but I can't help my sense of inferiority spreading through me like ink dropped on blotting paper. It swamps my abdominal cavity, it rises to the top of my skull, it runs into every single fingertip. I want something from Hemstedt. That makes me totally worthless. I twice imagine a shadowy figure approaching the glass door, and then a grey sleeve really does emerge from the darkness, a pale hand pushes the door open. Hemstedt comes in. He looks brilliant. Yes, I think brilliant's the right word. Slim and young and madly healthy and successful and charming and with a designer suit and money and all. By objective standards he's more desirable than ever. But I can't love him more than I already do anyway, more than I'd do even if he were hunchbacked and shabby and had a face with warts all over it. His beauty makes the hopes I won't admit to myself shrivel to nothing. I realise how repulsive my love is, how pushy and needy. I can see that no one wants to be loved like that. I fully understand it.

When Hemstedt comes towards me he does it so awkwardly that he almost falls over his own feet. That surprises me. Shouldn't only the one who loves, the unworthy, adoring worm, be clumsy with embarrassment? Can it embarrass a person to be loved? Or does he feel awkward being seen with me by the receptionist? You only have to look at me standing there, figure like a tree trunk, fat heart full of longing, outfit by Hennes. Hemstedt has managed to shed the unattractive skin of the petit bourgeoisie. I still don't know exactly what his job is, but he's obviously made it. I haven't.

It was through a miracle that I passed my school-leaving exams. The name of the miracle was the Reformed Upper School. We all had our passes more or less handed to us on a plate. Of course Little Doris's were the best results. So she got to make the closing speech at the leaving party, not that I heard it. I was one of those who expressed their reservations about the whole occasion by stealing the platter of fruit from the buffet and pelting each other with oranges, bananas and grapes outside the door.

For a long time I believed that the year after I left school was the best time of my life. Was it really? It was the most exciting, anyway. It was the time when I had most jobs, took most drugs, bought most records, kissed most boys, and went out almost every evening.

The others were all going to train for something. Little Doris was studying medicine, of course. Hemstedt said he'd like to be a civil servant in the penal system, but then in the end he studied business management. Almost half the boys did. As if all the differences between them so far had been just a game or a mistake, and now they remembered what they were really meant to be. If they didn't have to do army service first. The girls studied German and sociology, or went to language school. Language school was like army service for girls.

I was the only one who didn't aim to be anything. So I went on working in the dog-lead factory. If someone asked what I wanted to be I played dumb and assembled a couple of extra dog leads to calm myself down. For one thing, with average school marks of 3.6 I didn't qualify to walk straight into any really acceptable course of study, and for another I didn't know how you got yourself on a waiting list so that you might perhaps study German in two years' time or veterinary medicine in seven years' time. I could hardly go to my sister or one of my former fellow pupils and say, 'Please help me, I don't know how to register for a course. And while we're on the subject, I don't know how to get to the university by bus and train either, and there are any number of other things that everyone in the world except me knows about, and I just can't do them, and there are more and more all the time. Help me, oh do for God's sake help me!'

My last hope was a dramatic illness, maybe a brain tumour that would give me only two years to live. With any luck people would leave me alone for those two years.

And I no longer believed that anything really good would ever happen to me in bed, or that I might wake up in a boy's bed without instantly wishing I was somewhere nicer. Kisses were just the introduction to the vain attempts that boys made to sleep with me. What was the matter with them? They were always saying who they'd do it to; they kept making these allusions. Either the whole thing was a gigantic fraud, or it was my fault. It was only with me none of them could get it up. But they might have thought of that earlier! Why did they try it with me at all? Why did they put so much effort into ending up in bed with me? The ones who used condoms said it was the condom's fault, they couldn't do it once they had the condom on. It looked to me the other way round: they couldn't get a condom on because their pricks weren't hard enough. It all came to the same thing: a desperate boy who ended up needing me to jerk him off.

Hemstedt was now going out with a girl called Bettina who was even taller than me. I met her in the washroom at the Sitrone, where the floor was always flooded and where I borrowed her hairspray. The washroom outside the Ladies was a kind of meeting place, because it was quiet enough for you to talk. Boys came there as well when it was too filthy in the Gents, or when they wanted us to paint kohl round their eyes, and then they hung around for ever, watching us put make-up on and talking. We also swapped tablets. Bettina persuaded me to take Percoffidrinol, which worked just like Captagon but was cheaper. I myself didn't know why I took all that horrible stuff. It didn't give you even five pfennigs' worth of fun, and it certainly didn't expand your consciousness. When there were several people smoking a joint the mood was peaceful, sometimes almost solemn. But swallowing one of those pills was just shabby, sad, psychotic. You couldn't sleep all night, and you were terribly tense and wound up. As if someone had reached into your brain, grabbed all the nerve ends and wrapped them round his wrist with a jerk. It was a state of mind miles away from any kind of pleasure. All the same, most people I knew were taking Captagon and Ephedrin and Valium and anything else they could lay their hands on. I only knew that I *needed* pills. I'd have done anything not to have to be me any more.

Bettina was just swapping me a tube of Percoffidrinol for some Sedapon when she told me, in passing, that she'd taken Hemstedt's virginity the night before. She thought it very funny, and tossed back her smooth, dyed black hair. I'd have liked to stuff her head into a lavatory bowl. Instead, I drew her close and gently pressed my lips to hers. I couldn't see what Hemstedt saw in her. She was a loud-mouthed, terrifying girl and didn't even kiss particularly well. When I kissed her after that I made sure, if possible, that we were doing it where Hemstedt was bound to pass on his way to the Space Invaders game. Then he would slink past us like a beaten dog. I couldn't make out why he put up with it either.

My boyfriend of the time didn't catch on to any of this. He never noticed anything. He was always fully occupied distributing his fanzine. Ole was a good boy, a punk who'd passed his school-leaving exam, was waiting for his place on a course, and didn't even try to sleep with me. He'd given me a photo of himself lying among a lot of garbage on a wrecked armchair from the tip, but the room where he lived with his parents was as tidy as something in a furniture brochure. When I went to see him he always took a piece of kitchen towel and immediately wiped away the rings our glasses left on the table. His fanzine cost between one mark and one mark fifty – depending how rich you were – and was called *WhatAMess*. He always had four or five copies with him, and went about trying to sell them in bars and discos. Every copy had some small gimmick stuck to the cover, a plastic bag containing a tampon and feathers, or toenail clippings, or a tiddlywink, or a freshen-up cloth. The fanzine itself consisted of photocopied collages, reviews of records, and interviews written diagonally across the pages. All his own work. When a band came to play in Hamburg Ole was always off with me like a shot, trying to get an interview. We spent the day in record shops. I trusted myself to go in with him. Usually we hung about in the Below Average store, surrounded by pale and inhibited music lovers. Ole would flip through the sleeves with nimble fingers, finding records for me that I bought so as not to hurt his feelings. 'Amok' by Abwärts, or 'Umsturz im Kinderzimmer', where the most cheerful song was one that pleaded, 'Give Me Death'. When he visited me in my room at my sister's flat for the first time, he decided to sort out my record box, and he took out my Ideal LP and almost all my singles and chucked them on the floor. I'd already removed the Hit Fever and Pop Explosion LPs myself.

'That and that and that and that – they're all shit,' he said. 'I can't make out why you buy such things. I mean, it's sick! Don't you have any ears?'

Remain in Light, Scary Monsters, Monarchie und Alltag and the Street Level Sampler he let pass, with a sigh. Then he picked out the last LP between two fingers, howled, dropped it, and shook his hand as if he'd burnt himself.

'*Kate Bush*!' he screamed. 'You listen to *Kate Bush*?'

He laughed derisively, didn't wait for an answer, but to my surprise the record was the only one he picked up again. He put it back in the box.

'Oh, well, typical girlie album. Totally typical girlie album.'

Next day I took the Kate Bush LP out myself, and with a heavy heart I threw it away. There was one song on it, 'Army Dreamer', that I really liked, but I certainly wasn't going to have my record collection contaminated by a girlie album.

But however much trouble Ole went to with me, I knew that I'd always be a suburban girl who deep down preferred pleasing melodies and driving, stomping rhythms with a deep bass line. It was the fault of my bourgeois genes. I knew quite well that it was primitive crap, but I couldn't help it. At best, listening to music meant being alone for me, meant overwhelming passion, so it was difficult for me to judge a record by how abstract it was.

'A guitar solo – I really don't see the point of that,' said Ole coolly. I never saw him get excited except when he was chasing up members of bands after their concerts. Then he was like an eager little dog.

'Mufti!' he shouted. 'That's Mufti from Abwärts! Hey, Mufti!' And he left me standing, just like that, ran over to a big, bulky fellow and talked at him for hours. I could never make out why boys had no pride at all. That delight in humility, that unrestrained enthusiasm for other men. Even Peter Hemstedt wasn't proof against it.

'Look! That's Diedrich Diederichsen,' he whispered to me once outside the Broadway Cinema. I turned round. A young man rather shorter than me, in a coat like the one worn by the Coal-Stealer character in World War Two propaganda, was slouching over to the booking office, spreading glory around him.

'Oh yes?' I said, with no idea who Diedrich Diederichsen was, but trying to memorise what he looked like so that I'd know him again if I saw him. I would sleep with Diedrich Diederichsen. If Diedrich Diederichsen slept with me, I'd be worth more in Hemstedt's eyes.

Of course Hemstedt hadn't gone to the cinema with me on my own. Bettina was there, sitting between us and kissing his neck the whole time while she surreptitiously kneaded my thigh. A point came when I couldn't stand it any more. I jumped up and made out that the film was getting on my nerves.

'How can anyone put up with this, there's no plot, the man just keeps switching the radio on and off,' I said in far too loud a voice, and I stormed out.

Every time Hemstedt split up with one of his girlfriends, I went and asked him for a new tape. When I fetched it I stayed sitting in his room for a while, and if it was late enough we got into bed. When he had just split up with Bettina we even slept with each other. Oddly enough, I can't remember what it was like. Which is amazing, when it must have meant so much to me. I surely ought to know if I was disappointed, or if it was the best song of all. But whenever I try to remember my head is as empty as an unsaleable flat on a new housing estate: nothing in it, not a glimmer. He did manage to sleep with me, I remember that much, but it's as if I wasn't there myself at all, as if someone had just told me it happened and kept back the details. The other times we simply lay side by side and touched each other. I never stayed all night. Once Hemstedt had gone to sleep, I slipped away and went back to my sister's flat. (On my bike. By this time I'd driven the Karmann into the ground.) Of course I was no happier afterwards, I had no reason to be any happier, but I was very much alive, no doubt about it, and for the next few hours I'd escaped the numb emptiness that I usually felt inside me. In my room I'd put the tape in the stereo and then the vibrations entered my body, spread through me, went everywhere. The music was for me, it said everything that I couldn't say. I found myself in it, and all of a sudden my love for Hemstedt wasn't worthless any more, wasn't anything to be ashamed of. It was just as touching as those songs.

Hemstedt's ex-girlfriends always looked sad and disappointed when they found out that I'd slept with him. My conscience was clear. I knew they'd soon fall in love with another boy, and then another. And then they'd marry the next, or the next but one, and bring little replicas of themselves into the world. But a night with Hemstedt meant so much to me that all the right was on my side. And now I can't even remember what it was like.

By now I was throwing up five times a day. Usually I made myself, but sometimes it just happened, and in the end I felt sick at the mere smell of tablets, so I stopped swallowing pills. Oddly enough, I felt just as nervous without Percoffidrinol as with it. It made no difference at all. And I still had to throw up. I may have had a mild attack of food poisoning too. The dog-lead factory had fired me, my father was giving me 250 marks a month, 50 of which my sister took for the telephone, so from the twentieth of the month at the latest I was living on yoghurt past its sell-by date, rotting fruit and remains of sausage with a mouldy green shimmer. I got my weight down to sixty-seven kilos, my hipbones stood out again, and when I went to the Sitrone I wore a slinky black satin dress and large rhinestone earrings. I could have taken a different boy home every night, and I did too, but I tried either to get rid of them before we reached my door, or fob them off with a coffee. Sex just depressed me too much. I know all animals are sad afterwards, but I was always sad beforehand too.

And then an odd thing happened. As soon as I stopped wanting to sleep with boys, there was suddenly no holding them.

I would say, 'Of course you can come up to my room for a coffee, but I'm not going to sleep with you. If you'd like a coffee you're still welcome, but I won't be offended if you say no and make better use of your time.'

And they'd say, 'Coffee would be great.'

Later they'd put my hand on the bulge under their zips, they'd beg me not to be a cock-teaser, turning a boy on and then leaving him to his own devices, with a terrible pain in the balls. They were really hot for me. And now that they could finally get it up I didn't want to discourage them straight away. Besides, it's always easier to say yes than no. Except that now I was the one who couldn't do it. The boys didn't believe me, and tried again and again, and nothing discouraged their erections. They didn't stop until I began crying. Then they begged me at least to jerk them off. Or couldn't I give them a blow job? They begged like crazy. Sometimes I felt as if they had the same problem with sex as I had with eating.

'Just once, jerk me off just once.'

'If you don't want to do it to me then can I at least do it to you?'

I thought: I can't keep saying no. It's partly my own fault. Why did I take him home with me? I know how it ends when I do. I thought: it's not all that much to ask. I thought: then with any luck at least he'll go away at once. I thought: I really ought to be charging for this.

When my weight dropped to below sixty kilos I wouldn't go to bed with any of those boys any more. Another couple of weeks at the most and I'd have a lean body, a body worth admiring, a body in which I could dare to wake up beside Hemstedt, and the others wouldn't get to touch it. They were welcome to the one I had now, that horrible soft body, they could jerk themselves off on that for all I cared, it wasn't really my body any more. I withdrew from the present and concentrated entirely on the future. What did it matter if I had no job, or if Hemstedt had another new girlfriend? It would all pass over. Once I was slender my real life would begin, and everything would sort itself out.

Nothing sorted itself out. I kept waiting for a good opening, but the only openings were jobs with Otto Mail Order, White Rose Express Cleaning, putting safety belts together on the assembly line, delivering strings of beads for Bijou Brigitte Accessories, and back to the dog-lead factory. In the end I did as my father wanted and ended up in a college for trainee tax officers.

Tax inspector was my father's idea of a dream profession. I couldn't live his dream for him. I was reasonably good at the balance sheet aspects of tax law. They suited my obsessive character. But all other subjects instantly started that Egyptian execution movie rolling in my head. With a vengeance! I didn't get even approximately the idea of what they were talking about in any other branch of the law. The only attractive guy was sitting two rows in front of me. He looked like someone who went to discos a lot, had a taste for large cars and could kiss well. I couldn't imagine how he had fetched up here. Just before we were due to go and do practical work in various tax offices, he drove his Polo into a tree and was paralysed from the neck down. I didn't do anything so impressive. I just failed the exam. At first I felt positively euphoric. I didn't have to stay there any more! Then I was nervous again, because I didn't know what I was going to do instead. What am I going to do, I thought, what in God's name am I going to do?

I called my parents and said, 'Hi, Mum. I've got the exam results. I failed.'

'Oh . . . oh dear . . . too bad. Well, there's nothing to be done about it,' said my mother, and her voice was unnaturally high and breathless, but at the same it sounded as hollow as if she were standing in a cave.

'I could retake the exams,' I said. I didn't know why I said it, though it was true. 'Only I don't think there'd be much point. I don't understand what any of it's about.'

'Oh . . . well then . . . well, 'bye for now,' said my mother, hanging up. That was done. I was glad I'd got her and not my father at the end of the phone.

Half an hour later the telephone rang and my mother said, 'You must come home at once! We have to talk! You have to retake the exam! Or your father will kill himself! Come over here at once! Your father's in a very bad way. I'm afraid he may commit suicide.'

I got on my bike and rode to my parents' house. When I walked into the living-room my father was sitting on the sofa with his arms folded. He did look rather like someone about to commit suicide any minute. He said not a word. My mother did the talking.

'Now can you see how your father's feeling? We thought this was something to suit you at last. We thought you'd finally found your niche. We were so pleased. Why are you doing this to us?'

I'd have liked to give them a sensible answer. I'd have liked to say that being a tax officer wasn't such a great job as they thought, it was a horrible job that normal people didn't want to do, only people who'd been teased the whole time at school. I wanted to tell them that some of the students on that training course were already solving crossword puzzles in their early twenties, others were hopeless drunks, and the only candidate for a job as tax inspector who'd looked as if he occasionally had fun was now paralysed from the neck down, and the rest of us would all be paralysed from the neck down soon too. I already couldn't feel my heart any more.

But my father's face kept me from saying any of that. He really did look wretched. His life was already so miserable that nothing else should be allowed to go wrong with it. I simply couldn't bring myself to tell him it was just too bad, I could never catch up with everything I'd missed in the three weeks still to go before the retake.

'Okay,' I said. 'Okay, I'll take the exam again.'

'Oh yes, you will, won't you? And it will be all right?' cried my mother. My father still said nothing, just sat there with his arms folded looking out of the window. He wasn't so ready to believe me.

'Of course it'll be all right,' I said. 'I'll have to study hard, but I think I can do it.'

Then I went home to my sister's, found my backpack and began putting things in it.

Next morning I took the suburban train, went along the Hauptbahnhof line to Berliner Tor, walked up the road to the petrol station and jerked my thumb. I just went south, looking out of the truck windows and waiting until I liked the look of the landscape. I asked the driver to drop me at the Europa bridge. There was a footpath going downhill beyond the picnic area, and I went along it. It was a green path in partial shade, tall ferns growing on both sides and large rocks lying around everywhere. Soon there was a little brook that I could drink from splashing along beside the path or crossing it in wooden gutters. Just before the sun set I came to the valley. There was a hay barn not far from the path. I looked round to see if anyone was watching me, threw my backpack up and into the barn, and climbed after it. That night I slept well and soundly for the first time in ages. Next morning I went on along the valley, bought myself a packet of butter biscuits and a Rotkäppchen Camembert in a village super-market, and climbed another mountain. The path petered out halfway up, and I had to clamber up a steep slope on all fours. After I'd been climbing uphill for two hours through all the greenery, the fallen trees and the dappled sunlight, I finally came to a bright, sunny meadow. It was full of bell-flowers and other flowers that I didn't know, yellow and white, and a stream ran through the middle of the meadow, falling into grassy dips and leaping out again over moss-grown stones. And at the source of the stream I found a real waterfall with a little basin, just large and wide enough for me to bathe in. I drank from the waterfall, put on shorts, lay down in the meadow and spent the rest of the afternoon there. I didn't think, I didn't do anything. I just listened to myself and the trees around me. As a child I'd imagined I could sense what trees were feeling, only I couldn't describe it because it was completely different from anything that hu-mans and animals felt. The feelings of the trees weren't connected with any kinds of needs. They were just there, like a green, velvety humming. I'd always found the company of trees a great relief.

That evening I showered in the waterfall. It was so cold that I shrank to a tiny dot. I climbed into my sleeping bag, lay down among the bell-flowers and looked at the sky. No stars came out, but there was a crescent moon. Everything was all right; I wasn't even scared. Then there was a loud crash in the woods, and I was scared after all and lay there for hours, rigid, waiting for a wild boar or a lynx or a murderer to turn up. Dew fell on my cheap sleeping bag, which never had any real warmth in it. A label sewn to it said it was suitable for temperatures of down to minus twenty-five degrees. But that probably just meant you wouldn't actually freeze to death in it at that temperature, not that it would keep you warm at plus ten degrees either. I froze, and listened, like a little animal, to the cracking sound of steps in the woods, until at some point I fell asleep after all.

Next morning I bathed in the waterfall again and waited for the sun to be strong enough to warm me. The birds sang and twittered. I decided to stay here for ever. Never mind the wild boar. I would make myself a grass hut, drink water from the stream, and eat bell-flowers until I starved to death by slow degrees, and then I'd dry up like a lizard that's been run over and crumble to dust. I'd chew blades of grass until millions of viruses and bacteria had got into my jawbones and dissolved me from inside. Perhaps I could even survive somehow, perhaps I'd find a mushroom now and then, and a few blackberries. Then I'd stay here until I was thin, and I'd found my real self, and I'd really understood something. The sun climbed higher, it got warmer, and as I was rinsing out my socks in the stream I heard voices and laughter, and was just in time to hide in the bushes. Over the next two hours nine hikers in all came past. They picnicked by the waterfall, went to the loo behind the trees, and then climbed down the mountain again. Just beyond the waterfall, the only place I hadn't explored the evening before, a footpath led to this meadow. I gave up. I shouldered my backpack, climbed down the path, and set off home to Hamburg again.

At a service station outside Kassel I had to wait ages for a lift. It started to rain. Rain coming down from above, cars going past splashing me up to the hips with dirty water. At first I tried to avoid these fountains of mud, but soon I was dripping wet and looked so miserable and filthy that it wasn't surprising no one stopped. Then this big, dark-blue Mercedes came along. It slowed down and I jerked my thumb, just in case. The windscreen wiper swept to one side, and for half a second I clearly saw the driver's face. He stared at me, disgusted and indignant. As rainwater was covering the windscreen again, I could just see him bend his head and tap his forehead with one finger. A cold hand closed around my heart, and I promised myself never, ever to vote Christian Democrat.

Soon after that it cleared up. I went into the Ladies in the service station, changed my wet, dirty jeans for shorts, dried my face and combed my hair. Standing in the rain had left me exhausted. When I positioned myself by the entrance to the service station again, a truck stopped at once. The driver was fat and silent. Within half an hour I was asleep in the passenger seat. He shook me awake again.

'Too dangerous,' he said. 'You can go to sleep if you like, but not in front here. If I brake you'll go through the windscreen.'

He was right. There was just that giant screen in front of me. Nothing but glass.

'You can lie down on the bunk,' he said. There was a narrow bunk bed arrangement behind our seats. My backpack was on the top bunk along with all sorts of long-distance truck driver's stuff – maps, a spirit stove, thermos flasks. The lower bunk was empty. Once you were lying on it there'd be no escape: the other bunk on top, the metal of the truck's bodywork at the sides, the seats in front.

'No, no,' I said. 'I'll stay awake now.'

But soon I was drifting off again, and this time the truck driver braked and I really did shoot forward against the windscreen.

'Didn't I tell you so? Damn it all, I told you so. Get back there to that bunk and hurry up about it!'

I didn't think of wondering why he'd had to brake so sharply; I meekly crawled round behind the seats. It was still broad daylight. You didn't have trouble with truck drivers until it got dark. I wouldn't sleep any more now to be on the safe side.

I woke up to find the fat truck driver pawing my arm. He was sitting half between the seats, half on the bunk.

We weren't driving any more. There was a small, useless light in the cab. Otherwise it was dark.

'Nothing will happen to you,' said the fat truck driver. 'If you don't struggle nothing will happen to you.'

I knew that line already from *Crimewatch*. You're for it now, I thought. Now what always happens to female hitch-hikers in *Crimewatch* is going to happen to you. In six months' time some woman out looking for mushrooms will find you hidden under spruce branches.

'If you don't scream and don't struggle I won't do anything to you,' he said, raising my arm. What nonsense! He was already doing something to me. He put his other hand on my leg. I knew it was my own fault. 'She never would listen,' my mother would say, 'but that's no reason for anyone to feel sad – Anne never liked living anyway.' Now the driver was putting one hand on my breasts. I let him. The man weighed over a hundred and fifty kilos, and I was underneath him already. If I defended myself a fight would begin, and I couldn't win it. On the other hand, that very fact would be brought up against me later in court. If I ever got to see a court.

'So now?' said the truck driver. 'What will you do now if I just screw you?'

'Then one of us won't survive,' I snarled. It does no harm to have watched a lot of TV all your life. He laughed at me, but he'd retreated all the same, just the single centimetre I needed to see that the driver's window had been wound down a crack. He realised I'd spotted something, turned, and saw the crack too. Without moving from where he sat he reached for the button to raise the window, but the narrow triangle of space that opened up between his back and the back of the passenger seat was enough for me. I shot through it like a genie coming out of a bottle. The driver tried to grab my legs, I kicked, I suddenly got hold of the door handle, which I usually don't manage to do in strange cars until the third attempt, pushed the passenger door open and fell out. I hit my head on some protruding metal part, and then I was lying on the asphalt. A lonely parking place. There was a feeble street light, but no other car anywhere in view. However, I could hear the roar of traffic on the motorway not too far off.

'Bastard, arsehole, wanker!' I shouted.

He leaned over the passenger seat and looked down at me, but he made no move to leave his truck. I got to my feet.

'My backpack,' I said angrily. 'Give me my backpack! Come on!'

'You get in again,' said the fat truck driver. 'Look, you'll never get away from here. Get in again!'

'You fuck off!' I yelled.

'Oh, come on, you're just being stupid.'

He was acting as if we were old friends and we'd only been

having an argument. Perhaps he thought I really wanted to sleep with him and was just shy about it. You never know what goes on in such people's heads.

'Get in again, don't be stupid!'

'Fuck off and don't you be stupid!' I imitated him, and I picked up a stone and threw it at his truck. Then he threw my backpack out, closed the passenger door, and finally drove off. I memorised his number plate, but then I imagined myself turning up at a police station in those shorts, with my fat legs still showing their sunburn. I'd got fatter every day at that tax officers' college. I pictured the policemen looking me up and down. The mere idea of anyone wanting to have sex with me was ludicrous. I couldn't report this to the police, not the way I looked.

I sat down in the circle of light cast by the street lamp and waited. Although I'd escaped more or less unscathed, I felt ashamed and wretched. Two hours later a car turned into the parking place. A family in a Volvo. Mum, Dad, and two kids on the back seat. They stopped as far as possible away from me. While one of the boys was taking his trousers down, I went over to them and asked the husband to give me a lift.

'You can see the car's full, can't you?'

He didn't look as if he had ever given a stranger a lift in his Volvo. The woman looked alarmed, and one of the kids was on the point of bursting into tears.

'Only to the next service station,' I said. 'A man tried to rape me and then he threw me out here. I'll never get away otherwise! Please help me!'

The man and his wife looked at me with all the disgust I'd envisaged, but they gave me a lift after all. I sat in the back with the two boys. My backpack was in the boot. I put my hands over my ugly red thighs. Luckily it was dark in the car.

The whole family sat there rigid, no one said a single word to me. Not even the kids. They dropped me at the next motorway service station, and I went on to Hamburg in another truck.

When I started working as a taxi driver I still weighed seventy-four kilos. But I lost weight like mad in that taxi. I worked all night from six in the evening to six in the morning. If I could start earlier, or my relief driver arrived late, I worked even longer hours. I didn't eat anything while I was in the taxi. At first I couldn't eat because the radio in the cab made me so nervous. You had to listen the whole time in case they called the taxi rank where you happened to be, and then if you took on a fare you had to be there within three or four minutes, whether or not you had to look the street up on the map first, or there was a human chain barring the road as part of a peace demo. And when the passenger got in I had to find my way to somewhere new and completely different, and it was embarrassing if I didn't know it. But even after I'd got used to all that I didn't eat. I didn't need to eat any more. I was full. I didn't go to bed with anyone either. I had taken it into my head that I wouldn't age as long as I didn't have sex. Little did people know that every time they made love they were moving slightly closer to death. The trick was to leave it alone, not even do it to yourself, and then you could live to be old as the hills.

That first time in the taxi was the best I'd ever known. I was suddenly really alive. I was there! My mind was clear. This was the life, sitting in a Mercedes and driving through town all night listening to music. I'd finally arrived where I felt good. I'd always been looking for a place like that, and now it turned out to be not a place at all but a car. Movement was the only acceptable state of existence, music was the only comfort. Sometimes, when a particularly good song came on the radio, I switched off the cab's own radio intercom and turned off the light on the roof, and just drove around for no one but me. I felt happier and stronger the longer I drove, and when I felt strong enough I switched on the roof light again and picked up one of the dark figures by the side of the road.

'Since when have teenagers been allowed to drive taxis?' the passengers asked as they got in. And then they added, 'Not that I'd like your job.'

But it was a great job. The only drawback was the passengers, but they made up for that by paying. I earned at least a hundred marks a night. I stuffed all those hundreds into an old Macintosh tin, and there were more and more of them. In the end there were so many that I thought I really ought to buy myself something, and I got an old yellow Audi 100. I took a holiday for the first time in months and drove around town all night in the Audi. After a while it struck me that I was doing just the same as before except that it wasn't earning me any money. I sold the Audi again. The purring of the taxi, the sound of its tyres moving over wet asphalt, the dimmed light, the night programme on the radio, the un-friendly passengers and the knowledge that I'd be rid of them again in a few moments, sinking back into isolation, silence, darkness – that was all I wanted.

When my shift was over I got on my bicycle and rode the thirteen kilometres to my sister's flat. I went to bed at seven or seven-thirty, and I got up again at three in the afternoon. Then I heated up a can of green beans, ate them, watched a little TV and rode back to the taxi firm. I hardly saw my sister at all, and before long I weighed sixty-four kilos. But I stuck at that weight for weeks. I just couldn't get below it. It wasn't fair. I mean, a can of green beans has perhaps sixty-eight calories, and I was riding my bike for twenty-six kilometres a day. What more could I do to lose weight? Cut an arm off? Sometimes I ate a couple of biscuits too, but if I did I took a laxative directly afterwards. If I just went doggedly on in that way I was bound to get below sixty-four kilos some time. Physically, there was no possible alternative. This time I really would get thinner and thinner.

Then I met Felix. Felix drove a taxi too, and after six months he asked if I'd like to live with him. I took the chance to move out of my sister's place at last. Felix cooked and did the housework, and I began to eat and get older again.

'You don't have to drive a taxi,' Felix often said. 'You could just stay at home today. Do you need money? If you need money I'll give you some.'

Oddly enough, I got poorer and poorer the more Felix was paying for me. I didn't enjoy driving the taxi any more, I couldn't manage to work for twelve hours on end, and finally I even had problems finding my half of the rent. I got poorer and poorer, and wearier and wearier, and fell asleep at the taxi rank with exhaustion. If I hadn't been driving the taxi for two nights I couldn't imagine how I'd ever be able to use its radio or find my way around the streets. I was afraid of doing everything wrong. The real advantage of the job, which was that I could decide for myself when, how often and how long I'd work, had turned against me because my will-power was being progressively sapped. I couldn't even get around to leaving Felix. When I tried he just said no.

'Look at me,' I said. 'Look at me. I've put on twelve kilos since we've been living together. I'm unhappy. I don't want to sleep with you. I eat abnormal amounts every day, and if I didn't keep throwing up I'd be even fatter. I throw up at least twice a day. Don't you hear me doing it? You must be able to hear me. You can hear everything in this flat. Let me go!'

'No,' said Felix. 'I don't want to be without you.'

Then he started crying. I didn't know what he saw in me. He didn't know me at all, he hadn't the faintest notion who I was. I didn't even know myself. Perhaps there was absolutely nothing in me, and I ought to be glad that Felix was prepared to overlook my lack of personality.

One evening, by chance, Jost got into my taxi. He told me that, besides studying business management, Hemstedt had a job in a record shop now. I carried this information around with me for a few weeks, and when I'd lost six kilos I felt fit to go and look for Hemstedt.

I walked up and down outside the record shop for a while, then turned off into Mönkebergstrasse, bought a pair of green trainers, went back to the shop and checked my reflection in the window. I was wearing white army-surplus shorts with a very high waistband, and a striped sweatshirt in two shades of blue which kept slipping down over one shoulder. I'd grown my hair long again. I had tied it up with a scarf and backcombed the strands that stuck out. I tried smiling. Smiling was always a good idea. Except with me. With me, smiling distorted my whole face into a demonic gargoyle mask. I straightened out the corners of my mouth and my eyebrows again, and went through the door. The shop was a big one. You had to climb down a few steps to the sales areas, and from up on the ground floor I had a good view. Hemstedt was there, I spotted him at once, but I went on lurking near the door. For a long time I just watched him – his elegant movements, white shirt with khaki trousers, his relaxed arrogance in dealing with customers. He listened to young men asking for the records they wanted, his face unmoved, he walked fast but by no means hastily through half the shop ahead of them, took the desired LP out of its place with a flourish and offered it to the eager customer with two fingers, already turning away and calling something out to another salesman. This in itself made me so happy that I would willingly have stolen out of the shop with those images in my mind, instead of exposing myself to the risk of an actual meeting. But I didn't tear myself away in time. Hemstedt finally saw me, his mouth revealed a row of large white teeth, and he came towards me. The little muscle beside my right eyelid began to flutter, and when I noticed that it made me even more nervous. Out of pure compulsion I immediately began talking as fast and as volubly as if I'd swallowed two boxes of Recatol at once. I asked what he was doing these days, inquired after his friends, told him which of our former fellow pupils I'd met recently, in the middle of all this I asked him to record me another tape, I pressed my new phone number on him, privately cursing myself for doing so, talked and talked, asked why he didn't wear shorts in this heat, talked faster and faster, like the speeded-up version of an LP played at 45 r.p.m., and then something stuck in my throat, and I said, 'Well, I must be going now!'

Before Hemstedt could reply, I snatched up the bag with the shoebox and raced to the exit. Hemstedt walked beside me with his fast, long strides, and I was still muttering, 'Honestly, I can't think why you don't wear shorts in this heat,' as I picked up a single from the Top Ten display by the cash desks and slipped it into my mini-Görtz bag from the shoe shop.

A week later Hemstedt called me and said I could collect

the tape. I went out to see him in my taxi the same evening. He was still living with his parents. His father opened the door and took me into the living-room. Hemstedt was sitting in front of the TV set. His father took the newspaper off the table and went out with it. In the doorway, he turned and asked when Peter would be home the next day.

'Late,' said Hemstedt. 'I'm going to play table tennis.'

'Ping-pong,' muttered Hemstedt's father, closing the door behind him, 'ping-pong isn't a real sport.'

I sat down in an empty chair and watched the screen with Hemstedt. There was a show on. Finally an American singer introduced her new hit, and four young Germans who had reached the final stage of a dance competition breakdanced to it. It was not a good song for breakdancing.

'Look at them! Just look at them! Now the whole gang's going to join in,' said Hemstedt, laughing. The boys on screen raised their shoulders and bent their arms to look ancient Egyptian. One of them had a curiously old, pinched face, and Hemstedt said, 'He looks like E.T.'

'Two of the girls from the Funny Club bought E.T. dolls,' I said. 'I always take them home in the morning, and they put their E.T. dolls on the parcel shelf in the taxi.'

'I didn't see the film when it came out,' said Hemstedt, 'just a clip on TV. Of course I burst into tears at once. Although the clip came on without any introduction – I just saw the boy saying goodbye to E.T., and E.T. hugging him and stroking him with his long, spidery fingers. And that set me straight off crying.'

It's odd how moved you feel when a man admits to crying. Perhaps because they so seldom do. Like wrapping up presents. When a man gives you a badly wrapped present you feel special straight away.

I'd shed tears at the point where E.T. gets in touch with his space ship because he wants to go home, and the little boy says, 'You could be happy here. I'd look after you. We could grow up together, E.T.'

'I think bad, hard-hearted people are particularly mad about E.T.,' I said.

Hemstedt leaned over to me from his chair and gently stroked my cheek with the backs of his fingers. I once read a story where someone is hurt by a cactus. It's a very special cactus; if you get one of its prickles in your skin and don't pull it out at once, the prickle works its way right through your body of its own accord until it reaches your heart, and when it's reached your heart you die. It was that kind of touch.

'I sold your leather jacket to my brother,' I said. 'At a loss.'

Hemstedt stood up.

'Come on. The tape's up in my room.'

But as soon as we were in his room, and he'd given me the tape, Jost and Richard Buck came trampling upstairs, and Hemstedt immediately stopped talking to me. He just gave me apologetic glances. His friends didn't talk to me either. I sat down in an armchair and chewed a strand of my hair.

'What happened to Kathrin?' asked Jost. 'Are you still seeing her?'

Hemstedt handed Jost a letter that was lying on his desk. 'Here. She wrote me this.'

Jost took the note and began reading parts of it out loud. It really was a very silly letter. It said things that you just ought not to put into words. About feelings. I could hardly bear to think there were other girls suffering over Hemstedt too. My love was not only something sick and ugly, it was a love anyone could feel. All the same, I hated the fact that the boys were laughing.

'I once wrote you a letter myself,' I said. 'My God, am I glad I never sent it!'

'Why not? You should have,' cried Hemstedt at once.

I pointed to Jost. 'You can't be serious.'

'What?' said Jost, who hadn't been listening because he was still reading the letter. 'Here, you've got to hear this . . .'

I laughed before Jost could read aloud whatever it was we had to hear.

'When you laugh your whole face twists into one great grimace,' said Hemstedt.

'Oh yes?' I said. 'Is that so?'

Jost and Richard were watching me with interest now. They were waiting for me to laugh and turn my face into one great grimace.

'Thanks very much for the tape,' I said. 'I'll be off.'

I hated and loathed myself. I wished I could have snuffed myself out, my grimacing outer envelope and the disgusting, slobbering love inside me. Something like me ought not to exist. Do away with it, do away with it, do away with it, I thought. When I got into the taxi I took the tape out and put it in the player. I hated myself for that too. I turned into a road where there were no houses; three street lights and then the darkness closed over me. The music started. Angels' voices, but they were angels with bats' wings, they were singing outside the gates of Hell, with a sweet, unearthly menace, to the accompaniment of clashing cymbals. I turned the volume right up. The cymbals clashed again. And then a threateningly deep male voice said, 'The world is my oyster,' and followed it with such a ghastly, terrifying laugh that I turned the steering wheel the wrong way and ended up in the ditch.

'Hahahahahahahahaha . . .' went the voice. I climbed out and looked at the damage. I was stuck in that ditch, in the pitch-black darkness, and now a woman was singing.

'This is not a love song, this is not a love song.'

It was a voice with a really nasty undertone. You believed her at once.

'This is not a love song, this is not a love song.'

Yes, all right! For heaven's sake, I'd got the point already.

I called the taxi's radio operator and asked her to connect me up with five-double-eight on Channel 3, and when Felix came over the line I told him where I was and asked him to come and tow me out.

While I waited for him to arrive I went on listening to the tape. How could anyone as mean and horrible as Hemstedt record music like this? Music that showed me, very gently, how I'd betrayed my own wishes. Music that revealed the miserable nature of my life. How did you get into this mess, the music asked. You want to get out of it again, it added. Hey Joe, said the music – Joe was me – hey Joe, look around, you're about to lose something very, very important. Only I couldn't remember ever having had anything very, very important. In fact I didn't really exist at all. Whenever I was with a new man I became a different person. I was as empty as a mirror, and when people looked into it they saw something that could grant their wishes and satisfy their needs. Felix too loved something about me that hadn't been there at all at first, but he firmly believed he could find it in me until in the end it actually did exist. Whoever or whatever I was now, I had no right to take it away from him. He'd made it himself, so it didn't belong to me. Only when I was with Hemstedt did I feel I had a distinct outline and became an independent being. Perhaps it wasn't Hemstedt I missed at

171

all. Perhaps I just missed myself. I missed the person I was when I was with him.

When Felix arrived, it turned out that he didn't have to tow me out of the ditch. All we had to do was put the mats from inside the car under the front tyres.

Now that I didn't smile any more I kept getting into trouble in the taxi. I realised that men don't like gloomy women. They'd rather stand at the bar looking full of pain themselves, and then some beaming little tornado of a girl was supposed to come along and cheer them up. All the same, I'd always supposed that my smile was a free gift, something like a perfume sample given away in a pharmacy. But now drunks would suddenly put their faces very close to mine, saying nastily, 'Think you're something special, do you?'

Within four months I'd been hit in the face twice. I was beginning to understand why I'd always smiled before, and once I understood that then I *really* couldn't smile any more. When I looked round in bars and discos it seemed to me that every woman had a smile carved into her face. As if they were all members of the same horrible sect. Some had a happy smile, some had a tense smile, some wore a smile like a mask, and some smiled as naturally as if they'd been born that way. I hardly got any more tips, my financial situation was getting more and more complicated anyway, and then my mother called to ask if I would look after the dog for two weeks. By now my parents were cutting short the German winter, autumn or spring on one of the Canary Islands at least twice a year. And then, since I was the only member of the family not to have a proper job, it was always up to me to look after the house and the dog.

'Yes, sure,' I said. 'Of course I will.'

Only just at the moment I simply couldn't afford not to work for two weeks. Even under normal circumstances, when my parents went away I always had to borrow money from Felix afterwards, and I had my work cut out paying back my debts bit by bit for two months afterwards. I always felt wretched sleeping in my parents' house too.

'I'm so glad you'll have a chance to be out of the city and get your fill of fresh air here,' said my mother. 'You can convalesce from your TB.' I'd been diagnosed with tuberculosis of the lungs some time before. Of course at first I'd been pleased, but only until I landed in a dead boring sanatorium among a lot of asthmatics who breathed stertorously, and until I found out that there was a ward with barred windows for people with infectious TB who wanted to leave the place. The physiotherapist was busy trying to recruit me for the sanatorium basketball team when it turned out that my TB wasn't the infectious kind after all, so I could go.

'You only caught it because you're up all night, every night, and you live in that slum,' said my mother. By slum she meant the floor of the old factory where I lived with Felix. Advertising copywriters and editors were always ringing to ask us to let them know at once if we moved out, but my parents hadn't seen the movie *Diva* and didn't know the expression 'loft', and were convinced that we were living the life of social misfits.

'And because you never eat anything,' said my mother.

'Mum.' I said. 'Mum, I'm overweight. I eat more than enough.'

'Not the right things. You just munch bread! Anyway, I've filled the fridge for you. You won't even have to go shopping. I've left you sixty marks in my purse for emergencies. But the fridge is full to bursting. The money's only for an emergency.

I'm so glad that at least I won't have to worry about you for two weeks, I'll know you're having a nice holiday here.'

'Listen, Mum,' I said cautiously, 'it's a tie, looking after the dog. Of course I'm happy to do it, but it's not as if it's a holiday. I'm doing it for you. And I can't easily go two weeks without working, just like that.'

'You could if you had a proper job. Then you wouldn't have to live hand to mouth the way you do.'

'If I had a proper job I certainly couldn't look after your dog.'

'I thought you liked doing it. I thought you were fond of Benno.'

'I am fond of Benno. I just want you two to realise I'm making a sacrifice for you.'

'A sacrifice? Of course we don't want you making a sacrifice. Well then, we won't be able to go away any more.'

'Well, perhaps sacrifice is putting it too strongly . . .'

My mother turned away from the phone and called into another room, 'Dad! Dad, we can't go away after all. You'll have to cancel everything. Anne doesn't want to look after the dog. Do you think you can get the money back from the travel agent, or is it too late?'

'Oh, all right,' I said. 'I'm sorry. I'm not making a sacrifice. I'll be glad to look after the dog. I'm glad the fridge is full and I won't have to go shopping and I can stuff myself with food and convalesce for the whole two weeks.'

Two days later I drove my parents to the airport in their car.

I last saw Hemstedt in 1990. I'd made up my mind never to see him again, but it was practically inevitable that he'd cross my path some day. Since I drove a taxi night after night, year after year, just about everyone in Hamburg got into my cab at one time or another. Except for Diedrich Diederichsen. I'd always hoped I might have Diedrich Diederichsen as a fare some time, but instead I was always taking Alfred Hilsberg to the Subito.

Hemstedt appeared in front of my bonnet at six-thirty in the morning. In fact I'd already handed the taxi in, and now I was driving home to my new flat in a black Mercedes that cost a hundred thousand marks. After splitting up with Felix, and after a phase of love affairs that kept changing, I had met the owner of this limousine and had good sex for the first time in my life. It was true that I still couldn't remember what it had been like sleeping with Hemstedt, but I did know now that it couldn't have been all that great. That much was certain. Or I would have remembered it. Did I still love him? No, there was nothing there. Nothing at all. There'd never really been anything there either. I'd probably just fallen in love with the first man to cross my path who couldn't stand me any more than my father could. Hemstedt looked disparagingly at the Mercedes as he got in, and said, drawing his eyebrows together, 'Well, really, Anne . . .' but all the same I could see that its showiness was making him think.

'Where do you want to go?' I asked. He told me he'd moved into his own flat long before, and had been working for a foodstuffs company for years. I didn't understand exactly what his job description meant, but he was in the marketing department or something like that.

'There's no point at all in what I do really,' said Hemstedt. 'If the work doesn't get done it's no loss to anyone. I don't make anything, I don't repair anything, and whether I'm helping my firm to make a bigger profit is purely hypothetical. Quite possibly the whole job is a mistake.'

'Can't you leave?' I asked. 'Don't you want to look for something else?'

'No,' he said venomously. 'It's all I've learnt. There's nothing else I *can* do.'

We said nothing for a while. As we got near his place Hemstedt told me he'd joined the Young Socialists. I was absolutely flabbergasted.

'Slowly! Drive more slowly! Why are you racing along like that?' asked Hemstedt. Even though I'd been driving very, very slowly all the time, so that I could sit beside him for as long as possible.

'I'm the retribution of God visited on everyone not fit to be out and about,' I said, stepping on the gas.

'No, you're not. You're just totally antisocial!' said Hemstedt. 'Thirty! For God's sake, thirty! This is a thirty kilometres an hour zone, kids play here.'

'It's seven on a Sunday morning,' I said, 'there aren't any kids playing here, they're asleep now the way kids should be.'

'Asleep! Exactly!' he said. 'Hard-working people who want to lie in on a Sunday live here.'

I took my foot off the accelerator. It wasn't over yet after all. If it had been over I wouldn't even have stopped to give Hemstedt a lift. I looked facts in the face again: the expensive hundred-thousand-mark car I was driving was in shocking bad taste, so souped up and tuned and converted that it couldn't even call itself a Mercedes any more, and its star had been removed, like a dishonourably discharged army officer who loses his epaulettes. The man it belonged to was a conceited show-off who wallowed in my feelings of inferiority like a dolphin in the wake of a ship, and I had sex with him only because I was afraid I wouldn't ever get any otherwise. But really I didn't want anyone but Hemstedt. I even loved him for joining the SPD and making me drive slowly. His good Social Democratic heart beat for the hard-working populace and watched over their sleep. He probably thought about social improvements and a more equitable distribution of taxes all the time. What a pity my unhappiness wasn't the kind that any SPD reforms could have alleviated.

Hemstedt asked if I'd like to have breakfast with him. He looked tired and exhausted. His coat was all creased.

'Coffee would be lovely,' I said. I was wearing black breeches, black knee-high boots and a grey sweater, the kind of outfit in which you'd go upstairs two steps at a time. Hemstedt led me down a narrow corridor into his dwarf's kitchen. I sat down opposite him at the folding table. He made us coffee, then tipped something out of a packet into a dish for himself and poured milk over it. As he ate, I picked up the packet and looked at the picture on it – little cushions made of spun wheat.

'Is it edible?'

Hemstedt waved his spoon dismissively in the direction of the packet and went on shovelling the stuff in. In silence, he put two slices of white bread in the toaster and took a packet of butter out of the fridge.

'Aha, expensive Irish butter,' I said.

'Yes,' said Hemstedt, 'I can afford it now. It costs thirty pfennigs more, but it spreads more easily. That's worth it to me.'

'Do you realise that this butter has travelled hundreds of kilometres, and several tons of oil have been used to transport it just so you can spread it on your bread more easily?'

He shrugged his shoulders.

'Butter's the same everywhere.' I said. 'Cows eat grass and

give milk, and the result is butter. You could just as well buy Schleswig-Holstein butter.'

'Yes, but it doesn't spread so easily,' said Hemstedt.

I said no more. I'd said everything I had to say about butter. Hemstedt stood up.

'I've got to have a shower,' he said, and went out.

When I heard the water running I stood up too to poke about in his kitchen. I took the peppermill off the spice rack and hid it behind the coffee filters on the shelves opposite. Then I opened the fridge. It was empty except for six packets of Irish butter. There was a pharmacist's calendar hanging next to the fridge. This month's picture showed a rabbit in the grass, nibbling. I picked up the salt container and sprinkled a little salt on the floor.

'Save me,' I said to the Irish butter behind the fridge door. 'Save me, because I'm in a state of the utmost emotional need. Don't deliver me up to that conceited show-off with his pimp's car. He does things to me that make me sick. They frighten me. But you could save me.'

Hemstedt came out of the shower and stood in the kitchen doorway with only a towel round his hips.

'What are you doing clumping around my kitchen in your dominatrix boots?' he growled. Obviously he'd been doing some weights and now he wanted to test the result. That's why he was standing there half-naked – so that I'd see his body.

'I don't know,' I muttered.

Hemstedt disappeared into the next room. I imagined his body on mine, his hands on my face, his lips on my temples.

'Touch me,' I whispered to the Irish butter. 'Stroke my cheek like that again. Why can't you like me? What's so wrong with me?'

'Everything,' said the Irish butter.

Hemstedt came back in a white dressing-gown.

'I'm worn out,' he said. 'Don't take offence, but I'd like to get some sleep now.'

I quickly stood up and left. I tried to imagine how Hemstedt behaved when he loved someone. I had no idea. His love only ever took place in my absence. I got into my showy car again and drove off. At the next lights I started to cry. I cried so much that I had to turn right and pull in next to a shopping centre. I leaned over the steering wheel weeping and weeping. One of those thin, wretched-looking kids you saw all over town that year was standing at the bottom of the escalator in the shopping centre playing a piano accordion or a cheap synthesiser. The kid's poverty was not at all picturesque. He looked discontented and not quite right in the head. I wondered whether to get out of the car and tell him this was Sunday, and there wouldn't be anyone in the shopping centre at eight anyway, but perhaps he had his secret reasons for being there that only he understood. The discontented kid was playing his own version of 'Lambada' on his squeezebox synthesiser. It was the saddest 'Lambada' imaginable. Like the lament of a mangy bird.

The London sun flickers through the lobby, casting a green light. Hemstedt gives me a kiss on the cheek and smiles. The receptionist acts as if she were alternately busy with the phone and with the frill at her neck, but she never takes her eyes off us for a second. We're still standing by the glass door. Hemstedt hands me a set of keys and says something to me, but I'm far too nervous to be able to form words, let alone whole sentences, from the sounds and syllables coming out through those impressive teeth. It takes half a minute for the first word to register with me. It's 'island-hopping', and I'm not sure if there even is such a word. Then he says something about a yacht, and then the word 'business partners' comes up, and a sudden invitation that he couldn't refuse. It sounds like something from a boring TV series, how odd, I think, how odd, and only then do I realise what they mean.

'I brought my travelling bag in with me,' says Hemstedt, nodding to a colleague hurrying past. 'After work I'm going straight to the stadium, and after the game I'll be going direct to the airport.'

Is it always going to be like this? What curses were spoken over my cradle? And why wasn't there a single *good* fairy there to take the sting out of one of those curses? Hemstedt is telling me how he's been given a ticket for the semi-final, interrupting himself every time the swing door lets smart young men through and he has to reply to their greeting. Hemstedt says that the company has invited business partners of some kind – not the ones with the yacht – to the semi-final. They'll be sitting in a VIP block, and Hemstedt is one of the employees going along. What luck. Hemstedt is doing things just right. The whole trick is to get enthusiastic about something: football, horses, careers, record collections, stickers, market research, bridge-building, aquariums, island-hopping – whatever. Just so long as you can control it and it doesn't leave you too much time for thinking. You have to immerse yourself in your work and your hobbies, you have to tell yourself daily that what you're doing is madly important, and then you won't need to think about love or find out who you really are any more. I have no training, no money, no prospects and nothing to replace them. The only hobby I ever had was slimming. Someone like me is delivered up to love –

helpless as a kitten when it gets into the washing machine. I pretend I have a fit of coughing to get rid of the lump in my throat. While I cough I can hold my trembling chin still too. What did I expect?

I say, 'That's great. Wonderful. That's marvellous for you! And island-hopping straight afterwards! Wow!'

'Of course you can use my flat. Just put the key through the letterbox when you leave.'

'Yes,' I say, 'yes, I'll do that.'

'Well, I have to get back to work now.'

'Yes. Of course. Off you go. And thanks very much for letting me use your flat.'

My God, I'm making things easy for him again. He'll be gone in a minute and nothing will have changed.

'Wait a minute,' I say, as he's about to kiss me goodbye on the cheek. 'Why do you think I was fool enough to come to London? For the football? For the Crown Jewels?'

He shrugs and makes an exaggeratedly puzzled face.

'I curse you, Peter Hemstedt,' I say quietly, while looking so impersonally friendly that the receptionist will be bound to take our conversation for mere small talk. 'You'll go far in your horrible firm, you'll get to be head of some really important department or whatever else here you fancy, and you'll go island-hopping every year . . .'

'Hey, Peter,' calls one of three young men striding past, waggling his eyebrows in a meaningful way, and he raises his left forearm to shoulder height and taps his watch with his right forefinger as he runs by. So perhaps the eyebrow-waggle was meant as a reminder. Hemstedt watches him go. I ask myself again if he feels embarrassed to be seen with me. He hasn't yet said anything about the size I've grown to. And there's really no overlooking it. Even if you're totally indifferent to someone. Hemstedt turns his face to look at me again.

'You'll find an enchanting wife,' I rapidly continue my curse, 'a wife who looks like a model and has a university degree in one of the Romance languages. The pair of you will have a modern apartment in town and a wonderful house in the country, and your wife will make the kitchen curtains for the house in the country herself. You'll have two children, first a boy and then a girl, and when the children are past the most difficult stage you'll get divorced and marry an equally beautiful, well-educated and clever wife, but one who's fifteen years younger and is studying art history. And this time round you'll spend rather more time with the baby and rather less on your job, but of course you'll still be a terrifically important man, and you and your new wife will live in an even bigger house. So now you just listen to me, Peter Hemstedt, because here comes the worst part of my curse.'

Hemstedt leans politely forward to indicate that he's listening attentively.

'You'll be happy! That life will make you happy. You won't even notice what a horrible life you're leading. Even on your deathbed you'll think: well, that was all fine, couldn't have gone better.'

Hemstedt blinks briefly, then puts out his hand and touches my cheek, just to throw me off balance.

'Take your filthy hand away!'

'I'm sorry,' he says. 'But I've agreed to go already.'

He walks away, turning once more, the glass door swings shut, and Hemstedt disappears into the dark corridor beyond it. He's gone. The receptionist is staring at me. I nod to her mechanically, pick up my case and go out.

Hemstedt's flat is in an elegant part of town. Notices hang on the Victorian façades saying that a security service patrols here every hour. The door of the building is so difficult to open, even with a key, that I really wouldn't want to be a burglar around these parts. On the way here in the taxi I pulled myself together, but now that I look like failing to open the door a hoarse sob breaks out of me, followed by helpless whimpering. I tug and rattle at the door, whimpering to myself all the time. When the door finally flies open it's no comfort any more. Still whimpering, I heave my case up two flights of marble stairs and open the door of Hemstedt's flat – without any difficulty this time. It's huge. The entrance hall alone is at least fifteen metres long. It's completely empty and freshly painted. White. I put my case down and go into the first room. It's white and empty too, except for six massive cast iron lamps standing on the grey carpet. Grey. That's the second colour. There's fitted grey carpet everywhere. Lights like bull's-eyes with stout metal rivets are set in all the ceilings instead of lamps. The second room is the bedroom. A black steel bed, a black chest of drawers, a black curtain with a walk-in wardrobe behind it. Five suits hang from a metal rail, two blue, one grey, one black, one beige. One shelf of jeans, one of pullovers, one of T-shirts and two of shirts. White walls, grey carpet. A door leads straight from the bedroom to the bathroom. Yellowed tiles, a large mirror, and a bathtub with ancient brass fittings. I put my face under the tap, go back into the bedroom dripping wet, sit on the bed and take my boots off. It's not a double bed, but wide enough for two people to sleep comfortably in it. Sleep. Exactly. That's what I'm going to do now.

Normally my mother phoned only early in the morning when I was still asleep, so that I'd complain and she could say,

'What an awful job you have, keeping you out and about all night.' So I should have suspected something at once when she suddenly called in the afternoon.

'Anne?' her voice came through the receiver. 'Anne, I have to tell you something. It's about Benno.'

I thought I was going to be asked to look after my brother's dog again, but she went on.

'We're either giving Benno away or having him put to sleep.'

'What?' I said. '*What?*'

I knew the dog got on my mother's nerves because he made the place dirty and sometimes spent hours whining to himself. But this was going too far.

'It's no good. Now that your brother's moved out no one cares about him, and your father and I have all the work to do. And you don't want to look after him any more either.'

'Look,' I said, 'that's not true. I've had him every time so far. I've been to stay at yours at least twice a year to look after the dog.'

'But you said it was a burden on you. That dog's nothing but a burden on all of us.'

I couldn't imagine my mother really having the dog killed; after all, he was one of the family. On the other hand, she sounded grimly determined, as if she were actually intent on going through with it.

'You can't do that,' I said. 'I'll look after him. I'll look after the dog whenever you two want to go away. And if you want to be rid of him entirely I'll have him. You don't have to kill him!'

'You don't know what happened here,' said my mother. 'You weren't with us. Your brother was visiting with Susanne, and your father nearly went crazy. The poor girl was really upset. "Now I've finally retired, and I could go away," he said, "and I have this dog cluttering up the place." Your father is depressive anyway. He was so desperate, he'll kill himself yet. And let me tell you, my husband matters more to me than a dog.'

I could easily imagine my father's face as he said those words. It will certainly have been twisted again, showing that he could only just keep his rage under control, as if he might start weeping uncontrollably any moment. When his face was like that we all of us always did what he wanted.

'Take it easy,' I said. 'He'll calm down again. Look, I'll think of a way to fix it so that the dog comes to me . . .'

'You can't take him. What will you do when you're driving the taxi? We'll have him put to sleep, he's old anyway. I'm only telling you now so you can't complain later that we never let you know.'

'I'll think of something,' I said. 'I'll take him, I'll look after him. He's a healthy dog. The main thing is you mustn't kill him.'

'Well, we haven't reached that point yet,' said my mother. 'I only wanted to tell you.'

That evening I called my brother.

'What actually happened?'

'Oh lord, the old man's getting crazier and crazier,' said my brother. 'We had a bag of laundry with us. Mum wanted us to bring it. She called and asked whether I had any dirty washing. She positively begged to be allowed to do it. So I brought the bag along, and at the supper table the old man suddenly starts on about what an imposition it is, us still palming our laundry off on Mum. He just wouldn't stop. And all this time Susanne was there. She was almost in tears.'

'*The dog*,' I said. 'Didn't I just tell you they want to kill Benno?'

'Oh. Well, then the old man started carrying on about how he absolutely had to go away again. There's something sick about all this going away. He'll calm down. Talk about crazy.'

'They're serious,' I said. 'Mum said she's going to have Benno put to sleep. She's just been waiting for an opportunity to get rid of him.'

'Nonsense. She'll never do it. She's much too cowardly. She wouldn't dare ask the vet. Anyway, he's still my dog. And if he's really too much for the old man, then I'll shoot him myself. In the garage.'

'I'm going to take him,' I started again. 'There's no need for any of you to kill Benno!'

'You see about managing your own life,' said my brother. 'You've got your work cut out for you there.'

I made a list of all the things I had to do. First I had to ask my landlord if I could have a dog in my flat, as a special favour. If not I'd have to look for a new flat, and a job where a dog was allowed. Perhaps I could operate the radio for the taxi firm, or be an assistant in a pet-food shop. Perhaps I could move in with my new boyfriend if his landlord allowed dogs. Although we'd only known each other two weeks. It wasn't easy. I really did hope my parents would pull themselves together. On the other hand, maybe I'd get to have a dog now after all. Benno would sleep beside my bed and go everywhere with me. He would force me to change my lifestyle. Though who knew what good that would be?

Next day my mother called again at about four-thirty in

the afternoon. She was weeping uncontrollably. Her voice broke, and kept being interrupted by sobs.

'Anne? Anne, you mustn't be cross! Promise you won't be cross with me!'

'What's the matter?' I asked, but really I knew already.

'Benno's dead.'

'How do you mean, Benno's dead?'

'I took him to be put to sleep today.'

'You mean you had him killed by lethal injection.'

'You mustn't go on at me now! I feel terrible. Say you forgive me! Say you forgive me *now*!'

She sobbed again.

'No,' I said. 'I can't forgive you. You've killed him. You've killed a healthy dog.'

'Oh, oh . . . well, if that's how you see it.' And she hung up.

I hung up as well, and then I began to cry too. First I just sat there in silence while tears kept leaking unstoppably from of my eyes, but then I really got going. It was a totally disfiguring wail, all the dams breaking down, and it wouldn't stop. It just would not stop. I flung myself on the floor and howled and raged until the tears were running out of my nose as well as my eyes, there were strings of saliva hanging from my lips, and snot on my chin. I ought to have gone to get the dog at once. Why hadn't I fetched Benno at once? I howled and screamed till I ran out of air. I tried to make it even worse. I wanted an ambulance to come and take me to hospital. But it didn't get that bad. Suddenly my lungs opened with a crackle, and I could breathe again, and I had to get through to the end of that day on my own.

* * *

At night I dreamed that my mother was putting a wire noose around my neck and trying to strangle me. She was doing it in the bathroom, presumably because the tiles there could be more easily cleaned. Blood shot from the tap into the wash-basin. I was trying to crawl out of the bathroom on all fours, still with the wire noose round my neck, and my mother was walking beside me hitting me on the head with bowls.

First my sister rang, then my father rang, and then my brother dropped in. They wanted me to pull myself together and make it up with the family. My father had never before called me of his own accord, and it was so extraordinary to hear his voice asking for a discussion 'so that we can get this cleared up at last' that I promptly fell for it. But then all my father said was that I was psychologically unstable and took everything much too hard, and I'd have to learn to live with myself as I was. I didn't argue, but after that I didn't answer the phone any more. That was why they'd sent my brother.

'The old man's an incredible hypocrite,' said my brother. 'You should have seen him burying the dead dog in the garden. He cried and cried, he could hardly see out of his eyes. And next morning he went off with Mum, chirpy as you like, and bought a complete new three-piece suite for the living-room. They can finally throw out that stained sofa.'

Oddly enough, my brother wanted me to make it up with my parents all the same, or at least spend Christmas with them, and when I said no he said, 'You're as crazy as the old folk.'

Before he left, he remembered that he'd bumped into Axel Vollauf and was to give me his regards.

'He wants you to ring some time,' said my brother.

'Axel Vollauf? I don't believe it. What did he look like?'
'Same as ever. He hasn't changed a bit.'

But of course he'd changed. He had turned into one of those tall, thin types with endlessly long matchstick legs and a behind like a piece of soap. However, he still had the same old hairstyle, and the eyes of a panic-stricken deer staring into car headlights. We went to the Lullaby, a bar much frequented by taxi drivers because it stayed open until the small hours. Axel had become a taxi driver too, but I'd never come across him because he drove during the day. That night I told Axel that my parents had killed the dog, that I'd only ever had car mechanics and taxi drivers as boyfriends and I hadn't loved any of them, including the one I was with at the time, although this time he was a driving instructor, but I could never manage to break up with him, that I'd only ever had good sex with one man, and he had thrown himself into it so wholeheartedly only to dominate and torment me in the most private corners of my soul and my body, that I couldn't manage the simplest, most basic things, and that the only good bit of my life had been that time with him in the animal hospital, and I'd only thrown him out because his wild embraces got on my family's nerves.

'Yes,' said Axel bitterly, 'I kept on finding that not everyone liked my heartfelt hugs.'

I remembered how he'd nearly strangled me, but I thought it would be tactless to say so just then. Axel told me that he was in therapy now, and how it had been the best decision of his life, and when he was fourteen his mother had stripped naked in front of him and asked, 'Well, what do you honestly think I look like?' And he had said, 'Beautiful, Ma, I think you're beautiful,' but in fact he felt like running away. He told me he'd been in love with a woman called Andrea, deeply in love, but now he was over it, and he was still friends with her, and his circle of friends, consisting of this woman and a man, were his family now, his new little family, and he spent Christmas with them too, and he sometimes wrote articles for magazines about the Hamburg scene. He had just been planning an article about why women were suddenly using sanitary towels rather than tampons.

'This new trend for sanitary towels,' said Axel, 'I wondered if it might be to do with greater physical awareness, women treating themselves more gently and not wanting to stick things into them any more. But then my therapist said I'd better drop the subject, because it's really just to do with my own birth trauma, all the blood and so on.'

A clever man, that therapist, I thought, and the best of it was that apparently he talked in parables the whole time, like Kwai Chang Caine's teacher in the *Kung Fu* series.

Back when Axel was still in love with this Andrea, who didn't want anything to do with him, his therapist had told him the following story:

'Imagine you want to buy some rolls. You're ravenously hungry for rolls. And at last you find a shop, you go in and say: Ten rolls, please. And the shopkeeper tells you: Sorry, I don't sell rolls. This is an ironmonger's. I just sell nuts and bolts.

'So now you have three possibilities. You can come back every day shouting about wanting rolls, and some time, if you're lucky, you'll get on the shopkeeper's nerves so much that way that he'll decide to sell his ironmonger's shop and sell rolls instead. The second possibility, which is more to be recommended, is that you leave the shop again and look around for a bakery somewhere else. And thirdly, of course you could stop and think whether a few nuts and bolts might not come in useful. Whether maybe you're not so ravenously hungry for rolls after all. Whether nuts and bolts might not do. But if you think nuts and bolts will never satisfy your hunger, you'd better leave the shop and look for a bakery.'

His therapist had cured him of many unfortunate mistakes in his life by using such parables.

'When I helped people move house in the past, I always carried the heaviest crates on purpose,' said Axel. 'I thought I had to show I could do it. But now I know I'm not the strongest man in the world. Now I always pick up the lighter crates, and I'm not ashamed of it.'

I can't say I felt enthusiastic about this new form of masculine self-confidence. If there was one thing that had made the usual shortcomings of men palatable to me, it was probably that my car-mechanic boyfriends had always kept whatever cars, motorbikes and electrical household gadgets I had at the time in tip-top condition, and carried the heaviest crates upstairs for me. I didn't think one could just dispense with these favours without a clear increase in quality in other areas. On the other hand, had I been in the least happy with my car mechanics? Might not all my unhappiness be due to my always looking for this conventional masculinity, and thinking heartlessness was just a casual attitude?

'I don't see why you can't split up with your boyfriend,' said Axel. 'He just drives stupidly around the neighbourhood in his taxi listening to heavy metal. And do you have to be happy just so that a dim idiot like that can go on being happy, and stay with him although you don't want to at all? Or is that what you *do* want?'

'He doesn't drive a taxi, and he doesn't listen to heavy metal,' I said indignantly, but at the same time I had to suppress a chuckle of approval. For the first time ever, making the break myself seemed like something I could do. Yes I thought, yes, I'll leave my boyfriend. I'll tell him I don't love him and it will finally all be over. And then . . . Why shouldn't I put right the sad injustice into which my family had forced me back then? Why shouldn't I bring the love story between Axel and me to a happy ending after all, and heal our wounds? If we moved in together some day presumably I'd have to carry the crates with the LPs in them. But wasn't that worth it?

Just before sunrise Axel drove me back to my place in his little red housewife's car. He turned the engine off outside the door. The birds were already striking up. We looked at each other, and first we smiled, and then we were a bit embarrassed. Finally I asked if I could kiss him. I thought that was the idea. Why else would you turn the engine off?

But instead of leaning over to me, Axel widened his saucer-eyes in panic, pressed himself back in his seat and uttered a toneless 'Yes,' staring straight ahead. To be honest, I hadn't the faintest wish to kiss him now. The way he was behaving wasn't exactly sexy. On the other hand it might be even worse for him if I just left him there. It was a silly situation. I leaned briefly over and kissed him on the lips as fleetingly as possible. Even that was too much. For God's sake, what was the matter with him?

On our second meeting we went to the cinema. It was a movie set in Ireland. Someone bought a cow at auction, a chubby cow with a huge udder, without a doubt the animal that produced such particularly spreadable butter, and the hero of the film led her after him on a rope through a picture-book Irish landscape.

'How sweet!' squealed Axel.

I decided to think of this as a plus point. None of the men I'd ever been with before would have said 'How sweet!' at the sight of a cow, and I hadn't been happy with any of them. After the movie we went straight to my place. I was a free woman. I'd split up with the driving instructor two days before. Just by saying so. I hadn't even had to be unfaithful to him first. It had not been easy by any means, but all I felt now was relief.

Axel complained of the bright light in my flat, and asked for a candle. I fetched one. Don't laugh at the candle, I told myself, it must have been difficult for him to ask for it. Then we both lay on the floor and talked. The candlelight, I have to admit, did make it easier, and anyway I'd made up my mind that this time I wouldn't move as much as a finger, I wouldn't expect anything. Sometimes Axel reached his hand out and stroked my arm, and it looked as if this might turn into a nice evening after all, an evening when no one would act in a sick or nasty way, and we'd just be friendly. In retrospect it's always hard to say at what point the man you're planning to spend a nice evening with suddenly changes his mind about it. Perhaps it was the moment when Axel told me, 'I like the way your big bum looks in that skirt.'

'That's not exactly the kind of compliment one really appreciates,' I said.

'Why not? Because I said you have a big bum? But you do have a big bum. And I like it, too.'

'Would you mind changing the subject?'

'Why? Do you have a problem with your bum? I don't mind how fat you are.'

'Yes, okay,' I said, 'let's leave it at that. You like my big bum. No need to discuss it any further.'

I wasn't looking for the signs. I thought Axel was just particularly bad at paying compliments. That's what I wanted to think. I'd taken it into my head that we were two children who'd once been badly treated and who had now been given a second chance, and this time their love would triumph over all the malice and pettiness in the world. That's how I saw us.

'I'd like to kiss you,' said Axel, moving close to me. I stopped leaning on one arm, let my head sink to the floor, and closed my eyes. Nothing happened. I opened my eyes again. Axel was bending over me with his hands propped on the floor to left and right of my shoulders. His face wasn't twenty centimetres from mine, and it was not a nice look he was giving me, not the kind to make you feel good. I'd have to give him time. He was so terribly screwed up. Axel's eyes were the size of saucers, as always, and his face around them was rigid. But something began moving in his eyes. The pupils. They were going alternately large and then small again. He was looking at me with the large, velvety pupils of affection for ten seconds, and then – snap – suddenly he was darting glances of hatred at me out of little black pupils. Then – snap – the pupils were large again, and – snap – they were small. He did the whole thing ten or twenty times. It was really weird.

'What's the matter?' I asked.

'I don't know if I want to kiss you after all,' he replied.

I was not feeling particularly tough any more.

'Why are you doing that? Is it fun?'

'I don't have to listen to this,' said Axel, standing up. 'I'm not listening to any of that shit.'

I propped myself on my elbows, but I was still more or less lying on the floor. Why do people expose themselves to all the humiliations they should expect when they take someone else home?

'I could have seriously wound you up!' I shouted. 'Don't you think you're ridiculous? And I didn't. Why are you doing this?'

'You really do have a problem!' Axel yelled back. 'You have a real problem, but it's none of my business. You just leave me alone! Oh, well, I suppose there's no point in it any more,' he went on, perfectly composed again. 'Look, I'll write a phone number down for you. It's my therapist's number. You can call him or not, just as you like. I don't want any more to do with your sick fits anyway.'

'Stick your phone number up your arse!' I shouted. 'You idiot!'

'I'll leave the note on the table,' said Axel. 'And now I'm off. 'Bye.'

And he left, closing the door behind him. So now we were quits.

I couldn't really stand the therapist from the start. He was very tall and had long black hair which he tied casually back into a ponytail. I'd rather have had an ugly, clever-looking little man with tangled eyebrows. This one looked like the most desirable man at an open-air concert. This one looked like the sort who had always made my life a misery. It's a good thing, I told myself, if you have a negative transference or negative projection or whatever they call it at the start, then you can work it off on your therapist and afterwards you'll have made some progress. The therapy room looked the way I'd imagined it: woodchip wallpaper in mood-lifting apricot, two horrible sketches in watercolours of human bodies, and two comfortable armchairs opposite each other, with orange throws over them. Beside one of the chairs stood a box of Kleenex. The only thing I hadn't expected was the bright-yellow shelf of kitchen gadgets, which was dominated by a monstrous coffee machine, a gigantic metal thing that must have come from either some huge canteen or the Pentagon.

As I quite quickly found out, the main task of a therapist is not to think up concrete suggestions for his patients' problems, but to look at you the whole time as if he believes in you the way you'd like to believe in yourself. Mine did his job very well except that he had to make himself a frothy white coffee at the beginning of every session. The operation lasted at least three minutes, and the Pentagon coffee machine boomed, vibrated, spat and belched as if it might take off into the air any moment. You'd have had to shout to be heard while my therapist fiddled about with his cup, the adjustable outlet of the coffee machine and the foam nozzle. If he was trying to demonstrate my worthlessness to me this was quite a good way of going about it. Then he sat down with his coffee in the other armchair and looked at me expectantly, while his upper lip was already feeling its way to the rim of the cup like a greedy Shetland pony's.

At first I thought he was trying to annoy me, or find out how long I'd put up with this outrageous conduct. But he just went on the same way. He wasn't trying to annoy me. He simply liked pouring coffee down himself while he listened to the depressing twaddle uttered by his patients. Finally I did a sum and told him out loud that since his fees were a hundred and twenty marks an hour, that frothy coffee was costing me, or rather my health insurance, at least six marks.

'What role does money play in your family?' asked my therapist. I shrugged. Whenever I told him something about my family I suspected I was lying or exaggerating wildly the whole time, probably to make myself seem important. It had always been the way I'd described, but not all the time. Anyway, it hadn't been as bad for me as it must sound to an outsider, but sort of normal. And if anyone had a problem with money it was my therapist. No sooner had my health insurance agreed to pay the bill I'd run up so far than he raised his fee by another twenty marks an hour. He claimed in all seriousness that it would be good for me to pay for at least part of my therapy myself.

'No,' I said, 'it'll just be good for you,' and off he went about my problem with money again. Finally he looked at me seriously and said, 'Do you know I like you very much? I think you're a very nice person.'

'That's your job,' I said, 'that's why I and the poor health insurance company are paying you a hundred and twenty marks an hour.'

It was true, too.

'You and your damn problem with money! You really think that, don't you? You think I'm lying to you?'

'Oh, come on,' I said, in conciliatory tones, 'that's how the world works. Salesgirls in boutiques say: that really suits you. Tarts say: ooh, aren't you strong! And therapists say: you're a nice person. And anyone who believes that sort of thing isn't very bright. I mean, did you ever tell one of your patients you couldn't stand him, he was boring and stupid, and you hated the thought of your session with him?'

In answer to that my therapist claimed that there were no boring people – the way parents always claim to love all their children equally – which in turn made me suspect that he had either never met an interesting person in his life or was shockingly undiscriminating. To be honest, I slightly despised my therapist for it, while my therapist said that to despise someone was just a defensive attitude to ward off the fear of rejection. Because besides money, we also argued about the way I always described him as my mad-doctor. He said that was derogatory, but I thought the term therapist was much worse.

If I didn't want his friendship I was at least supposed to *feel* something. It wasn't enough for him if I just said something was depressing me. My mad-doctor wanted to see me cry. I tried to explain that my problem wasn't feeling too little, it was that I couldn't help feeling what other people were feeling too the whole time. But he didn't understand that.

'People who don't feel pain can't feel happiness either,' he said. It sounded logical. But of course the theory worked only if there was some prospect of happiness. I don't think he'd thought of that. What eventually came of it was that I got worse at pretending. While I once hardly batted an eyelid if something was on my mind, now even tiny things gave me a lump in my throat and my voice broke treacherously. That was no help; it was as if he were sending me out unarmed among gunslingers.

After the tenth session my therapist began hugging me when I arrived and when I left. It was horrible, but I let him do it a few times so as not to offend him. He hugged all his patients. When I left at the end of my hour and the next patient came in they fell into each other's arms immediately, clutching and hugging one another forever. The time came when I asked if we couldn't drop it, and he said he had already noticed that I didn't really like it, and after that he left me alone. Only now I kept feeling that he was just waiting for me to hug him some day after all. He wasn't so keen for the hug itself, but he was keen for me to *want* to do it. For some reason that mattered to him. And I didn't want to keep disappointing him, so sometimes I did it, as if I felt like it all of a sudden. And sure enough, he looked much better as soon as I'd hugged him.

After a year I wanted to stop the therapy, but I still hadn't learnt how to make the break. I didn't know how to tell my therapist without hurting his feelings. Our discussion ended with me signing up for one of his workshops. The workshop lasted five days and took place in the converted farmhouse in Lower Saxony where my therapist's ex-wife and their son also lived. On the first evening the group met in a kidney-shaped annexe that positively oozed orthopaedic charm with its light wood panelling, parquet floor, ergonomic floor cushions in turquoise and violet, and a pile of woollen blankets. The windows were hung with heavy blue linen curtains to protect us from the eyes of interested neighbours. We sat down in a circle, and then we all had to say who we were, what we did, what we hoped to get out of this work-shop and if there was anything we were afraid of. There were twelve of us – not counting the therapist – seven men and five women. Five of the seven men were taxi drivers, one was a computer engineer and one taught sociology. Four of the five women taught sociology, and I was the fifth. Unlike me, the others all seemed to know each other to some extent, and had hugged and kissed cheeks in greeting. Some had even tra-velled together.

'Normally people aren't supposed to know each other at a workshop,' our therapist explained cheerfully, 'but I take no notice of that.'

When we came to what we hoped for and feared, almost

all of them hoped to get further with their psychological development, and were afraid they might find out something about themselves that they'd rather not have known. I hadn't really been afraid at all, at least not until I overheard the conversation between my therapist and his son in the hall.

Because before we marched over to the kidney-shaped temple, we'd been standing around briefly in the hall of the main house, and my therapist's son had come in to take a disgusted look at us. He was about eight years old, in jeans and a Jurassic Park T-shirt, and he had a plastic machine gun over his shoulder. My therapist had knelt down to give his son as enthusiastic a hug as he usually gave his patients.

'Hey, what have you got there? Wow, a real gun!'

He crouched down behind his son, reached over his shoulders for the machine gun, and aimed at an imaginary target with him. They both closed one eye, which the sociology teachers and taxi drivers thought so cute that they had to grin.

'Well, what do you think?' my therapist asked his son. 'Who shall we shoot, then? Shall we shoot Mummy? Oh yes, the two of us could shoot Mummy! What do you say?'

The other workshop participants, apparently well versed in their therapist's arguments over his divorce, laughed understandingly, while the eight-year-old gave a miserable kind of grin for his father's sake and hunched his back in embarrassment, as if he wanted to disappear into himself. I felt the same. I'd have liked to drive straight home, draw the curtains and put a biscuit bag over my head. But I'd driven a taxi for a week so that I could afford this workshop, and I'd paid for it all in advance. If I knew my therapist he'd never refund the fee for the course; instead he'd start a discussion about my problem with money. So I said and did nothing.

After me it was the computer man's turn. He had dried spit in the corners of his mouth, and he too hoped to make some advance in his psychological development here. Then he added, with a shy laugh, that he hoped he might meet someone special here too. The others smiled knowingly to themselves.

Next morning I realised why they'd all smiled in that silly way, and why there were such a surprising number of men at the workshop. There probably aren't many opportunities for getting to know someone as easily and naturally as at a therapeutic workshop. It's because of all those exercises you're made to do in couples, and you sometimes get physically very close. For the very first exercise, we were to choose partners. While the others were still wondering whether to be bold enough to choose someone, or wait until someone else took pity on them, I got to my feet and asked Frank, one of the taxi drivers, if I could sit with him. Frank was masculine in an old-fashioned way – like the star of some action film with car chases from the seventies. That rather careworn, dried-up face with sharp folds beside the mouth, those eyes that looked injured and aggressive at the same time. No, life hadn't let him off lightly, but he had never complained, it could only be chance that had brought him to this workshop. Although the jeans he wore had a curiously silly cut. I'd noticed it before when I followed him into the group room. They sat much too high above his hips, and narrowed in where a woman's waist would have been.

In the exercise you had to sit opposite your partner and look at his or her face for five minutes. How long do you usually look into the eyes of someone you don't know? Four seconds? Four seconds is probably too long. Frank was glaring darkly at me, so as not to seem needy. I, on the contrary, gave him a gentle smile. Luckily I'd practised a gentle smile by now in front of the mirror. If I left my bottom teeth covered by my lower lip, and just showed my top teeth, if I froze the part of my face round my eyes and carefully pulled the part from the cheekbones to the upper lip upwards and outwards, then I could manage something that would pass as a conventionally nice smile. I looked Frank deep in the eyes, smiled, let my gaze wander to his mouth, assumed a serious expression, plunged into his eyes again and smiled until my bottom jaw felt numb. He had more difficulty, but then visibly thawed out, and when the exercise was over, and we were all sitting in a circle again saying how we had done and what feelings it had set off, our eyes were still searching for each other. When my therapist asked me how it had been for me, I just said, 'Lovely.' When he asked Frank, Frank said, 'Okay.'

It was really simple. Anyone who can't pick someone up at a workshop had better move to some form of society which goes in for arranged marriages.

After that we had another break, and everyone went out into the garden to smoke. They stood around, grown men and women, each of them thinking secretly that he or she was the therapist's most interesting patient. A funny sort of ambition, to be the nuttiest nutcase. Although when I looked at this miserable gang in that light, in all probability I was still the most interesting patient myself. I heard the sociology teacher Brigitte telling the sociology teacher Maria, 'I could never again have anything to do with a man who has no experience of therapy.'

'Oh no,' said Maria, 'I wouldn't like that either. Imagine having to begin at the very beginning.'

Two locals approaching the property walked along the fence staring at us. To them, we were all crazy, of course. In the village the farm was probably known as the loony bin or the funny farm. The others let the locals stare. They seemed to think as little of it as the colonial masters thought of the glances of their native servants.

I paired off with Frank for the next two exercises too. But in the afternoon he wasn't quick enough, and Ronald the taxi driver asked me first. Ronald was strikingly tall, had receding hair and a hot temper. This time we were to say in turn how we saw our partner and what we concluded about him or her from it, and it didn't matter if it was particularly convincing or complete nonsense.

Ronald put his head on one side and said, 'I can see little lines round your eyes and I conclude that you're a warm-hearted person who likes to laugh.'

I said, 'You put your head on one side and grin at me and pay me a compliment that isn't really a compliment at all, and I conclude that you think you can have it off with me.'

'I see your eyes twitching,' said Ronald. 'You're nervous, and I conclude that you're afraid of me.'

'Ha, ha,' I said, though we weren't supposed to react. 'I see that you're bringing your face closer and closer to me, and baring your teeth when you talk to me, and I conclude that you're insulted because I've given you the brush-off, and you wish I was at least afraid of you.'

'I see your eyes flickering even more, and I conclude that you don't feel able to cope with this situation but you want to give the impression that you don't mind what I say.'

'I see that you've grabbed my wrist and I conclude that you can't control yourself for toffee, and if you don't take your paw away at once I shall throw something at you!'

'You just try it, you silly cow!'

That was the moment when our therapist intervened.

'Stop that now! Everyone stop. What's going on back there? Ronald, let go of her at once! Is that clear? At once!'

'She insulted me!'

Ronald's eyes were glazed as he complained of me to our therapist. I gave him my best controlled smile and massaged my wrist. Shut up any twelve apparently civilised adults together under conditions like those of a youth hostel, and within twenty-four hours they'll all have regressed to the level of twelve-year-olds.

On the last evening we had the so-called Truth Round, in which we could all say what we still had on our minds and hadn't trusted ourselves to say before.

'I wanted to say I've fallen in love with Brigitte. And I also wanted to say I'm afraid of Anne.'

'So am I,' 'So am I,' said two others. I was astonished. I couldn't think of a feebler, more miserable person than myself. Obviously I was credited with abilities which I'd known for ages I didn't possess.

It probably ought to have made me stop and think when Frank came into my flat, and the first thing he did was take the glass front off my TV screen and scrub it with glass cleaner. But to be honest, I was pleased. Afterwards the screen was fantastically clean. My God, what a great picture I suddenly had, with such clear colours!

The name Andrea came up relatively early. Andrea was his great love. She had nearly destroyed him, she'd walked all over his golden heart, she was a slut, a tart, she'd even said he'd abused her, but it was only that her skin was so sensitive it bruised the moment you held her arm a little more firmly. Apparently her eyes were the basis of her sexual power. According to Frank, Andrea was just under one metre seventy tall, but through some kind of gymnastic trick she could manage to look up from under her lashes even at a Lilliputian. She had the kind of look to which every man was delivered up helpless. So she had got Frank into bed again and again. But not any more now! Now he had seen through her. He was finally over it.

'Andrea?' I said. 'You don't mean the Andrea who was once with Axel Vollauf, do you?'

He did. She was exactly who he meant.

'He said he was over it too.'

'Him?' cried Frank. 'Never! He'll never get over her in a hundred years. They're always sitting around together in their little family or whatever they call it. The other man in it is crazy about her too, of course. It's a totally sick arrangement. If Axel had got over her he'd have left her long ago.'

The image of this ominous Andrea came up again and again as time passed, shimmering in all its different facets. Bernhard, Frank's best friend, had been with her once too, and had gone through all his friend's misery with him afterwards.

'Of course she isn't as bad as he paints her,' Bernhard told me. 'In fact she's really to be pitied. Something horrible happened to her once. I think she was gang-raped by several Bundeswehr soldiers. I don't know the details, of course, but she hinted at something like that.'

Frank, on the other hand, told me that her father had probably abused her, while back in the taxi drivers' bar Axel had speculated that she had been raped by her first boyfriend.

Andrea's fate had set them all wishing to be her saviour and rescuer, although none of them ever thought of inquiring into it more closely.

'So now she makes all men feel randy without doing anything with them. Once it comes to the point she backs out,' said Bernhard. Of course he too was deep in the it-used-to-be-very-bad-but-now-I'm-totally-over-it phase. A phase with which I was only too familiar, and which immediately precedes the okay-so-now-it's-total-surrender-and-I'm-unhappily-in-love-for-the-rest-of-my-life phase. Bernhard's trousers had the same unflattering cut as Frank's. Frank had seventeen pairs of those waist-high of trousers that made a man's hips look like your auntie's behind. He never wore anything else. Andrea had made them. As well as having scarred hearts and unflattering trousers, most of Andrea's former boyfriends also shared the same therapist.

'I think even Frederic once had something going with her,' said Frank. Frederic was our therapist's first name.

'Yes, that's correct,' said Frederic, when I confronted him with it.

'But you can't do a thing like that. Everyone knows a therapist can't do a thing like that.'

'I think I acted correctly,' said my therapist. 'It happened when I was starting out and I'd just opened the practice. And when I realised that I'd fallen in love with her I broke her therapy off at once . . .'

'. . . and slept with her,' I finished for him, although I didn't know that for sure.

'She wasn't my patient any more then.'

Point taken.

'But she's still here with you.'

'All this was eight years ago. And two years ago she started a new course of therapy with me.'

'Do you think that's a good idea?'

'I'm not in love with her any more. It was a beginner's mistake. I very quickly realised what had happened to me . . .'

'And now you're over it?'

'Completely,' he said.

That wasn't the first time I thought that I really ought to change my therapist. I had been thinking about it when Frank, who was partly in therapy because he found it so difficult to ask for what he wanted and get it, was helping Frederic to redecorate his flat, and Frederic was paying him only half as much an hour as he paid the other workman there. But when I contemplated changing my therapist – was there a professional list of them somewhere, and would my health insurance go along with the change just like that? – the complications seemed to me insuperable. So I stayed on another year with Frederic.

At my second workshop Axel Vollauf was there. I had known in advance and signed up all the same. Or maybe that was why I signed up. It was the first and biggest mistake. After that one thing led to another.

A bookseller whose phone number my therapist had given me drove me down in his small car. The bookseller was dark-haired, and his name was Winfried. He was attractive in a rather dusty way, and he was cleverer and nicer than I'd ever have expected someone taking part in a workshop to be. But he was a worse driver than my mother. Even when we were starting off he scraped a hubcap along the pavement, on the motorway I had to grab the steering wheel several times to turn it the right way – he thanked me effusively every time – and as we turned into the car park of the funny farm he ran into the hedge.

Axel was already there. He was standing in the hall with his luggage and he'd brought his substitute family along: the legendary Andrea and a man called Olaf. I knew from Frank that each of them had been in therapy for at least five years. They spoke of the workshop as simply 'the shop'.

'Hey, are you back at the shop again, then?' called Andrea, very much the woman of the world, to a red-haired girl. I could tell it was Andrea at once from the way she looked at me: as if we'd been to kindergarten together and we'd been enemies even then. She was much prettier than I'd expected, so beautiful that you could have sold cosmetics with her face and car accessories with her body. She had long black hair, and teeth as large and regular as Peter Hemstedt's. She was three classes above Axel, Frank or this Olaf who was still in tow. Why on earth did she mix with these screwed-up nutcases?

That evening I played a dice game with Axel, his little family, Winfried the bookseller and a man called Guido, who looked like the young Franz Josef Strauss and kept twitching when I spoke to him. I normally despised such parlour games, and I still did, but I wanted to get to know the bookseller better.

My bookseller project fell through next day during the first exercise in pairs. This time you couldn't choose your partner. We had to stand in two rows several metres apart, and then walk towards whoever happened to be opposite. Andrea got the bookseller. I had to go through the exercise with Olaf. It was up to him to see how close he'd let me come to him. He made a lot of fuss about it, yelled, 'Stop,' when I'd only taken my first step – thought hard, then said, 'Come closer slowly – slower than that,' and shouted again, 'Stop! Get back, get back!' Then he let me come closer all the same, and in the end I was about two metres from him. When we changed roles I didn't have to spend long wondering how close I could tolerate Olaf. I let him come to within a metre of me, stopped him there, and then it was all right. The passengers sat a metre behind me in the taxi. If something was a metre or more away from me, by now I didn't feel it any more.

In the next round we all had to say how we'd felt during the exercise.

'I'm amazed that Anne let me get so close to her,' said Olaf. Then he tried to make eye contact with me, but I just looked over his shoulder at the bookseller.

Andrea said, 'Oh, I don't really want to say anything about the exercise. I'd just like to tell Winfried he has a lovely smile. When he smiles there's such a dear little dimple in his right cheek.'

The bookseller blushed a rosy pink, and after that he was lost to the world. Like a blind elk, he'd blundered in front of her gun. It was a real shame. The bookseller was the only clever, interesting person in this whole gathering, nice, educated, discriminating – but of course he was powerless against Andrea.

The afternoon session was tough going. Frederic was going to a lot of trouble to upset someone, but for one reason or another we all sat about lethargically on those round cushions, and when he asked us something we gave monosyllabic answers or remained obstinately silent.

'How about you? How are you doing, Anne?' asked Frederic.

'Me? I'm fine.'

'Are you sure? Are you sure there's not some problem you'd like to address?'

His question was perceptibly more nervous now.

'No,' I said. 'No, I'm fine.'

It was our therapist's job to be a step ahead of us all the time, anticipate our emotional downs, trigger them, stage them, and then catch us as we fell. Presumably it was a good feeling to hold all the strings, to be the only one in possession of all the background information and such great, healing knowledge, and then to withdraw into proud isolation at the end of the workshop. But this time it didn't get going properly; nothing worked. Frederic got more and more annoyed, snapped at Axel when he was whispering to Andrea, and finally ended the session early.

Since I now saw no good reason to waste the second evening playing dice, I approached Silke, a woman who had said in the opening session that she wanted to learn to say no at long last, talked her into lending me her car, and phoned my ex-lover Rita. Ex-lover may sound like a drastic change of orientation (and it had been quite a shock to Frank), but I should add that Rita was one metre ninety-two tall and a car mechanic by trade. The affair didn't last long. I had a guilty conscience the whole time because I'd had to be big and fat and unhappy before I even thought of trying it with a woman. It's exactly when you turn away from men that you ought to look perfect, matching their expectations and longings in every particular. And then, when all the men are crazy for you, only then do you say, 'Sorry, guys, that's not the way I imagined it,' and let a woman love you as you've never been loved before. Someone like me was no loss, but only confirmed the prejudices about ugly, liberated women who can't get a man. Anyway, I wasn't sure if I really fancied women. As long as all concerned kept their clothes on I was full of longing and desire, but the moment anyone undressed I always felt much less lesbian. Perhaps the only reason I liked being in the Camelot so much was that the women there wore normal clothes. They didn't have bows in their hair and little frilled collars, or appliqués on their sweatshirts, or sweet little teddy-bear earrings. They looked like grown-up people who did proper jobs in the daytime. Although the S & M lesbians were an exception when they dropped into the Camelot in the early hours of the morning, coming from their dark, mysterious parties, and staggered around the dance floor in shiny boots with their shaven skulls and fishnet vests over bare breasts. Rita sometimes went to the Black Parties too. She'd promised to take me to the next one, but then the workshop intervened. 'I'm coming with you,' I told her now over the phone. 'This place is a total washout.'

I drove fast towards Hamburg in Silke's Polo. First I went to my flat to change. The question of what to wear gave me quite a problem. Apart from my rather brutal-looking black biker boots I had nothing suitable for a sadists' party. Finally I put on black trousers and a close-fitting black denim shirt.

Rita was wearing thigh-high pirate boots with close-fitting elasticated trousers, and a leather corsage so tightly laced that she had difficulty getting into the Polo. We set out around ten. The whole thing took place in a gloomy, ramshackle villa that looked like the Munster family's residence. Torches were burning to right and left of the heavy front door. First we sat in a room like a bar, and apart from the fact that everyone wore rather odd clothes the whole thing was a bit like an old school reunion. There was giggling and whispering in the corners of the room, although gloomy sadists' music came from the loudspeakers, a slow, theatrical melody with a refrain in which a woman's voice kept saying desperately, 'No, I don't want to,' and a deep male voice replied, 'Yes, you do, come on!' The way to the torture chambers lay behind a blood-red velvet curtain, but no one was allowed in yet. I told Rita about the workshop. And Andrea.

'At least three men I've been involved with have gone to bed with her too. And they're all still in love with her. Like all the men at the workshop. Even my therapist has been to bed with her.'

'Poor girl,' said Rita, 'she must be terribly unhappy.'

'There, you see?' I said. 'Just as I thought. Now you've gone and fallen in love with her too. I knew you would!'

I leafed through a magazine that was lying around, called *BlackAndBlue*.

'Sadomasochism on a voluntary basis is all very well,' wrote Anton F. from Eppendorf on the Letters page, 'but which of us real sadists could pass up the chance to torture someone who doesn't want to be tortured and get away with it? Suppose the political and legal situation allowed you to train a maid and beat her? Who'd say no on moral grounds?'

'I expect you think masochists are nicer people because they don't hurt anyone, right?' said Rita when I showed her the letter. 'I'll tell you something: masochists are just bone idle. Masochists who want to be given a good seeing-to are two a penny. But just try finding good sadists. Everyone's after them, the heteros too.'

A waitress came and put two beers down in front of us. Her black T-shirt said THERE MUST BE PUNISHMENT across the front. Before we could finish our beers things started to kick off. A second woman, whose T-shirt said THIS HURTS ME MORE THAN IT HURTS YOU, pulled back the red curtain and unbolted the citadel door behind it. One by one all the women went into a hall which was draped with black fabric. Organ music boomed from huge speakers. In the cavern-like lighting I saw a wooden cross big enough for Jesus Christ, and a human cage with tea-lights all over the bottom of it. Rita suggested looking round separately. I wasn't enthusiastic, but she was already off down the right-hand exit.

'Torture is no joke,' I shouted after her before turning left. Torches lit the narrow passages leading you from one room to the next, or sometimes up a blind alley. I saw a long, worm-eaten wooden table in a large hall. On the table, for totally inexplicable reasons, stood a silver dish full of potatoes. Here I met Pony, a friend of Rita's. I'd seen her before at the Camelot, and hadn't liked her. Pony was wearing black leather trousers that exposed her behind, and to balance it she had shaved her skull bald. I was grateful to meet anyone at all I knew.

'Pony – hey, Pony, for God's sake tell me what they do with the potatoes.'

'Oh,' she said in a much deeper voice than usual, 'you can do all sorts of nice things with potatoes.' And she smiled the superior smile of an initiate and left me where I was. I stumbled on along the passages. There still wasn't much happening. Most of the women were just cowardly voyeurs like me. In a small chapel with church windows made of coloured paper a girl was being whipped by a woman who looked as if she was concentrating, but in my opinion she didn't really have her mind on the job. There was another room where the onlookers were crowding round a hammock in which a naked woman was being penetrated with a dildo by four others. I went back to see if anyone was doing anything with those potatoes yet, and saw a camping tent I'd missed earlier on my way through. It stood in the far corner of the potato room. I slipped in and found myself watching another remarkable scene. Three ladies having tea. They wore sixties dresses with amoeba patterns, they were sitting around a folding table, pouring tea, waving their cups in the air and helping themselves to biscuits. Dear nice aunties. Only there was no talking. There couldn't be, what with the booming organ music. A fourth chair was still empty, standing a little way away from the table. That suited me nicely. My back was aching again, and there was nowhere else for anyone to sit down here. I was the only spectator. The women in the auntie-style clothes put their cups down, and now I saw a thin, naked girl who had probably been waiting in the background all along. One of the aunties beckoned her over, pulled her on to her lap and started first kissing the girl and then biting her. The others watched in silence. After that the girl had to lie across the second auntie's lap, and the second auntie picked up a carpet-beater from the floor and spanked her with it. Then she turned the carpet-beater round and stuck the handle up the girl's behind. It was nightmarish. I felt like getting up to go, but there was no way I wanted to attract the attention of these frightful women. Only when the curtain parted again and more people came in did I dare make my escape.

'My word, that was truly horrible,' I told Rita when I found her and Pony under the wooden cross. 'The other things going on here are more or less a Punch and Judy show, but that carpet-beater really got to me. My knees still feel weak.'

214

The cross still wasn't occupied, and a naked woman was crouching in the cage. A wardress stood beside it in laced boots, leather panties, a leather harness round her ribcage and a mask. I knew the woman in the cage by sight, again from the Camelot. Her name was Gabi, and she was always trying to please people somehow, but no one wanted anything to do with her.

'When did she have herself locked in there?' I asked.

'Half an hour ago,' said Pony. 'If you give the wardress five marks you can do anything you like to her for five minutes.'

'But no one comes along wanting to torture her,' said Rita, and the two of them fell about laughing. They had to prop each other up.

'No one comes along.'

'Someone ought to go in and at least whip her a bit or something,' I said. 'You can't just leave her hanging in the air.'

'You do it,' said Rita.

'I can't. I don't know how. You go. I'll give you the five marks.'

'I'm not touching her. Not for a hundred marks.'

'Me neither,' said Pony, 'it's her own fault. Last time she tried to be sold in the slave market, and no one wanted her then either. Not even when the minimum bid went down to ten marks.'

They laughed so much that they had to hold on to each other again.

'It's time I was getting back,' I told Rita. 'I've a long way to drive. You can go back with Pony.'

Only when I was in Silke's Polo again did I notice how my knees were trembling. I made up my mind that the Black

Party was all ridiculous pretence, but my knees were trembling all the same.

Just after Lüneburg I felt unwell. I stopped, got out, and threw up on the verge. I was back at the funny farm at around five in the morning. My contact lenses were so dry that when I took them out I almost tore my corneas away with them. I lay down in bed. At first I couldn't get to sleep, then I dreamed of the carpet-beater scene. Everyone else got up at eight. I waited until they'd finished showering and were having breakfast, and I had the bathroom all to myself. I couldn't even contemplate putting my contact lenses back in. I had to go downstairs with glasses on. When I reached the kidney-shaped temple the others were already sitting on their round cushions. As I looked for mine, my therapist's glance followed me. It was the look of a man concentrating on an insect with fly-swatter raised. But it was still Olaf's turn. This morning he was wearing trousers that had clearly been made by Andrea, and he was talking about the Disney film *Bambi*. A girlfriend had talked him into going to see *Bambi* with her, and apart from the fact that all the animals were so sugary sweet he almost got diabetes, there'd been Bambi's horrible parents.

'Bambi's mother kept on about his wonderful father who had such great antlers. It reminded me of my own family. My mother was always telling us what a great person our father was. The fact is, Bambi's old man never shows up. He doesn't care about anything. He just stands around on some mountain crest all the time displaying his antlers to the countryside.'

Andrea was sitting opposite me, working on the bookseller by lowering her eyes, looking suddenly up at him and immediately away again, then looking down to the floor.

When her big brown eyes met his there was something heart-rendingly injured and pleading in them. When her eyes happened by chance to meet mine they went cold as wet socks.

'Those fucking roe deer,' said Olaf.

'White-tailed deer,' I told him. 'They're white-tailed or Virginian deer in that Disney adaptation. Hence the big antlers.'

'How are you feeling this morning?' Frederic asked me. 'How was it in Hamburg?'

Of course I hadn't said I'd been to an S & M party.

'Fine,' I said. 'I feel fine. Absolutely terrific.'

In fact I felt as if I were made of candyfloss, and anyone who wanted could pull a bit out of me and run off with it.

'Are you denying that there's something between you and Axel which urgently needs to be discussed?'

'I know what you mean,' I said. 'I know, and you know, and half the present company is equally well-informed. However, I've decided not to mention the subject. And I really don't have any problem with that.'

My God, now I was using the same language as my mad-doctor.

'Why,' asked Frederic, 'don't you want to talk about it?'

'Look,' I said, trying to make concessions, 'it's just sad, that's all. I remembered Axel as my childhood friend, standing beside my bed with a bunch of parrot tulips. I've been thinking all this time that the one good thing in my life had been destroyed. But that was just a load of shit. There was never anything good there to be destroyed.'

That lump was back in my throat again. Why hadn't I just kept my mouth shut? Large chunks of candyfloss blew away. Frederic – back in his element at last – turned to Axel.

'And what goes on inside *you* when you hear that?'

Axel shrugged.

'Can't say. Don't want to either. It's not really anything to do with me.'

'And how do you feel, Anne, when you hear Axel now?'

'That,' I said, 'is exactly the reason why I don't want to talk about it. Why should I give him the satisfaction?'

'Anne,' said Frederic very gently, 'how do you feel about it? Listen to what's going on inside you, see how you really feel.'

He was keen to get some success at last.

'Please don't try that on with me,' I said.

'Take a look at Axel,' said Frederic.

Axel looked elsewhere and let the air audibly out through his lips. His eyes were a normal size, his face was relaxed. He was feeling great.

'Why don't you just say you're sad?' Frederic asked me even more gently.

Well, I don't know if *sad* was the right word. Because at that moment I started bellowing. I bellowed and howled, I lost face entirely, scraps of candyfloss flew in all directions, and surging grief broke over me like a wave over a sand-castle. There wasn't much of me left at all. I didn't know where this vast weight of pain came from or what had set it off. Presumably the pretence of sympathy in my therapist's voice; he got at most people that way. I tried to concentrate on the bottle of mineral water beside me. I only had to knock the glass bottom of it off on the floor and then push the jagged edges of the remains into my face and twist them around. If I looked the way I felt, maybe I could stop crying.

'I didn't expect this just now,' said Frederic at last, rather helplessly. 'I didn't know you'd react so strongly.'

I tried to answer, but I could only manage the howl of a medium-sized dog. I was a shipwrecked mariner tossed around in the raging sea of pain, with waves of shame washing over me the whole time, a hurricane of helpless rage whistling in my ears, and clouds of total abandonment darkening the sky. If you can't even trust people when you're paying them a hundred and twenty marks an hour for it, then who can you trust?

'Is there anything I can do for you? Is there anything you'd like?' asked my therapist.

'Yes, I'd like to be dead,' I croaked.

'And how do you others feel about this?' he asked, turning to them. Why couldn't the bastard give it a rest? Why did he have to keep making everything even worse? I couldn't understand it. I just could not understand it.

'Well, it's getting on my nerves,' said Andrea. 'It really gets me down, that ridiculous suicide threat. She won't do it. And I know why it annoys me so much, of course. It annoys me because I've done the same. Because I keep saying I'll kill myself too, and then I don't. It's so ridiculous.'

She looked shyly at the floor, and when she raised her eyes again she met the concerned and tender gaze of the book-seller.

Now Olaf spoke up. 'It's always the same,' he said, leaning back. 'The women who seem so strong at first always pipe down later. I wish I knew why.'

'Yes,' agreed Guido, 'I've noticed that too. I noticed how hard and cool she seemed at the beginning. I knew at once she couldn't keep it up. It was all pretence.'

There was no stopping them now. While I went on howling and bawling to myself, one after another of the men said he'd seen from the first that I was pretending to be something

I wasn't. Only the bookseller kept quiet, because he was a good, kind-hearted person, and because he was probably wondering all this time what could have happened to Andrea that was so bad that she'd wanted to kill herself.

'I'm really surprised that you reacted so violently,' said my therapist at last, once I'd stopped howling. 'I don't know – can I let you go for the break in this state?'

He needed his frothy coffee, and was sick and tired of the whole thing.

'Of course,' I yelled, 'what else are you going to do? Carry on like this for all eternity?'

'But you won't do something to yourself afterwards?'

He was smiling, the bastard.

'No,' I said, 'no. Well, Andrea has already very neatly analysed that I don't intend to do anything to myself.'

'Good, then let's break for lunch and meet again at three.'

They all went off to lunch in their stockinged feet. I didn't really want to go until they were out of the room, but I saw my therapist watching me, and if I stayed until the last he'd misinterpret it as a sign that I wanted to speak to him alone. So I quickly got to my feet, went out with the others and picked up my shoes. I passed the dining-room, made out I was going to the dormitories, but then turned and slipped out of the front door. I hurried through the garden, went into the barn where my therapist kept his car and looked to see if there was a rope there, but it was one of those tidy barns and contained only the car, a shelf full of screwdrivers on the wall, and a spare petrol can. I didn't want to burn myself, so I went out again and over to a little wood. It was a deciduous wood, all slender young trees, none of them more than ten metres tall, with stinging nettles and undergrowth among them. I left the path and made my way through the bushes.

Like I said, it was only a small wood, surrounded by fields and houses, you couldn't lose yourself in it without being found very quickly. I went as far in as I could and looked for a stone. There were plenty of stones; the region was known for its dry and stony soil. All the same, it took me quite a time to find one that was the right handy size. I sat down on the ground and leaned against a birch tree. I imagined what the others would say when I'd killed myself. I always liked imagining such things as a child. Of course Axel would feel enormously flattered, or at least I'd have felt flattered if someone had killed himself over me. Axel could easily drop that kind of thing into conversation later when he met a woman, and then he could gaze very sadly into the void. That would put the new woman in her place all right. Andrea would lean on the bookseller's shoulder weeping desperately and sob, 'It's my fault. I drove her to it when I said she wouldn't kill herself.' And the bookseller, overwhelmed by his own happiness, would take the woman who had revealed his strength to him in his arms, pat her shoulder and say, 'No, no. You couldn't help it. You mustn't think such things.'

Axel and Olaf and all the other men would cluster around her too, and Axel would say, 'Anne was totally nuts anyway.' And then Frederic would stand up and tell them, 'It's no one's fault. If someone really wants to commit suicide no one can stop it. A suicide will always find ways and means. And what happened here just set it off. If she hadn't killed herself here she'd probably have done it in six months' time, for a similarly insignificant reason. She has no one to blame but herself.'

But his neighbours probably wouldn't see it the same way. If a patient committed suicide here there'd be no end of talk. If my therapist went to the bakery conversations in the shop would die down at once, and everyone would turn to look at him. I felt very sorry for him standing there in the bakery. It hadn't been at all easy for him to be accepted in the village. He had put up with all the derision bravely, and when his neighbours saw that the funny farm was in fact doing very well, and he could afford to build on to it and renovate it, he'd thought he could feel something like respect from them at last. And now it had all come to nothing, just because of an idiot with weak nerves who couldn't wait to kill herself until she got home.

I picked up the stone and brought it down on my skull. Of course I hadn't hit hard enough, because I didn't really wanted to commit suicide, I just wanted to be able to persuade myself that I was trying to commit suicide, only I couldn't manage to. Otherwise I could have taken the spare petrol can after all. But at least I wanted to feel pain and have blood running down my face. That was more difficult than I'd expected. I hit myself with the stone again and again. Then I collapsed against the tree and knelt down with one arm round its trunk. Still with no blood on my face. There were good reasons why suicides in general prefer the rope, sleeping tablets or jumping off a bridge. What I was doing called for too much determination. I crawled around on all fours looking for a bigger stone. I threw it up in the air and tried to imagine I was heading a football. At the fourth attempt I made contact. It hurt so much that I immediately realised that I no longer wanted to die that day. I hauled myself up by the white tree-trunk and waited until I'd stopped feeling dizzy. Then I took the stone, kissed it, put it down beside the birch tree and made off in the direction of the funny farm. As I walked along, four bumps came up on my skull. Like a cartoon character. I decided to spend the rest of the lunch break in the shower. That way I needn't see anyone or speak to anyone. Of course the showers were always accessible, like the six-bed dormitories, they weren't even separated by sexes, but I took such a long, hot shower that a wall of steam rose around me.

When I went back to the kidney-shaped temple my skin was red and swollen. I really did hope that my therapist could solve the whole thing for me. I had the humiliation behind me, now came understanding. He had broken me and now he would put me back together again. I'd find out why I'd had to cry so much, he'd ask me the right questions, he'd ask Axel the right questions, and I'd find out something about myself which would make it all worthwhile. You always think things will turn out all right in the end. I wonder why?

Frederic sat down in the circle with the others and me and asked how I was feeling.

'You can't seriously be asking that,' I said, feeling for the biggest bump with one hand. The pain was breathtaking. As long as I could give myself that kind of pain I'd get through this without having to shed any more tears.

'You're looking good,' said Frederic. 'All soft and relaxed. Don't you think so too?' he asked, turning to the others.

'Yes. All soft,' said Guido.

'I think so too,' said a woman called Grit.

'I think it did her good,' added Olaf.

'She seems . . . kind of less tense,' said Andrea.

I fumbled around in my hair, setting off a firework display of pain in my skull.

'Broken,' I said. 'The word you're all searching for is broken.'

My therapist turned to the bookseller.

'You once had a great weeping fit here, do you remember?'

'Yes,' said the bookseller. 'I remember it very well. I'm glad it wasn't me this time.'

My therapist talked to the bookseller and then to Olaf. So I'd been dealt with. The workshop was functioning again, and my therapist was in charge once more.

I had no intention of spending that night in the six-bed dormitory, so I brought my bedclothes downstairs and snuggled under the pile of red blankets in the common room. I switched on the CD player. Grit's *La Traviata* CD was still in it, and I set it to repeat-play over and over again.

At around eleven Olaf came in. I'd expected him to come. 'Can I lie down there with you?'

I didn't say anything, and he crawled under the blankets with me. He stroked my head and my back. His hands were big and warm, his touch was comforting. I just had to forget who was at the other end of his arms. He kissed my face, my temples and my cheeks and then my throat. His breath brushed over my skin and made me shudder. I'd never get anything but men like Olaf. It was completely unimaginable that a nice, clever man would ever be interested in me. Perhaps I'd manage to hang myself some day, if I could only be sure that someone would cut my body down and lay it on the floor.

The door opened for the second time and Andrea came in.

'Oh, sorry,' she murmured. 'I just forgot to take my blanket with me.'

She picked up her blanket and disappeared again.

'She's jealous,' said Olaf when she'd gone. 'She didn't come in by chance. She can't bear me being with you. She's afraid of getting old,' he went on, when I didn't say anything. 'She's beginning to lose her power to attract, and she knows it.'

He was trying to get into my good graces by running her down.

But Andrea would never lose her power to attract him. Olaf would never get over her; he'd still be begging for a smile from her in the old folks' home. He was a failure, and repulsive, and he was the only person in the whole world ready to take me in his arms. He kissed my mouth – he kissed well – and it was almost as if we loved each other.

'Hey, you do that nicely,' said Olaf, 'I'd never have thought it of you.'

When I wake up the afternoon sun is shining in my face. I blink. Who am I, where am I? I'm lying in Hemstedt's bed, so much sunlight, blinking isn't enough so I turn over, there's another white pillow over there. Like a reflex action, I stretch out my arm and my hand strokes the cool, smooth fabric. I watch it for a while, but then I imagine David Peskow sitting alone in *my* flat on *my* bed and stroking *my* pillow if only I'd let him – a perfectly revolting idea – and I snatch my hand back as fast as I can. David Peskow is the same kind of depressed, gloomy person as me, and he was in love with me for at least ten years – until I got really fat. Then I was rid of him. So I know about it from the other side too. I know what it's like to be loved immoderately and have no answer to it. David Peskow thought I'd be the means of helping him to escape the darkness and hopelessness of his own existence. And for a while I really did want to save him. Any common viper could have done it better. For to be honest I shared David's poor opinion of himself. I only had to look at the limp way he stood, his neglected clothing, the hangdog look in his eyes – one couldn't fancy him. As soon as he said something I snapped at him. Did he just say 'we'? What made him think he and I were a 'we'? I despised him and tormented him, and at the same time I wallowed in his love like a pig. You have to remember what the flight attendants say: first find your own oxygen mask and put it on before you think of helping other people.

I yawn, and try to stretch, but I can't bring my shoulder blades together any more because of the two rolls of fat between them. In the shower, which has no curtain, I avoid looking in the big bathroom mirror. I can't bring myself to look at my naked reflection in a mirror. But even if I see my reflection fully clothed, it's immediately obvious; *that's* all over. I don't even need to think about sex any more.

I nose around the bedroom like an old maid, working my way round to the black chest of drawers. What sort of underpants does Hemstedt wear? Black. I take a pair out, put it on my head and go out into the hall. He's crazy, giving me the run of the flat! The hall is lined with built-in cupboards. I open the first. It's empty. The second is empty too. So are the third and the fourth. And the fifth, sixth and seventh are empty, empty, empty. It's rather uncanny. Eight built-in cupboards, seven of them empty. When I open the eighth, a brown and white St Pauli scarf and a brown sweater with a skull and crossbones are in there on a coat hanger. There's a brown and white woolly bobble hat in a compartment underneath. I reverently take the underpants off my head. I assume it's a male thing, feeling that you belong. Men can't help relating everything to themselves, particularly the success or failure of football teams. I don't feel that it's got anything to do with me, even watching the TV news, and I'd sooner drive donkeys than sit in a stadium shouting encouragement at someone who doesn't know my name. Oh well, time to get out of here.

It's coming home,
it's coming home,
it's coming,
football's coming home – but apart from two young men wearing scarves and silly squashy hats in the English colours there's no indication of the coming semi-final. The sun is shining, I wander across Trafalgar Square with my hands in the pockets of my hip-length jacket. The jacket is almost a kaftan; otherwise I look really bad in trousers. Once I'd reached a hundred and ten kilos I began to pant and waddle as I walked. Surprisingly, now that I'm really fat people don't stare at me and pass comments nearly as much as they did when I was almost slim. If I make my way through a supermarket turnstile which is much too narrow for me, people sometimes take offence, but the men and boys who used to call things after me about my arse don't even notice me now. Their glances slide past me, or even through me as if through a ghost, which from their point of view is what I am now. It's a relief, but at the same time this lack of interest is unsettling, because I don't know if I have anything else to offer apart from my body. Still with my hands in my jacket pockets, I stumble over a pigeon and fall full length. Now I have as much attention as anyone could want. Tourists of all nationalities watch with interest as the fat lady who's had an accident mops the blood off her chin with a handkerchief. But as no one wants to share in the attention I'm attracting, I have to struggle to my feet by myself. When I push off from the ground it's not my whole torso moving, it's my old, slender self bending inside my body as a wave of fat ripples

up my ribs and climbs to my armpits. In order to stand up again I practically have to dive into my own body.

It's pleasantly cool in the entrance lobby of the museum. A black-clad security man asks to see my shoulder bag, puts a cautious hand into it and gives it back to me. I walk round a group of little girls in black school uniform, sitting cross-legged on the floor, one white knee-high sock over another, drawing Rousseau's tiger in their sketchpads with wax crayons, I wander past crazy sunflowers and dotted landscapes, before stopping in front of a gigantic painting of a sad historical event. It shows, very realistically, the execution of seventeen-year-old Lady Jane Grey, queen for nine days. Lady Jane is kneeling in a dark dungeon, wearing a very elegant, radiantly white and incredibly spotless silk or taffeta dress. The artist has used rather gloomy colours around the queen and her dress; the walls of the dungeon are the same dull grey as the plastic bags they use for collecting body parts after a plane crash. The ladies in waiting and the executioner are dressed in black and red, and you can't help thinking that the young queen's white dress will soon be soaked with blood. Lady Jane's eyes are blindfolded. She is trying to do everything properly, groping with childlike docility for the block where she is to lay her head. No one feels happy about the whole occasion, certainly not the broken-hearted ladies in waiting, and not the old man who is guiding her towards the block either, touching the puppy fat of her arms in a paternal and concerned way as he does so. Even the executioner is sad, if only in the autistic, illogical way proper to an executioner's sadness. He has a rosette on one sleeve, the kind you get at gymkhanas, only bigger. You immediately feel that he will do his job well, and Lady Jane won't suffer for long. But perhaps that's the worst of it – it will be over so quickly, and that bright radiance hasn't the slightest chance against all the darkness around it.

After standing for half an hour I have Achilles tendons as thick as ropes. I cut my museum visit short, buy the *Daily Star* at a kiosk, make for the nearest café and order three slices of gâteau and a pot of tea. The ladies at the table next to mine turn quite pale. I look right into the depths of their shrivelled little hearts. Two slices of chocolate gâteau at 730 calories each, they're calculating, plus one slice of strawberry gâteau with whipped cream, that's at least 560 calories. As if she needed it! And at the same time envy rises in them.

Yet the three slices of gâteau that bother them so much are nothing. If I put my mind to it I can consume five chocolate bars and follow them up with a sixth, and then I can eat a bag of crisps and a packet of biscuits, and finish it off with four cheese sandwiches. After that second workshop I gave up not just therapy but any attempt to diet. I've reached a point where I don't believe in anything and anyone except a chocolate bar. It's like an intoxication, you're falling and you can't stop, and naturally I get fatter and fatter. Exactly what I was always afraid of has happened. Sometimes I watch myself stuffing my body to the point of unconsciousness, and I ask: what's the matter with you? Aren't you fat enough yet?

A hundred and seventeen kilos – a woman who doesn't have a boyfriend now isn't going to get one. A woman who's on her own now will be on her own for a long, long time. When I read about people who weigh three hundred or four hundred kilos, I never think: how can they? I think: how come I don't weigh that much yet? After I've been bingeing I feel sick, bloated, as if I'm filled right up with glue, with

229

stinking black slime flowing through my veins instead of blood. But that's not the worst of it. The worst of it is that a time comes when even I can't eat any more. There's a point when no more will go in. I can't even force it down. And then I'm so scared that I don't know what to do. If I don't eat it's as if a large brown wall were moving steadily towards me. As long as I'm eating, the wall stands still.

I reach for the second piece of gâteau and unfold the newspaper. 'WATCH OUT YOU GERMAN SAUSAGES. TONIGHT EL TEL'S BOYS ARE GOING TO SHOW YOU WHAT IT MEANS TO GET A GOOD KICKING IN THE STRUDELS.'

The right-hand side of the front page of the *Daily Star* is reserved for a half-naked blonde with heavy eye make-up and a lion crest on her panties. The panties are as radiantly white as the dress worn by young Queen Jane for her execution. 'HANS OFF, FRITZ!' says the wording on the blonde's shoulder. 'YOU'VE GOT YOUR OWN PAGE FRAU BIRD INSIDE.' I go straight to the German pin-up on page 3. She is about as fat as me, and she wears a cheap platinum-blonde Gretchen-style wig, a large, grubby flesh-coloured bra, and Bavarian lederhosen with home-made straps of painted strips of fabric. Her calves are laced into army boots. In her right hand she holds a peculiar glass with a handle which, with a little English imagination, might pass for a beer tankard. In her left hand she holds a whole loaf of bread, split like a roll and filled with an entire large pork sausage. The caption underneath says: 'MEIN GOTT! SHE MAY LOOK LIKE YOUR WURST NIGHTMARE, BUT TODAY YOUR FAIR PLAY *DAILY STAR* STRIKES A BLOW FOR ANGLO-GERMAN ACCORD BY PROUDLY PRESENTING OUR VERY FIRST PAGE FRAU GIRL:

LEDERHOSEN LOVELY BRUNHILDE GROSSENTITTI BOOBS MIGHT NOT SEEM SO WUNDERBAR TO REGULAR READERS THOUGH SHE IS A HUN-EY.'

When I set off back to the flat at around seven, the streets are full of men and women wearing top hats decorated with the Union Jack and carrying English flags and pennants. They are all as cheerful as if they'd won already. At the thought of going back to Hemstedt's minimalist flat and lying down in his black bed, I just feel exhausted. As if I'd come to the end of a long and hopeless road. Love is not something I can still hope for. Love is something I missed out on way back in the past. I might just as well follow all these hopeful people into a pub and watch the German team, minus Jürgen Klinsmann and all the other injured players, being paid back by Pearce, Platt and Gascoigne for the 1990 World Cup and the Second World War. 'DON'T MENTION THE WAR – WHY NOT, FRITZ, YOU STARTED IT.'

The nearest pub is already crammed full, as presumably all the pubs will be, but none of the customers who want to come in and make their own contribution to the victory are turned away. A great, a fateful encounter is about to begin, and it's meant to demoralise the loser's whole nation. Once again my body is a problem, because I can't just push past people, I have to ask them to let me through. Surprisingly, there's a big gap right by the bar. So big that even I can stand and move about comfortably there. Everywhere else is crowded, but I'm able to order my beer straight away. Only when the match begins do I realise why. I'm standing right under the TV screen. To see anything of the game, I have to lean over at an angle with my head tilted right back. I stay in this position, and of course I'm supporting Germany, but only because it would be even sillier not to. In 1990 I was sitting in front of the TV with a taxi driver and his two friends, watching the World Cup final. One of the friends, who was a teacher, happened to mention that he really wanted Argentina to win.

'You don't get the point of the game,' said the other friend, a reporter on *Welt am Sonntag*. 'The point of a football match is to support your own team. Every Argentinian supports Argentina, every Frenchman supports France, every Colombian supports Colombia . . .'

'Never mind that,' said the teacher. 'I'm against Germany.'

'They won't forgive you for Auschwitz, all the same,' said the taxi driver.

And his friend the reporter went on, '. . . and every Icelander supports Iceland, and every Italian supports Italy, and every Fiji Islander supports Fiji, and every Guatemalan supports Guatemala, and . . .'

'And don't for heaven's sake start on about some brilliant, stylish African team,' said the taxi driver, but the reporter just went on.

'. . . and every Cameroonian supports Cameroon, and every Norwegian supports Norway, and because of that every German had better support Germany, and a German who doesn't support Germany doesn't get the point of the game.'

I'm just sipping my beer when the rejoicing of the pub customers breaks against me like a wave, hesitant and almost questioning at first, and then again two seconds later, properly this time. Not three minutes into the game, and England are already in the lead. I've never before been aware of the feelings of so many people at the same time: thanks to Shearer everything's going to be all right. It can only be all right now, surely? Three minutes and we're already in the lead. Oh, Shearer, Shearer, Shearer! All their emotions are bent on the point where I'm standing, under the TV screen, and their horror when Kuntz equalises less than quarter of an hour later hits me like a punch in the stomach. Kuntz, Kuntz, Kuntz, I think as enthusiastically as possible, to arm myself against their surge of disappointment, but I clench my fist only briefly so as not to attract attention. On screen the German fans are doing a ritual dance, swaying in bear-like fashion from foot to foot and raising their right and left fists alternately to the sky with arms still bent, drawing down invisible threads of energy, weaving them into a lucky carpet. The tension among the pub customers makes the beer glass shake in my hand. A hopeful roar in unison that dies away before it has fully developed. The ball hit the post! And then more despair, despair as Germany scores another goal, oh, such despair, but immediately mingled with hope. Was that a foul? Surely it was a foul! The goalie says it was a foul. The referee says so too. Foul! Foul! People breathe again, clutch their hearts or foreheads, stagger back and fall into their friends' arms. The relief of the whole pub washes round my feet.

When the penalty shoot-out begins I'm already bathed in sweat; the nape of my neck is tense. England kicks and scores, Germany kicks and scores, England kicks and scores, Germany kicks and scores. A goal and rejoicing, a goal and disappointment, a goal and rejoicing . . . the ball keeps flying into the upper right-hand corner of the net. On the TV screen, the exhausted and resigned remains of the two teams are sitting on the turf, they can't do any more, they don't have to do any more. A single man will decide between victory and defeat now, the first one not to score, and it will all be that man's fault. Gascoigne scores a goal and assumes the attitude of a gymnast doing floor exercises and landing after a triple twist. Perfectly done. Then he yells and races towards the spectators; someone must once have blamed him for something, and now, whatever it was, it has to be taken back. Ziege. Ziege scores, and no one can tell from his expression what he's thinking. Sheringham. Sheringham scores a goal. Into the right-hand corner of the net again. Sheringham raises his fist in the air. Kuntz. Kuntz has it easier than anyone else, because he's already shot two goals, although the second was disallowed. But for him these penalties wouldn't be taking place. But for him the German team would already have lost. No one could even really blame him if he missed. Kuntz kicks and scores. To the right; all the balls seem to be swinging to the right. Kuntz clenches his fists at chest height, without excessive emotion, a man who knew in advance he'd get the ball into the net. Southgate. At first sight Southgate resembles Sheringham, or no, he doesn't. He's younger. And better-looking. Southgate is afraid. The fear of the goalkeeper during a penalty shoot-out is as nothing to the fear of the man taking the penalty. The others were all afraid, but they had the knack of mingling their fear with something else, anger or a sense of duty or concentration. Southgate's fear simply feels like fear, and he is beginning to think. He thinks that because all the goals have swung right so far, the goalkeeper will fling himself to the right this time. Southgate doesn't shoot as he had intended. Southgate shoots left. Left is a mistake. In helpless fury Gascoigne throws his water bottle to the pitch. England's hope destroyed with a single shot. The despair in the pub presses me up against the bar. Southgate feels nothing. Southgate feels nothing yet. Only now is the despair slowly seeping into him, he mechanically mutters something, presumably something like 'Shit', and he realises that he is the unluckiest man in the whole world and even his own mother will shun him. He thrusts his bottom jaw out slightly, but he doesn't shed tears. I wish I knew how he manages that. Andy Möller takes the next penalty. If he shoots a goal this will be his victory, his European Cup. The horror in the pub is boundless. They all try to hope, but no one doubts that Andy Möller will get the ball into the net, and he does. Oh, not again! They bury their faces in their hands. Andy Möller runs to the side of the pitch, preens in front of the spectators like a small, stout cockerel, puts his hands on his hips and moves his head to left and right in triumph. But the people around me are much too shocked to feel indignant. The champagne ready on ice has lost its sparkle. That was it. Another case of: 'Oh, so near!'

Half the customers leave the pub directly after the end of the match, the rest go over to the bar, they intend to stick together in their time of trouble and get drunk in company, and that gives me the space I need to get out of this place without having to apologise to anyone in broken English. Both fat and German, that might be a bit too much just now. Outside. Men propping each other up and patting one another's bowed heads. Failure weighs heavy on England. It wasn't just the team, it's their own fault too because they didn't believe strongly enough, didn't shout loud enough, weren't there at the stadium or didn't wear their lucky jackets. One young man wrapped in the English flag is leaning against a wall and sobbing his heart out. But what's his pain compared to what Southgate must be feeling now? How many years of psychotherapy does it take to get over missing a goal like that?

And I, the beaming beneficiary of the victory that Andy Möller has just won for me, go back to Hemstedt's block of flats, master the recalcitrant front door, climb the stairs to Hemstedt's flat, go in, close its door behind me, undress without looking at myself, shower, put my pyjamas on, clean my teeth and go to bed. And compared to Southgate I'm happy.

Around midnight, or at least I feel it may be midnight, I hear sounds at the door. First I think: Hemstedt. Next I think: burglars! How did they manage to get past the front door of the building? Then I remember Hemstedt mentioning something about a woman lodger who's gone away. When there's a knock at the bedroom door I know it's Hemstedt.

'Hello,' I say, sitting up quickly. Luckily I'm wearing my blue and gold striped pyjamas, in which I look almost passable.

'Hello,' says Hemstedt, leaning in the doorframe, a decorative silhouette. 'Sorry to wake you, but I need something from my wardrobe.'

'I thought you'd be on the plane by now.'

'Missed it. The traffic was solid. By the time my taxi reached the airport the flight had left.'

'What will you do now?'

'I'm catching the next one tomorrow.'

I can't blame fate. Fate has done what it could. It's Hemstedt.

'I can sleep on the sofa,' says Hemstedt diffidently, going into his walk-in wardrobe and stripping to his underpants there. They're black, like all the others in his chest of drawers.

Stay here, I want to say. Don't go away tomorrow! I have

so many things I want to say to him, but I just ask how the match was, and of course the match was great, because Germany won, and since they won it doesn't matter how.

'Didn't they lynch you? You must have been surrounded by Englishmen!'

'I was with the people from my company, and I know them all. Though one of our business partners did say he'd knock my head against the wall if I went on shouting so loud.'

'Why were you shouting so loud, then?'

'Because we won,' says Hemstedt happily, and goes into the bathroom. He gives me time to admire his body. It's not for me he's kept himself so fit, but I'm allowed to look. While he showers I wonder if he's waiting for me to offer to let him sleep with me in his bed. Something about him suggests that he is, and of course I'd like to sleep beside him, but there's always my neglected body, bulging out of all my clothes except my pyjamas, and he simply can't want that. I shift my weight, heavily, and let my legs dangle over the side of the bed. My fat moves in ripples under the fabric and comes to rest, quivering. The man showering in there is handsome, athletic, successful. I'm just a fat woman without any self-confidence who should have stayed at home. Hemstedt comes out of the bathroom, steaming slightly, and does the number with the bath sheet around his hips again. I want him to sit down beside me, and I'll put my head on his lap, and I want him to put his hand on my head, and then it will be all right at last and I'll die very quickly, before he thinks better of it and takes his hand away again. Hemstedt turns at the door, looks at me and goes out without a word. A moment later I hear music from the living-room. I get out of bed and put on the black dressing-gown that he took out of the wardrobe and then didn't use after all, and I steal out into the hall. Hemstedt has left the light on. I so much want to go to him and touch him, but the weight of my body keeps me where I am, heavy as lead. That body is the reason for everything I never did. I lean against the wall. The music that has just begun is dark yet soft, with a driving, stomping native American rhythm beneath it. It's that one, wonderful, unique song, it enters me, it's in me, it floods through me, makes me light and draws me out into the hall. The hall broadens out into a kitchen, and beyond the kitchen is the living-room. The kitchen walls are ochre, not white. On the work surface by the cooker stand a coffee machine, a lemon squeezer and a kettle – all Alessi. I knock over one of the three tall stools in front of the kitchen counter with my fat hips, and it falls to the terracotta tiles with a clatter. If you've put on as much weight as quickly as I have, it takes a time to get familiar with your new dimensions and be able to shunt yourself around easily.

Hemstedt opens the living-room door and stands aside to let me in. He's naked except for one of the pairs of black underpants that he seems to keep deposited all over the flat. The folding sofa-bed has been pulled out and made up with a sheet and a duvet. It stands by itself on the floor. The right-hand wall consists of shelves full of records, CDs and tapes. A small bookcase with four shelves stands by the left-hand wall. Out of sheer embarrassment I go over to it and look at the contents. Mostly mainstream masculine literature, *The Time of the Assassins, Hollywood Babylon, Compulsion*, but also *The Mists of Avalon* and *The Big Summer Holiday Book*. I take out *The Big Summer Holiday Book* and hold it out to him.

'What's this in aid of? How can you put a thing like that on your shelves?'

'Why not?'

'How can you ask that? It's like having K-Tel's Pop Explosion LP in your record collection.'

'It was a present. I don't have many books, so I just added it to the others.'

I take a book by Hermann Hesse, *Readings for Minutes*, off the shelf and throw it on the rug together with the *Summer Holiday* book. Hemstedt stations himself beside me and looks at me.

'I don't read them anyway. I never get around to it because I'm at work every day until nine in the evening. I don't even get around to listening to CDs any more. I keep buying new ones, but I don't listen to most of them at all.'

'This book – and this one – and that one. They're all crap!' I throw more books on the floor. '*The Mists of Avalon* – you might just as well go out and buy an Enya CD. Don't you notice anything? I really don't know why I love someone like you. I suppose you probably never noticed that I love you either?'

'Yes,' says Hemstedt, 'yes, I did get that. I noticed that you kept turning up at my place. I thought it was very flattering. It was, too.'

'I know,' I say, 'but there's no need to pride yourself on it. It's nothing to do with you being so lovable, it's because of my unresolved childhood problems. Well?'

'What do you mean, *Well?*'

'Is there any hope?'

'No.'

'That's what I thought.'

'Do you still dream about me?'

I put the book I've just taken out back on the shelf and slowly turn my head to Hemstedt. I look him in the eye.

'I've never dreamed about you. I don't dream at all. I don't even sleep. I've never slept a night through in my life. Why can't you love me?'

He shrugs his shoulders.

'I think I used to be afraid of you.'

I ought to have been prepared for that. But I'm not.

'You always said such harsh things,' he goes on. 'It was rather intimidating.'

I pick up *The Mists of Avalon* and put it back on the shelf. 'And now? Are you still afraid of me now?'

Hemstedt puts out his hand and strokes my throat up to my ear with two fingers and then down again. It's probably the only part of my body that's still slim.

'You probably think I've got terribly fat,' I say, 'but that's only the way it looks. Inside I'm thin and vulnerable and desirable. It just doesn't show.'

'Come on,' says Hemstedt, taking my hand and leading me over to his folding sofa-bed. His naked torso brushes my towelling-clad arm. How late is it now? Two in the morning? I take the dressing-gown off, pick up the only duvet and wrap myself in it at once.

'Right, so you look great,' I snap at him. 'But has it ever done you any good? I mean in absolute terms. Is your life satisfactory? Are you happy?'

'No,' he says peaceably, 'not really.'

'I expect you think it's a great achievement to look the way you do, but really you're just too cowardly to match your fellow men in being fat and ugly.'

'Could be,' says Hemstedt, and he lies down beside me and puts a hand under the duvet, and then tries to push it under my pyjama top too.

'No,' I say, 'no! I don't want you to touch me there. Can't

240

you just hold my hand? Don't touch anything under the duvet . . .'

Hemstedt pulls the duvet a little way down and looks at me. There is no malice in his eyes. They're like window-panes at night, where your reflection looks much better than it really is. I can hardly bear the way he's looking at me. Hemstedt puts his arm round me – he has to reach a shamingly long way to do that – and lies half on me. It's good to feel him, but how much better it would surely be if I was thin and I could feel his body properly, not just through a double neoprene fat-suit. I weep. I weep because I was once a young, pretty, slim woman and I never knew it. Even then Hemstedt didn't love me. And if it wasn't my body that made me unattractive to him and still does, then it must be something more basic, and I'll never be able to change that at all.

'I love you so much,' I say. 'I wish I didn't, but there's nothing I can do about it. I won't bother you, I'll go home tomorrow, then I'll be gone.'

'No,' he says, 'you must stay here. Anyway, I'm off tomorrow myself.'

He's learned a few things, he kisses well now, he holds my upper lip in his teeth while his tongue moves over it, puts his large mouth on mine and touches my heart. He wants to impress me. He doesn't want me to be sorry I ever fell in love with him. He really does kiss surprisingly well, even if you can tell how keen he is to be good at it. Everything I ever wished for is lying beside me, only the wish seems to come from a dark place far away and out of reach. The tears just run out of my eyes. They won't stop. The final is cancelled because of flooding.

'That's enough crying,' he says at last, kindly and just a tiny bit impatiently. 'You can take a break now and smile.'

'I can't smile,' I weep. 'You once said when I smiled my whole face twisted into one great grimace.'

'Did I really say that? Yes, sounds like me. Forget it.'

Hemstedt takes me in his arms again and rocks me gently back and forth. He's rocking a huge giant dolphin in his arms. I don't want to know what it looks like. That's the worst of it: if you're fat nothing you do can be nice or loving or romantic. Nothing. Ever. The sight of you spoils it all.

'I'm sorry,' he says, although he doesn't understand anything. 'I'm sorry you're so sad.'

He goes on rocking me, and he kisses me all over my face and breathes a little faster. I put my fat arms round him, round his body that's so young and so handsome and so obviously not made for me. I think of the elegant, self-controlled women who walked past us at his office, and it makes me feel desperate.

'I'd like to sleep with you,' he says, 'but only if that's what you want too,' and he kisses me again. He kisses so well, and it doesn't matter that he knows it. Hemstedt lets go of me and takes off his underpants without embarrassment. I don't look. He fumbles around beside the sofa-bed, there seems to be a place for condoms there, and then he pulls my pyjama trousers down with one hand. I put my hands in front of my face. It's so dreadful. Pity, the word goes through my head. He just wants to sleep with me out of pity. Any moment he'll look at me and see what he's really doing. Without my trousers on everything is against me. Hemstedt parts my legs, kneels between them and carefully takes my elbows, so that I lower my hands and open my eyes. Simply and naturally he takes his pink-wrapped prick in his hand, feels around a little with his fingers first, and then he's inside me. I hold tight to his shoulders, my hands slide down his spine, wander up his ribs, feel the hard stomach muscles. I press close to him, feeling his life and strength.

'Anne,' he says gently. 'Anne . . .' And he strokes my face.

Only now do I arrive in the present, only now do I become real, and the terrible void stretching out behind me is nothing to do with me any more. In my head a whole field full of parrot tulips opens its flowers, and my soul reaches to the stars. It's fusion, it's megalomaniac wish fulfilment, transfiguration, regression, loss of myself and its opposite – all the wonderful states of mind that our therapists warned us against are here. Of course all the therapists are right, it's much more sensible to spare yourself pain, delusions and obsessions and conduct your relationships with other people in a calm and rational manner. Except that then, of course, you can never feel what I'm feeling now.

Later Hemstedt gets up to put another CD on. Then he goes to the window and looks out. I prop myself on my elbows. There's a thunderous noise to one side, because the speakers are on the floor, and a sad man's voice sings, 'Don't try so hard to be different.'

'Southgate,' I say. Southgate's fate doesn't have very much to do with the text of the song, but all the same Peter immediately understands what I mean.

Later still, when Peter is asleep, I imagine him going out to buy fresh rolls for us next day and being run over by a car. That would be a nice ending. I'd spend the rest of my life mourning him. It's the best ending I can imagine. Not even in my wildest dreams did my imagination ever run to picturing a life together with Hemstedt. I want nothing more than to be with him, but that doesn't mean I'd be able to sustain it. Peter is breathing quietly. I'll always love him. There's nothing to be done about it. This was the night I've been living for. Now there won't be anything else. Of course he won't go out for rolls in the morning. He'll get up early and phone to find out the time of the next flight to Italy. The best idea would be to kill him while he's still lying beside me. I could steal into the kitchen and pick up an Alessi kitchen knife. With my forefinger, I touch the place on his ribcage where I'd position the point of the knife. Peter sleeps deeply and steadily, without moving. The only problem is that I really do love him and I could never hurt him. When I take my finger away again, he moves in his sleep, breathing in and out hard, and something slips off the bed to the floor. I grope for it. It's my pyjama trousers. Carefully, I get up and put them on. Then I go quietly back into the bedroom, get dressed and pack my bag.

ACKNOWLEDGEMENTS

My thanks to Doris Engelke, Wolfgang Hörner and Christina Hucke for their patience and confidence, Karin Graf for enlightenment on the difference between good and bad sex, Thomas Meinecke for advice on music history, Guido Schröter for advice on football, and Friedemann Sittig for information about English newspapers.

A NOTE ON THE AUTHOR

Karen Duve was born in 1961 and lives in Hamburg. She has been awarded numerous awards for her short stories. Her first novel, *Rain*, was published by Bloomsbury in 2002. This is her second novel.